## CAN THIS BE LOVE?

She backed against the desk and looked into the laughing eyes of the Colonel.

"Come here," he was saying. "I can't talk to you when you're so far away. You're sweet and warm and alive, Cindy. I loved you from the moment we met. Believe me?"

His unsteady voice drew her like a magnet. She found herself leaning forward, her lips soft and warm against his.

Then she wrenched herself free. This was the man who travelled under an alias, who had lied to her and deceived her!

Bantam Books by Emilie Loring
Ask your bookseller for the books you have missed

*Rose*

# TO LOVE AND TO HONOR

## Emilie Loring

BANTAM BOOKS · TORONTO · NEW YORK · LONDON

TO LOVE AND TO HONOR
*A Bantam Book / published by arrangement with
Little, Brown and Company, Inc.*

*PRINTING HISTORY*

*Little, Brown edition published November 1950
2nd printing .. October 1951*

*Grosset & Dunlap edition published February 1952*
2nd printing . December 1952     5th printing . November 1955
3rd printing . November 1953     6th printing ... October 1956
4th printing . December 1954     7th printing . December 1957

*Excerpts appeared in* GRIT *magazine and*
THE PITTSBURGH PRESS, *May 1951*

*Bantam Edition published March 1963*
2nd printing ...... June 1964      9th printing .November 1966
3rd printing ...... June 1964     10th printing . December 1967
4th printing .... August 1964     11th printing . February 1968
5th printing . November 1964     12th printing . December 1968
6th printing ..... April 1965     13th printing ... March 1969
7th printing .... August 1965     14th printing .. October 1969
8th printing ...... July 1966     15th printing ...... July 1970
*Bantam new edition published October 1974*

*Bantam Books are published by Bantam Books, Inc. Its trade-
mark, consisting of the words "Bantam Books" and the por-
trayal of a bantam, is registered in the United States Patent
Office and in other countries. Marca Registrada. Bantam
Books, Inc., 666 Fifth Avenue, New York, New York 10019.*

PRINTED IN THE UNITED STATES OF AMERICA

# TO LOVE AND TO HONOR

# ONE

She was waiting at the Gift Shop for the films she had left to be developed when she became aware of the man standing beside her looking at bracelets. Sharp-eyed, rapier-tongued Ella Crane, the saleswoman, was expatiating on the charm and desirability of an ugly super-expensive silver band. As she went to the window to get another tray sympathy for the woman who was about to receive the atrocity overcame Cindy Clinton's caution.

"Not that one," she whispered. "It's been here for ages."

He turned. The clearest gray eyes she had ever seen keenly interrogated hers. Suspicion softened to a smile, the smile spread to a mouth which revealed a flash of white teeth in a bronzed face. His black hair was faintly dusted with white at the temples. Fine hands. Strong, with an intaglio seal ring on the left little finger. Thirtyish, she thought, and seen lots of service.

"Thanks," he whispered, then as the saleswoman returned with more bracelets:

"You know Sally, give me a break," he appealed to the girl beside him. "Which one shall I select for her? I'm sold on this silver band with the turquoise. Think she'd like it?"

Indignation that she was being ignored straightened the mouth of the saleswoman to a thin line. The imp of mischief in the girl's make-up, poised on tiptoe for a take-off, prompted her reply.

"Which Sally?" she inquired thoughtfully. "You know

1

so many. Is this for a young, middle-aged or elderly Sally? Dark or fair?"

"Blondish, but not so much gold as in your hair. Her eyes are blue, yours a velvety brown. After that comparison, you should be able to advise. Does age count in selecting a bracelet? I thought women loved 'em all." Obviously he was enjoying the game she had started impulsively and now was ready to drop.

"Better settle on the silver with turquoise. You like it. When I make a present I give something I want myself, terribly. We'll take a chance your Sally will approve." She collected package and change. "By, Ella. Have fun," she called over her shoulder as she started for the door. Before she reached the bicycle outside the man was beside her.

"Hold on. Give me a chance to say 'Thank you' for helping."

"Hmp! That's the neatest pickup I ever saw." The acrid comment of Ella Crane in the shop doorway, who thought she had been eased out of a sale, was intended for the girl's ears and reached them. Her face reddened. She tilted her chin and looked up.

"Our acquaintance, if you can call it that, ends right here."

"Have a heart. I'm a stranger in a strange land. A trifle early in the afternoon for the cup that cheers, but, have tea with me, will you? I've been abroad for several years and have acquired the tea habit." He glanced at the bow of broad green ribbon, the exact shade that striped her blazer, which tied her hair at the nape of her neck, at the enormous tawny zinnia at the belt of her white pedal-pushers and grinned.

"Perhaps you would prefer a chocolate-malted, ice-cream soda, or one of those loathsome drippy things called Popsicles?"

"Again, no."

He watched the bicycle till it was out of sight, then returned to the shop.

"I'll take the bracelet with the turquoise," he said. "Have you a box for it?" His smile and purchase placated the irate saleswoman.

"Sure. I didn't know but what you'd gone along with her. That Sally business didn't fool me. It isn't like her to make free with a strange man. She never forgets she's a married woman."

"That kid *married?*" His voice and eyes registered amazement. "I've decided to select a couple more bracelets."

"There's plenty here. She's not a kid, though she was dressed like one. The top of her head came 'most as high as your ear, and you are tall. She's twenty-four. Can't say she's much married. She came here summers for years, lives in the family homestead, The Castle. All of seven years ago her folks moved to the West. Her father went into business there and we heard he made and lost a fortune. Like any of those?"

"I'll take this plain one. Give me time and I'll select another. Might as well do my Christmas shopping early. I have a lot of girl cousins who like bracelets."

"There isn't another customer in sight. Take all the time you want."

"Thanks. It's a toss-up between this twisted one and the band with the pendant. What's this on it?"

"The old church—you'll see it in the village. It's one of the sights of the town. We have post cards of it, too."

"Sounds interesting. What did you mean when you said that the girl who was here isn't 'much married'?"

"It's the town romance. Folks just ate it up. Her father and his lawyer tried to keep it quiet but the news leaked out. It was a marriage by proxy."

"*Proxy?*"

"That turned your face red. Not going to have a stroke, are you?"

"No. Surprise has been doing that to me since my service with the airlift. I'm here for a vacation to get straightened out and to write a book on the job I've been doing."

"Are you a novelist?"

"Nothing so thrilling. My work is technical. I couldn't believe my ears when you said marriage by proxy. I thought those happened only in movies and novels."

"You're not a newspaper reporter, are you?"

"No. As I told you I'm a flier just out of the service. Safe to tell me anything. I'll have this one, too. You're so entertaining chances are I'll stand here buying bracelets as long as you'll talk. It sure is a treat to meet an intelligent woman. Marriage by proxy. I'll be darned. How come?"

"This was the story that drifted here. Cindy Clinton's father and another man were in the oil business together. They held a lot of patents about machinery that's used in drilling, they'd leased a piece of land and planned to dig and experiment. Looked as if there'd be some mix-ups in the future, I know nothing about law, they got the idea that if the son of one married the daughter of the other, it would hold the property together. Only trouble was, the son was still in the service and couldn't or wouldn't get leave to come home."

"Do you know where he was serving?"

"No, that was all of three years ago. Folks heard he was in the Navy. Her father got sick and was going to die, and he and his partner called in a lawyer to see what could be done. I heard they even consulted a bigwig in Washington. The result was a marriage by written contract, though the folks here call it proxy. That's the story."

"For the love of Mike, do you mean that the son never had seen the girl? That he consented to marry her sight unseen? I can't believe it."

"Looks that way. Folks heard he said he didn't care. He'd probably never get out of the service alive—they were so secret about where he was, we suspected he had something to do with those terrible bombs—if the girl was willing they could suit themselves. There was a lot of money at stake. Most men would sell their souls for money." Her sniff was drenched with contempt.

"Come now, Miss Ella, I heard the girl call you that, I've seen a lot of men during these last years and I can't think of one who would sell his soul for filthy lucre."

"Perhaps I did put it a little strong. Anyway, if he was after money, folks say there's an even chance there won't be much. Now the other partner has gone too. There has been litigation over some of the patents and leases. I guess it's an awful mix-up. It's three years since the marriage, he's never appeared and she's been advised she can divorce him for desertion. She has a lawyer working on it."

"Why come back here? There is always a Reno."

"She has kept her residence here because of the homestead, ever since she went West. She's had a Maine lawyer advising her. Counselor Armstrong—they tell me that's what lawyers are called in New York—is awful smart."

"Has he an office here?"

"In the summer. There's a little white house right beside his family home, the yellow colonial house, White Pillars, that sets back from Main Street. His great-grandfather was a judge, and it was his office. Seth uses it for business."

"Is he here now?"

"Heard he arrived yesterday, that he has come to put through the divorce. He's a widower. I hear that the Western lawyer who acted as proxy is on the way here. She's a very attractive girl."

"I could see that. I'll take these. That will make four. My cousins will think I have acquired a bracelet complex on the other side." He drew money from a billfold, and watched her put the silver bracelets into boxes and wrap them before he asked:

"Where is this Castle, where Cindy Clinton lives?"

"How'd you know her name?"

"You called her Cindy Clinton, didn't you?"

"Perhaps I did. Her real name is Cinderella—named for her great-grandmother Clinton, but she's still Cindy Clinton in this town. We never think of her married name."

"What is it?"

Her small eyes sharpened to glittering points.

"I've forgot."

"You mean, you have talked enough?"

"That's right. Folks say my tongue's hung in the middle and goes at both ends, when I start. Here are the boxes. I've tied them with ribbon. Hope your cousins will be pleased. You asked where The Castle is." She

came from behind the counter and followed him to the
door.

"See that point of land that juts out into the sea?" He
nodded. "It's divided by a little cove, called Pirate's
Cove, can't see it from here. The Castle is on one point.
It's one of our show places. The big drawing room is
full of what summer people call collectors' items. The
Clintons have owned it for generations. Years and years
ago, an Englishman, Sir Aubrey Reade, built it. The
story is that he was the younger son of an earl, ran away
because he mixed in a revolution; that early in 1800 it
was a smugglers' hide-out; that on stormy nights you can
hear doors opening and shutting and the sound of heavy
footsteps tramping up the secret stairway to the turret
room. A visiting newspaperman wrote up the story, and
last summer a movie company came and used The Castle and grounds for a picture. It hasn't been released
yet. I was talking with Cindy about it just before you
came in."

"It's a thrilling yarn. I noticed a quiver in your voice.
Do you believe that heavy footsteps tramp up the secret
stairway to the turret room?"

"There's never smoke without some fire."

"Which means you do. How does the present owner
react to the ghostly sounds?"

"She laughs. She isn't so much pleased, though, when
some folks insist there's smugglers' treasure buried on
her land, chances are that some day someone may com-
mence digging. The house has been added to a lot since
the first owner's day, but in the main house the big
staircase, cornices and carved trim about the fireplace,
and the old kitchen are just what Sir Aubrey brought
over."

"Sounds like a museum piece. I'd like to see it."

"It's opened when other houses not so old are on view
for charity. Going to stay long?"

"That's on the knees of the gods and the progress I
make with my work. What's the low-spreading house on
the point beyond The Castle which looks as if it had
come FOB California?"

"That's Rockledge. Rented for the summer by a rich

woman, they say she's silent partner of a big cosmetic outfit."

"She'd need to be rich to keep up that place these days. Thanks for everything, Miss Ella. You'll be seeing me again."

After he left the shop he looked down at the bulky package in his hands.

"What in time will I do with this collection of bracelets after I send one to the sergeant's wife? Cousins! The only ones I have are several times removed. They would be surprised."

# TWO

CINDY'S FACE burned as she pedaled swiftly toward home. She was aware that the man had watched her take-off. Smarty. He had noticed the big bow on her hair and her bobby-soxer ensemble and pretended he thought her a schoolgirl. He hadn't been fresh or wolfish, just having fun. Perhaps the broad ribbon was too youthful for a gal twenty-four, but what else could one do when one detested a mane and was undecided whether to cut or not to cut? Wobbling was out. It would be cut tomorrow. Of course she shouldn't have spoken to him. Why care if he bought that hideous bracelet?

As to that why dwell on a mistake this heavenly day? Early August at its hottest and most colorful. Sumac against stone walls was beginning to show scarlet tips. The sky was a cloudless turquoise, the sky shaded from faint emerald on the sandy beach through rich jade green to ultramarine, to indigo and then to purple where it met and fused with the sky. A stiff breeze was capping in-rolling breakers with fleecy foam and shaking spicy fragrance from the tips of balsams and pines. A few raucously mewing gulls swept low over the beach tormenting a foolish brown setter that raced back and forth, back and forth in a frenzied, futile pursuit.

He was outstandingly good-looking, darn him, her thoughts deserted the beauties of nature and returned to *homo sapiens*. No hat, which fact made it safe to assume he was not a transient passing through the town, his reddish sports coat and beige slacks suggested vacation.

8

His handkerchief scarf had been a mixture of the two colors. Snappy dresser. A newcomer at the Inn? She laughed as she visualized the seasoned dungarees and shorts of the masculine old-timers.

Who is Sally? Trying to place a Sally in the community absorbed her thoughts till she reached the door of the rambling stone house with towers and turrets, the main body of which had been on the point of land jutting out into the sea longer than the oldest resident could remember.

She parked her bicycle against the iron railing at the side of the five stone steps, stopped to look across the lawn to the harbor, its shore fringed with lobster, fish and boat headquarters, its still water dotted with craft of many sizes and designs. Sir Aubrey had turned his back on the lonely expanse of ocean and had faced his house toward the color and incessant activity of the harbor. Between the shore with its boathouse and pier and The Castle was a lawn smooth as green velvet. The real-estate broker had been right, this was one location in a thousand. She had been offered a small fortune for it. Ought she to sell? She wondered as she entered the house through the tall classical doorway with its richly carved hood.

The long hall, with spiral staircase and Persian rugs on the waxed floor, was cool and shadowy in contrast to the blaze of sun outside. She backed up against the door and drew her hand across her eyes. Had they played tricks or had she seen the figure of a man, hat drawn low, dark against the sunlight sifting through white slats, slip out of the door which opened directly on the patio?

Of course it was her imagination stepped up by the talk she had had with Ella Crane about the movie company which had photographed the place last summer, and the write-up about the smugglers who, at times, could be heard tramping through the rooms—if ghosts tramp.

She caught a glimpse of herself in an overmantel mirror as she passed the arched opening of the ornate drawing room. Her costume was on the bobby-soxer

side. "Chocolate-malted? Ice-cream soda? Popsicles?"
Humorous guy, wasn't he?

She followed the sound of a male radioed voice.

"The wind-up. The pitch! Foul ball!" The shouts of a
crowd yelling itself hoarse. Sarah Ann Parker, a rabid
baseball fan, was listening to a game.

She passed through the old kitchen with dark hand-
hewn beams, Dutch oven with a long-handled warming
pan and glints of shining copper, open cupboard, but-
terfly-pegged floor of wide boards, pumpkin yellow walls
and matching cheesecloth hangings at the two twenty-
four paned windows, and entered the spotless, modern
white one with its electric equipment. A man's voice,
cracked with excitement, yelled:

"Two and two. Two men on base—two out and—"

The radio clicked off.

A tall, bony woman in checkered gingham, red as the
spots on her high cheekbones, her graying sandy hair
drawn back by a pearl comb with painful tightness
which lifted her eyebrows, pulled off her bone-rimmed
glasses. They hung by a spec-band as she declared:

"Thought you was never coming home, Cinderella.
Where you been all this time?"

"To the village. Um-m, luscious smell. What's bak-
ing?" Cindy inquired and perched on a high white stool.

"Brownies. You said you loved 'em. Want to know
somethin'? A message came for you, that's why I was so
anxious for you to get home. Counselor Armstrong
phoned he'd be along about four-thirty to talk with you.
I figured we'd better give him tea, he bein' the one
who's takin' care of your case."

She drew a pan from the oven, turned it over on a
wire cooler, pulled off the buttery waxed paper which
lined it and began to cut the nut-enriched chocolate
sheet into squares. She rapped the fingers reaching for a
piece.

"Don't touch it now, Cindy. 'Twill crumble 'fore it's
cool."

The girl wrinkled a charmingly modeled nose at her.

"You're a tyrant, Sarah Ann Parker."

The woman's face crinkled in as near a grin as her tightly drawn skin permitted.

"I've been housekeeper here years enough to watch the cooky jar and cakebox when you're around, child." The smile faded. "There was days, though, when you was off in the West when I would have baked from sunup to sundown if I could have had you back and known you were safe and happy. Your Pa had queer ideas 'bout bringing up a daughter, thought she ought to learn to look out for herself."

"The experience didn't hurt me, Sarah. As the days went on I learned that the ideas and ideals which Mother instilled for eighteen years made a sound foundation on which to build a design for living."

"Want to know somethin'? I think your Pa must have been crazy as a coot when he cooked up that marriage between his daughter and Kenniston Stewart, a man neither of you had seen."

"He hadn't seen him, but he knew he came from fine families on both sides, and you know father was a stickler for family, Sary."

"You're telling me, but I still can't understand why you did it, Cindy."

"I did it because at the time it seemed the right thing to do, and also, I'll confess to you, Sary, I had the silly idea it was romantic. His father sold me on him, told of his son's tenderness and devotion to his mother; of the boy's habit of bringing home lost dogs and cats to care for; of his success in athletics while he kept his scholarship high until he became my dream man. I was starting my sophomore year at college. My imagination, apt to work overtime, visualized Ken Stewart's return—in appearance a combination of Gary Cooper and Walter Pidgeon, at that time my favorite movie actors—saw him fall desperately for me, I for him, and we'd live happily ever after."

"Hmp. Things don't often work out that way, Cinderella."

"You're telling me. Long before the contract went through, the girl grew older and wiser, and wished she'd never heard of Kenniston Stewart. There were documents to be mailed back and forth, license regulations to be checked and followed; doctor's certificates O.K.'ing blood tests, it was made as difficult as possible and everything had to be kept hush-hush because our hero was on secret business."

"Didn't you know what he was doin'?"

"Yes, but I was sworn to secrecy. Every move was checked by Father's lawyer to be sure the contract of marriage conformed to the law of the state, that it couldn't be declared illegal. Dad and his partner suspected there would be financial wolves lying in wait to pounce if they saw the smidgin of a chance."

"An' after all that you're settin' out to break it. Ain't that human nature. What's that fella Stewart say about it?"

"He wants the annulment as much as I. He consented to the marriage to help his father, wrote that it was ten to one he wouldn't live through the work ahead. He was a major in command of a tough situation—he didn't say at the time what. His father told me. He wrote he thought me a grand person to help out, that if he lived he would aid in every way to annul the marriage—Dad's lawyer made me burn that, said it might invalidate the contract, that attorney was the original sharp-eye—added, 'If you're in love with someone *don't* do it, let the business go to'—you wouldn't approve of the word he used, Sary."

"Your pa and his have been gone more'n a year. Seems if he might have come home and straightened out that business mess. Want to know somethin'? Perhaps he's got a girl where he is he's plannin' to marry."

"I hope he has. All right with me. We have exchanged letters during the years. I did all the bookkeeping for the business from the time it was organized, I settled the estate of my father and his and submitted verbatim reports to him. Deposited his share of the income, kept records and forwarded monthly statements. The lawyer wrote him that he ought to be here to attend to the sale of the property. He long-distanced that he couldn't come, that whatever I decided would be all right with him. Atlas upheld the heavens on his shoulders, I've been holding up an oil property on mine. If we ever get rid of it I'll sleep for a week."

"Who's Atlas?"

"A mythological Greek. I suspect that the outfit which wanted to acquire our holdings when Dad was alive is behind this offer. I'm holding off, I scent a crooked deal. I wrote Ken Stewart months ago. It's too big a responsibility for me to handle alone. He has to sign the deed of sale, the would-be purchasers are not satisfied with my signature, although he gave me power of attorney. No answer."

"Want to know somethin'? Perhaps the poor boy is dead. He wrote he thought he'd never come back, didn't he? Perhaps you don't need no divorce."

"I might have to wait seven years to be sure before I was free. I would be practically an old lady, Sary."

"Sure 'tain't because you want to marry one of the lawyers, the Western fella, Slade, or that Hal Harding who's been on your trail ever since you've come back? I'd die, Cindy, if you took up with him, a twice-divorced man—besides that, folks is saying he's what they call 'pink.' "

"Relax, Sary. I don't intend to take up with anyone at present. I'm getting an annulment for separation in the state where I've kept my residence for years. I intend it to be the most legal release a woman ever had. That's the story, incredible as it sounds." She slipped off the stool.

"I'd better get a move on and dress to receive Counselor Armstrong. I've corresponded with him, but never met him." She visualized the man in the shop. "Is he tall and tanned and devastatingly good-looking?"

"You talking 'bout Trader Armstrong? That hands me a laugh. Sakes alive, child, don't you remember him? His family's lived here 'most as long as yours."

"I haven't lived here for years except for a short time in the summer, remember."

"You're right. Trader—that's what he was called when he was growin' up in this village, 'cause one time he owned the marbles of every kid in town—is bald and short and broad and bouncy, if you get what I mean. Powerful smart, though. He was born here, keeps up the family place fine, went to college, then to New York. Married young, she died when her baby come, so'd the baby. He never took another wife. He's made a big name and a lot of money, folks say. His sister Alida married Lord Barclay—a real lord with a fortune he'd made in this country. She was a beauty, still is, she arrived with him. I hear she's brought a cook and two maids, looks like she's figurin' on doing some entertaining."

"Did she bring the fabulously rich and titled husband?"

"Sakes no. He died long before the war. He'd just been made a citizen when Burke's Peerage began advertising for him in this country. He wouldn't go back, let the title and estate go to a cousin. Lucky, that kept his fortune here. Trader always was terrible proud and fond of Ally. During the war and long after she worked with our army in hospitals abroad. Folks call her Lady Barclay, though she insists she's plain Mrs. Neil Barclay."

"Sounds as if I had a good man to work for me."

"He's good, has a license or whatever he has to have to practice here, and an office. Town talk is, he's got the Congressional bee in his bonnet. Run along and get dressed. Get off them pants. 'Tain't fittin' for a girl your age to be runnin' round in them."

"There's something in what you say, Sary." Cindy swallowed a gurgle of laughter as the ice-cream soda invitation flashed through her memory. "I hasten to make myself beautiful."

"Guess you won't have to work too hard at it. I've got the table set with the Lowestoft and the best silver in what you've called the pat-i-o, since you come back from the West."

"You're a dear to take so much trouble." She paused in the doorway. "Know a gal among the cottagers named Sally? Blondish?"

"Sally? Only Sally I know is Mrs. Drew, the woman who last May leased the newfangled house on the point matches this across the cove. You can see it plain from that seat on our point. I sit there a lot to watch what goes on. She's a sort of blond and claims she's a widow. Town talk is she's lookin' for number two. Want to know somethin'? Every little while a big boat drops anchor off Rockledge shore an' signals. I guess she goes off in it. So kind of mysterious it gives me the hibby-jibbies."

"This is a mysterious neighborhood Sary, if you believe the smugglers' legend. That reminds me, did a man call just before I came—to sell something?"

"I didn't see one."

"Have you been here all day?"

"Except for a few minutes after lunch when I run across the inlet in the dory—that Evinrude motor sure makes it easy—to Mis' Drew's. Hal Harding came through the garden looking for you just as I was leavin'. When I told him I expected you any minute, he said he'd hang around till you came. Guess he got tired of waiting. He was gone when I got back. Who do you think is parlormaid at Mis' Drew's—Rena Foster."

"Wasn't she a waitress at the Inn? Didn't she leave under a cloud?"

"That's her. Nothing was ever proved against her, though. She was always a flighty piece."

"Apparently you don't approve of her. Why did you go to see her?"

"She phoned and asked if I'd come over and tell her how to make hot mushroom *canapés,* said she'd heard mine were out of this world. Poor thing, she's tryin' to earn a living. I'm glad to help her. Why'd you ask if I'd been here all day?"

Cindy disciplined a laugh. Praise of her cooking is Sary's Achilles heel, she thought before she answered.

"I saw a man—near the house. Had an idea he might have been here. I'm so used to having men, sometimes women, want to talk business with me that I see them in my dreams."

"I hope when you get this law case settled folks'll let you alone." Sarah glanced at the banjo clock. "Most

four-thirty. New York lawyers won't put up with bein'
kept waitin', Cindy."

"You're telling me about lawyers. Believe me, I've met
a grist of them during the last three years. I'm on my
way."

# THREE

SHE RAN up the stairs to the accompaniment of a raucous voice:

"The wind-up, the pitch! Two *balls!*"

Sarah listening to the game again. This part of the country had gone baseball mad.

She showered, then dressed in her room with its cool ivory walls and sea-green hangings and cushions, where sunlight glinted between Venetian slats. Her mind was busy lining up questions to ask Counselor Armstrong. "Trader," Sarah had called him. The nickname grated. Reminded her too much of the gang which her father and his partner had suspected was out to acquire their oil holdings. She had been assured by the broker who was handling the sale that the present buyers had no connection with the former outfit, but, suspicion that they had made her hesitate about selling. Ken Stewart had given her power of attorney. It was too big a responsibility to shoulder. Why didn't he come home and share it?

Allah be praised, the sale couldn't affect the annulment. Hal Harding, about whom Sarah Ann Parker was having a brain storm, had recommended Armstrong when she had asked him the name of a Maine lawyer. He had advised her to have the divorce put through in her home state, he should be an authority, he had had two. If she were in a rush, he would suggest Reno.

Not in that much of a rush, she told herself as she fastened her hair at the neck with a long silver arrow. Neither was Ken Stewart, apparently. Months ago she

17

had written him she had been advised that an annulment of the marriage now would in no way threaten their inheritance, would he co-operate?

He not only would but with bells on, he had cabled. Go to it. He wasn't even interested to see what the girl he had married was like. Not too bad, she decided as she critically inspected her reflection in the long mirror. The leaf-green cotton taffeta frock, with the soft yellow velvet ribbon belt into which she had tucked a few calendulas, brought out the sheen of her hair and the brown of her eyes, the golden tan of her skin.

"He'll never know what a charmer he lost, will he, gal?" she queried aloud and wrinkled her nose in self-derision at the looking-glass girl. "Hal Harding appreciates you, lady."

Her eyes shadowed, her smile vanished. Hal was terribly likable, but he was making life difficult. He had waylaid her in the village this morning to tell her that he was planning a gala outdoor roast at his place, on the day her annulment was granted, to celebrate her freedom. Darn. Everyone in town had known of what they called "the proxy marriage," now talk of the annulment was crowding the air waves.

"I don't want a celebration," she protested under her breath as she went slowly down the stairs. "It's a poisonous idea to make whoopee over a broken marriage, even if it's only a written contract like mine. I won't stand for it."

Seth Armstrong rose and came forward with pudgy hand outstretched in greeting when she entered the patio. He was neither so short, bald nor stout as she had imagined him from Sary's description. A little bouncy, but nice manners. A boutonniere of deep blue bachelor buttons adorned the lapel of his expertly tailored gray sports coat, his white trousers were immaculate and creased to perfection, his eyes were pale, but keen, his voice was a trifle unctuous, the waxen whiteness of his plump hands was accentuated by a huge sardonyx ring. The big seal on the bracelet man's finger had seemed to belong; for some remote reason that on Armstrong's seemed out of character. Not especially attractive, but trustworthy, she decided.

"At last we meet, Mrs. Stewart. It is a pleasure I have long anticipated. I haven't seen you since you were little Cindy Clinton."

Mrs. Stewart. It was a shock to hear the name again. Since her return to The Castle two months ago she had been Cindy Clinton to neighbors and friends.

"Thank you, Mr. Armstrong. I am afraid I have given you a lot of trouble by asking you to come here, but I am eager to get this annulment business behind me. I hope you drink tea?"

She seated herself at the glass-top table which held the antique Sheffield tray with its equipment of silver and Lowestoft and the hot-water kettle spouting pearly steam. He drew a chair beside her. She wondered if his thoughts were as large and smooth as his white hands.

"Certainly I drink tea." He had a curious habit of inflating and deflating his cheeks before speaking. "My secretary serves it for me in my New York office each afternoon at four. Lovely place you have made of this spot between the two slanting ells."

Cindy's eyes followed his as they traveled round the enclosure, open on the fourth side to a superb view of the ocean. A velvety lawn was broken in the center by a small pool carpeted by green pads and pink and white lilies between which flashed an occasional streak of gold. The spray from a small fountain shot up into the sunshine, glittered like yellow diamonds before it dropped back. Beyond that a putting green extended almost to the shore.

Against the gray stone walls of the house, perennials put on a flower show of gorgeous color; humming birds poised above red and pink hollyhocks; a bee reeled drunkenly from out the depths of a mammoth regal lily; a great yellow moth fanned black-streaked wings on the tall, light-blue spike of a second-blossoming larkspur beside a rosy clump of phlox; a cloud of small yellow butterflies hovered above the orange king and lemon queen calendulas. On a window ledge a cat, black as the wings of a dragonfly hovering above a clump of tawny zinnias below her, regarded with blank topaz eyes a robin cautiously bathing in the shallows of the pool. Green chintz on white wicker chairs matched the lawn in shade. A light salty breeze shook fragrance from the flowers and spicy scent from a windbreak of balsams. Cindy's attention returned to the man beside her.

"It is nice here. Sarah Ann Parker has been a wonderful housekeeper and friend. She kept up my garden while I was away. Is your tea the right strength?"

"Perfect. This toasted *canapé* is tops. What's the spread?"

"Mushrooms. Try one of the lobster salad rolls. They are something to write home about. I can say that as I didn't make them."

"No, thanks. I am reserving space for the brownies. I'm a chocolate addict."

Gourmand, I'll bet. He actually licked his chops when he looked at that plate, Cindy thought.

They chatted about local matters till, after asking permission, he lighted a cigar.

"Now, may we talk business?" Cindy inquired eagerly. "I am anxious to hear a report of what you have accomplished."

"No more anxious than I am to get ahead with the matter." He drew a sheaf of papers from an inside pocket of his gray coat. "At long last I have succeeded in getting an answer from your husband."

"My husband! Glory be, I had almost forgotten I had one. I haven't, really. We'll have the table cleared, you may want me to sign something. Signing papers has been the major occupation of my life these last years."

She tinkled a small silver bell. Sarah Ann Parker emerged with a promptness that suggested she had been watching from the windows of the kitchen in the east ell.

"How's tricks, Trader?" The familiarity of the woman's greeting deepened the red of Armstrong's already sufficiently ruddy face. "I hear Ally's come for a visit with you. How is she?"

"Fine. Still young and smart for your age, I see, Sarah Ann." His unctuous voice had sharpened to razor edge.

Holding the laden tray Sarah paused halfway to the door which opened into the kitchen.

"Smart? Why not, Trader? I'm only sixty, five years younger than you. Wearin' bach buttons in your coat—bachelor buttons an' you a widower. Kinder got the signals mixed, haven't you, Trader?" She winked broadly at Cindy. A moment later the door to the kitchen closed with a bang.

"That seems to be that," Armstrong breathed a sigh of relief. "Even as a girl Sarah Ann Parker had a tongue sharp as a serpent's fang. Age hasn't dulled it. My sister, Alida Barclay, wants to meet you, Mrs. Stewart. She will call, after which we hope you will dine with us."

Having observed the social amenities he drew a letter from a long envelope, tried to tilt back in the chair, which refused to tilt, and laid the paper on the glass table.

"This is from Kenniston Stewart in answer to my letter asking if he would consent to the annulment of the marriage."

"*Consent*? That was a silly question to ask. He wants his freedom as much as I want mine."

"Asking his consent is a matter of form to be filed with the records of the case."

"Does he say why he didn't answer my question, shall I sell the oil holdings?"

"Read the letter aloud. I'd like to hear it."

Cindy picked up the sheet of paper, skipped the formal beginning, read:

I have been away from the base on an assignment, have just received your letter and Mrs. Stewart's [so he thinks of me as *Mrs.* Stewart, that's a laugh] re the sale of our holdings. I am in no position to advise. Fortunately a fellow officer, an engineer and authority on patents who knows something of the country in which our property is located, is returning to the States. I have appointed him my proxy to relieve her of some responsibility. He has a power of attorney, which automatically cancels the one I gave to Mrs. Stewart. He will confer with her and with you. Whatever he advises is my decision. I trust him implicitly.

As to the annulment, I am all for it. It was a crazy contract. I will sign any papers that will annul it, but, I suggest that it wait until *after* the property is sold—if it is sold. The marriage was cooked up to protect the holdings, I think it should hold, while we own the property. However, I will leave that to the judgment of you and Colonel Bill Damon—Bill, not William—who has been commissioned by me to decide that matter also.

Yours truly,
*Kenniston Stewart*

"I won't delay the annulment." Cindy crushed the letter in her hand. "Who does Ken Stewart think he is? My overlord? Forward the papers he should sign, Mr. Armstrong. If he doesn't reply wouldn't it mean, case uncontested? I've seen an expression like that in accounts of divorce trials. If he thinks I'll let this other man decide what I am to do, he has another think coming to him. What is this deputy's name?" She smoothed out the crumpled sheet. "Colonel Bill Damon. Ever hear of him?"

"No, I doubt if we do. A man who has been abroad for years won't bother himself with another chap's troubles, he'll have plans of his own. We'll proceed with the annulment—and the sale of the property. I'm boarding a plane tonight for the oil holdings, be back in a week. You have the power of attorney Stewart sent you. That's good till this other shows up, if it ever does."

"Ken Stewart advised the sale first. If he isn't sufficiently interested to come home—don't tell me he couldn't get leave after all these years if he wanted it—and attend to the matter himself, I will take over. We'll crack that marriage contract first."

"I agree with Stewart. The sale first. You have an excellent offer. If you wait you may lose it. Are you sure you want to sell that valuable property?"

"Yes. I think you should know that Kenniston Stewart loaned his father and mine the capital—he had inherited his mother's fortune—with which to lease the land, develop their patents, buy the needed tools, and drill test-wells. As fast as income came in Father would deduct what we needed for living and pay the balance into Ken Stewart's account. Since he died I have done the same, until now my share is free and clear of indebtedness to him."

"You've been very wise for one so young, Mrs. Stewart."

"I couldn't bear the thought of owing money. This letter has steeled my decision. The annulment of the marriage first. I won't wait a minute for that deputy of Ken Stewart's who may never come. I—What is it, Sary?" she asked of the woman who appeared at the door.

"There's a man on the phone who wants to speak to you. Says he's a friend of your husband, says his name is Bill Damon."

Surprise brought Cindy to her feet. She looked inquiringly at Armstrong, before she said crisply:

"Tell the gentleman that I am too busy to see him now or *ever*."

# FOUR

WITH a 35 mm. camera containing color film hung from her neck, Cindy paused before she entered the Club bathhouse to change her violet and white checked playsuit for swim clothes. She drew a deep breath of the briny air straight off the ocean. What a day. The sandy beach curved in between two low promontories walled by jagged brown boulders. The white frilled tide flowed and ebbed lazily. Far out beyond a stationary float breakers broke whitely against a reef with a rhythmic *Boom! Boom! Boom!*

Life and color everywhere. A balloon man surrounded by near-naked youngsters occupied stage-center, his green and red and yellow spheres bobbing and tugging at their strings against a backdrop of clear blue sky and malachite sea. Children digging. Building. Licking arsenic-green Popsicles. Dogs watching hungrily. Gay umbrellas. Canopied chairs. Figures outstretched on the sand in colorful scraps of clothing staring up at the sky through the black lenses of sunglasses. Man and woman pacing the beach, her multi-colored parasol a moving splash of vivid color. Gypsy in enormous hat peddling baskets. Stout woman with ankle-length skirt wading. Diminutive black cloud of sandpipers on the wing. Girl in crimson one-piece bathing suit on the step of a pavilion applying lipstick. Flashy man in black-and-white check suit, soft hat drawn low over one eye ogling her. Human interest. They were both facing her. Something familiar about the tough guy. She focused her camera on the couple and snapped it. The man must have heard the click, for he eyed her with a baleful glare.

Little boys tumbled in and out of the lifeguard's dory drawn high on the beach. That lifeguard. Jim d'Arcy. His first season here. Bossy creature. Female admiration had gone to his head. He rated admiration. She would hand him that. Tall, slim, straight as an arrow. Lean hips. Brief sky-blue trunks on a perfect body beautifully tanned. With wings on his white cap and at his heels, his right arm raised, his left upholding a caduceus, he would be Giovanni di Bologna's bronze Mercury come to life.

She made a little face in his direction. She had had two tilts with him since her arrival. Twice he had followed her in his boat to remind her that swimmers were not allowed beyond the float, as if she hadn't just realized that she was out of bounds. Of course he had been in the right, but his manner had infuriated her.

She entered the bathhouse barely avoiding collision with a woman going out. She looked after the as-near-as-nothing-as-the-law-allows clothed figure with its unbecoming rolls of flesh and shook her head. After spending hours on this beach, observing the swim clothes many women wear, no one ever will convince me that my sex is vain, she told herself.

Her .cap matched the string of large turquoise-color porcelain beads at the base of her throat, as in a white sharkskin suit with a brief pleated skirt she ran toward the shore. As she passed the pavilion she heard the girl in the red swim suit say:

"I'll try. Give me time—"

"Shut up," a low voice warned.

The black-and-white check man and the girl whose pictures she had snapped were quarreling. Evidently they were pals and she had thought he was being given the come-on, Cindy decided before she waded into the water and struck out for the float.

"Come back!"

A man's shout. That pesky lifeguard again. She wasn't anywhere near out of bounds. She glanced up at the plane only a trifle less blue than the sky, deafeningly thrumming above her head.

Another call. What did it mean? She raised her shoulders from the water and looked ahead. A motorboat just beyond the float was making a beeline for her. Was the person at the wheel stark *mad?* She looked again. There was no one at the wheel. The boat was running amok, was headed for her with diabolic intent.

Memories of stories she had heard of swimmers beheaded or rendered footless by a propeller blade, panicked her, paralyzed her arms and legs. She must make the float. Her haven seemed miles ahead in a rough jade-green sea.

"Steady. Take it easy!"

The voice rose above the hum of the oncoming motor. An arm seized her and dragged her down, down, down. Instinctively she closed her lips and eyes. It seemed but an instant before she rose to the surface and a breathless voice encouraged:

"It has gone over us. You can make the float. Only a foot ahead."

A huge wave made by the careening boat, a hand on her wrist, and another under her armpit lifted her to the rough boards. She clung to an iron ring. The lifeguard had disappeared. She'd never call him bossy again. Had he gone under? Had he been struck by the propeller while saving her? She flung herself flat and reached down with one hand.

"This way. This way," she called. "Grab my arm and I'll pull you up."

A black head appeared. A voice shouted.

"Get back. I'm all right. Hold on. Another giant swell coming."

One hand gripping the iron ring, the other clutching the edge of the float with all her strength, she clung while the water swept over her and knocked the breath from her body. She opened her eyes as a man with her blue cap in one hand pulled himself up beside her; sat back on her heels, shook water from her hair, and looked up into clear gray eyes in a tanned face. The bracelet man.

"You? I thought it was the lifeguard. Thank heaven you're safe. If anything had happened to you because you came to my aid—"

"Forget it. Here's your cap. O.K?"

"Yes. Still a trifle jittery. I was frightened. I had visions of appearing in the future with my head tucked under my arm like the headless horseman when in pursuit of Ichabod. Don't look at me as if you suspected I'd gone haywire. Talking like a house afire helps me relax. It seems painfully inadequate to say 'Thank you.' I wouldn't have made it without you."

"Stop imagining gruesome possibilities. The crazy craft is now shooting toward the open sea. Just escaped piling up on the ledge. Out of our lives forever."

"How far will it run?"

"Till the gas gives out."

"What do you suppose became of the skipper? Drowned?" She shivered.

"It is more probable that a new owner, wet behind the ears, started the engine, then stepped out of the boat for something, and the cagey thing shot off on a little joy ride of its own. Why didn't you turn back when I shouted?"

"I thought it was the brand-new lifeguard getting bossy. We have had two showdowns. I've been bathing on this beach all my life, it's more fun than going in alone off The Castle shore. I thought the hum I heard was from the plane overhead."

"I was the lifeguard, pro tem, while the boy went for his lunch. Ready to go back?"

"I'll sit here and sun for a while. Don't let me keep you."

"Thanks for the suggestion, but I like to finish a job I start. You are still shaking."

She had hoped he had not noticed her poorly suppressed shivers.

"It's a silly reaction I have after fright. I acknowledge I was scared stiff. I couldn't move. It really doesn't mean a thing. It's just the way I'm made." She kicked the water into foam to emphasize indifference.

"If you feel that way about it I'll go. I can see Jim

d'Arcy's white cap. He's back on the job. I'll leave you and report to him." He dived.

"Don't—" she snapped her lips together before the word "go" escaped. The thought of being left alone panicked her. Never before had she been afraid of the ocean. Slowly she pulled on the turquoise blue cap. The yellow beach where the tide ruffled whitely seemed miles away. Could she make it?

A brown hand with a seal ring gripped the edge of the float. A sleek wet head appeared. A shoulder with an ugly jagged reddish scar followed. White teeth gleamed in a strongly lined bronzed face.

"How about it? Ready to be good and come along with me?"

"Am I? Watch me. Just watch me." She slid into the water.

He fitted his stroke to hers. They swam toward shore side by side till they could touch the sand with their feet, then waded in. They walked up the beach to the music of "Good Luck and the Same to You" coming from a portable radio.

"I saw British Tommies marching to that tune just before I left London," he said. "Better stop a minute. You are still breathless."

She sank to the sand beside a colorful plaid beach robe, and pulled off the turquoise blue cap.

"The stiffening appears to have oozed from my knees temporarily. I'll sit here till it returns to normal. A million thanks for your help. Don't feel you must wait for me."

"When I go in for a rescue stunt I hang around till I am sure my patient is O.K." His straight body was as brown as the lifeguard's, his trunks as blue as the sky. He pulled on the gay beach robe. "As you see, I like exuberant colors. With your permission." He dropped down beside her.

"We're about the only persons left on the beach except d'Arcy and the girl in the red one-piece snuggling up to the man in the loud suit," he observed.

"I snapped a picture of them, they seem so out of character on this beach. Later they were quarreling as I passed. They seem to have made it up now. I have the most curious feeling I've seen him, the tilt of his hat, before."

He laughed.

"Sure you have. In the movies. That is bad boy Humphrey Bogart's tilt to the fraction of an inch." He drew a package of cigarettes and a lighter from a pocket in the beach robe and offered them.

"Have one?"

"No, thanks." She waited until he had blown a smoke ring or two. "Did your Sally like the bracelet?" she inquired.

"Sally was improvised at the moment to give the hatchet-faced Ella the impression that you and I were old friends. I bought it to send to a homesick woman overseas."

"You didn't fool Ella Crane for a minute. She fancies she's psychic. She has been owner and head bottle-washer of that shop for years. It is not only a listening post, it is a major clearing station with broadcasting facilities for town gossip. That woman has seen me grow up and never lets me forget the fact."

"Then you are grown-up?"

She liked the way his eyes which could be piercingly keen collaborated with his mouth when he smiled.

"Certainly I'm grown-up. I have been handling business affairs for three years and not a child prodigy, either. I am a certified accountant."

"Fancy that. What's happened to your hair since yesterday? Your head is covered with short curls."

"I had it cut this morning. Fortunately it has a natural wave." She ran the fingers of her right hand through the wet hair. "It will look more presentable when it dries."

"Even wet it has a golden glint. I thought the chatty Ella called you Cinderella. Right?"

"Right. It is my name, worse luck. Now don't quip, 'Has the Prince found your slipper?' It was amusing the first time I heard it, but it has lost its rapier edge."

He threw back his head and laughed a spontaneous

laugh of genuine amusement which made one think,
"What a bright girl am I."

"Good line. Sorry I didn't think of it first."

Stretched out at length, resting on one elbow, he began
to scoop, mold and pat the sand till it assumed outlines.
Fascinated she watched his long, supple brown fingers
add a tiny turret to the structure.

"As there is no Prince in the offing, another castle for
Cinderella," he explained.

"It's a masterpiece. Even to the little windows. Pity
the tide will wash it away."

"The castle for my Cinderella can't be washed away.
It will be built on a rock."

"Are you—" she remembered the jagged scar—"were
you an architect before you went into the service?"

"As an avocation only. I have helped my friends when
they made over old houses. Sometimes I help them in
other ways, also—I was off to a good start as a consulting
engineer when Uncle Sam called me."

A quizzical light in the eyes that challenged hers when
he said "Sometimes I help them in other ways, also"
clanged a warning. She sprang to her feet.

"You are Bill Damon," she accused. "Why didn't you
tell me?"

# FIVE

HE SWEPT the little castle flat and rose.

"Why should I? You refused to speak to him when he phoned. I couldn't very well stop and introduce him when that boat was shooting for us, could I?"

"I still don't want to talk with you."

"That's just too bad. Because I am in this town to stay and we are likely to meet. Remember I told you that when I started a job I hung on till it was finished?"

"Are you referring to the job for Kenniston Stewart?"

"That is one of them."

"Why doesn't he come home and settle the matter himself?"

"Why are you so bitter against Ken? Is it a defense mechanism? Not in love with him, are you?"

"In *love* with him. That's the funniest thing I ever heard. I've never even seen a picture of him—and you may be sure he never has seen one of me. I refused to send it, not that he asked for one, it was his father's suggestion. Didn't the chatty Ella tell you the story of my life? I'll bet she did, pulling out all the stops. I'm the town's Exhibit A. Haven't you heard about me from the man whom you are here to represent?"

"Yes, but I would like your side of it. I want to be absolutely fair. Why did you do it?"

"Do what? Marry Ken Stewart or start the annulment?"

"Let's take first things first. Marry?"

"At the time it seemed the valid solution of a problem. He and I consented to help his father and mine.

31

Because looking back it seems a cockeyed proceeding doesn't alter the fact that it appeared to be the only way out then."

"Sit down again, *please*. Be sensible. Let's thresh out this matter of your aversion to Bill Damon and get it behind us. I'd like to be friends. Believe it or not, I've seen enough fighting to last the rest of my life."

After an instant of hesitation she sank to the beach. He dropped down beside her and clasped his brown hands about his knees. Her eyes were on her fingers, through which she sifted sand.

"This is a lot more comfortable," he approved. "Now that the smoke of battle has cleared, I can see no reason why you and I should be enemies, even if you detest the man whom I am here to represent. I can't make a move till I know your side of it. First, having decided it was wise to contract the marriage, why dissolve it? You and Ken still hold the property."

"Apparently Ella Crane omitted the fact that the ardent bridegroom has not been interested to return to this country and take his share of the business load."

"Maybe he realized that you were under emotional pressure, that as nothing could be done about your freedom till the property was settled, he was giving you a clear uncontested plea of separation. The three years since the signing of the marriage contract were up a week ago, weren't they? Looks to me as if he has given you a chance to make a watertight case by keeping away."

" 'Want to know something?' That's a quote—I can't think of him as being so understanding. Mr. Armstrong told me yesterday that Ken Stewart is as eager to have that marriage annulled as I am."

"Who is Mr. Armstrong?"

"My legal adviser."

"The proxy?"

"Good heavens, *no*. There *wasn't* a proxy. The deed was done by signed contracts." Her mouth widened in a smile. "Tom Slade who was in the office of the lawyer who represented Father's interests is tall, slender, lithe, blond and terribly good-looking. The New York-Maine lawyer is broad and short and ruddy. Understanding, though."

"How did he know the sentiments of the indifferent husband?"

"They have corresponded. Counselor Armstrong—as he is called here—showed me a letter yesterday in which Kenniston Stewart reiterated his eagerness to dissolve the tie that binds." She hummed the last words to the tune of the hymn.

"You don't believe in the inviolability of contracts, do you?"

"It would be rank sentimentality if I believed in the inviolability of this one. I go through a form of marriage to save Father's business, the son of another man agrees to co-operate to save his, naturally, as he had advanced the capital to make that same business possible. After the contracts are signed, sealed and delivered, Tom Slade slips a ring provided by the distant groom's father on my finger, orates theatrically, 'With this ring—' I stopped his quote right there—and the deed was done."

"Where is it now?"

"The ring? In the safe in my workroom."

"Why aren't you wearing it? You are still Mrs. Stewart."

"I've worn it for three years. I'll so soon be free, I've shed it except for formal occasions. And now for the soap-opera touch. After all the scheming of the two fathers, the messing up of the lives of their children, there is the possibility that the holdings will be sold for a song because of faulty registration of patents and leases, but of course, Ken Stewart has briefed you on that. You're here as his deputy."

"Who discovered they are faulty?"

"The parties who wanted to buy."

"You said that Counselor Armstrong has been corresponding with your husband recently?"

"My husband? Your mistake, there isn't such a person."

"This marriage is a joke to you, isn't it?"

"And why not? A girl and man who never had met

make a *mariage de convenance*. It is no longer a neces-
sity. In fact the groom had intimated he is interested
elsewhere."

"Could it be possible that you are also?"

"Not only possible but probable."

"You are a hard-boiled female."

Her brown eyes widened in amazement.

"Why should I pretend affection for a man with
whom I put through a business deal because of a pas-
sionate desire to ease the mind of my father who, I
knew, hadn't long to live? Not for a minute. I'll save
that for the one I love."

"Tom Slade or a man named Harding?"

"What do you know about him?"

"I had quite a visit with the talkative Ella."

"That, *mon brave,* ends the Information Please quiz.
Good-by and I mean good-by." He caught her hand and
held it so that she couldn't rise.

"Just a minute. You can't give me the brush-off. I've
fallen hard for this village. I intend to remain here until
I've finished my book—and Ken Stewart's business. I'm
here to represent him. I can make the going rough for
you. I hold the power of attorney. Better be good. I will
phone for an appointment with your lawyer for this
afternoon to present my credentials."

"He's away. He has gone to check on the oil property.
He won't be back for a week."

"Too bad, it postpones your freedom just so much
longer. I'm glad he is looking over the holdings. He will
be able to understand my figures. I have been deputed
by Stewart to make sure your interests are protected in
the sale, if there is one, so there will be no chance of
unpleasant repercussions—"

"No chance that I may sue him, you mean."

"That is unfair. You want the annulment to go
through without a flaw, don't you?"

"Since my talk with Counselor Armstrong yesterday, I
want it more than ever."

"Good. Meantime, can't we be friends? There will be
many matters of business to discuss. I would be mighty
uncomfortable to feel that you hated me."

"I don't hate you. Work fast to get me free and you'll be my dreamboat."

"Thanks for the smile. With the aforementioned incentive your affairs will have my immediate and undivided attention. Ella Crane told me that THE PROXY in capital letters is expected here. Right?"

"Haven't I made you understand that there wasn't a proxy? My word, you won't drag in Tom Slade as my reason for wanting the divorce, will you?"

"Certainly not, it is a clear case of desertion, though I think a situation like yours and Ken's is called separation. I wish you would stop talking about divorce, you are after an annulment. We'll take up that after we settle the business. I went over the Clinton-Stewart oil holdings before I came here. No flaw in the leases. The registration of the patents is unimpeachable. I threshed out that matter with the Court. My mind is stuffed with figures and facts."

"What is he like?"

"Who? The Court?"

"Kenniston Stewart, of course." She became intent on the flow of sand between her fingers. "Has he—does he—do people know he is married?"

"You switched subjects so fast I lost my bearings. *Know?* That's the funniest question I ever heard." His spontaneous laugh deepened the color in her cheeks. "You don't think that a marriage by proxy—"

"By written contract."

"Written contract, could hide its light under a bushel, do you? The families of officers had just begun to come over when the news broke and did the wives eat it up. 'So romantic,' they agreed over the teacups."

"Does he—does he act like a man who is married?"

"Now just what do you mean by that? He wears the ring you sent him on—"

"I *never* sent him a ring."

"He thinks you did. I wonder if his father provided a ring for him as he did for you—poor old fella—trying to inject some sentiment into the cut-and-dried arrangement? Next question in your What-is-he-like quiz."

"You think this situation is a huge joke, don't you?"

"I do *not* think it a huge joke. Neither does Ken Stewart. I wish you took it as seriously as he does. Just what more do you want to know about him?"

"Is—is he—wild? That's a terribly old-fashioned word, I got it from Dad."

"If you mean by 'wild' does he drink? He doesn't. He cut out that entirely when he began to fly. Gambling doesn't interest either of us."

"Does he—does he take out girls? Does he appear to be terribly in love with someone?"

"Cinderella Clinton—Stewart, he and I have been on the same job for weeks and months and years. There has been no time for either of us to be 'terribly in love.' You don't realize—"

"Hi, Cindy!" She sprang to her feet in response to the voice.

A fair-haired, hatless man in gray flannels followed his hail as fast as he could make it with his feet sinking into the sand at every impetuous step. He caught the girl's hands eagerly extended.

"You're terrific in that white swim suit, lovely. The three years are up and here I am." His jubilant smile changed to a scowl as he became aware of the bronzed man in the plaid beach robe standing beside her. "Who's your friend?"

Cindy glanced up into the keen eyes intently watching her. Something in them sent the color in a pink tide to her hair, caught at her breath. She put her hand to her throat as if to relieve the tightness.

"He isn't my friend. He claims he is here as my almost ex-husband Kenniston Stewart's trusted adviser. He has put on a good act but not *quite* good enough. I'm wondering. Let's go, Tom." She linked her arm in Slade's and with a flippant nod to the man regarding her with inscrutable eyes took a step forward.

"Just a minute!" She stopped at the sharp command. "A few moments ago you declared I was Bill Damon. Now you intimate I am someone else. Better hop off the fence and decide who I am. It will make a heap of difference in your future. Good morning."

She watched him as he strode toward the bathhouse before she turned puzzled eyes to Slade.

"Now I am mixed up. Who do you think he is, Tom?"

"How would I know? Never laid eyes on the fella till a minute ago. If you ask me, I'll bet he's a guy horning in for a take when the oil property is sold, like one of those five-per-centers being front-paged in Washington. Jupiter, why the heck are we spending a minute on him? Hustle into some clothes and we'll go somewhere and celebrate."

Cindy hustled. Inside the bathhouse she frowned at her locker. It was scratched around the keyhole as if a knife had been applied. She unlocked it quickly. The contents had not been disturbed. Who would try to get in? For what? She had a sudden vision of the baleful eyes she had met when she clicked the camera.

The man in the black and white checks. Had he tried to get the film? He wouldn't be allowed in this locker room. The girl? She had said, "Give me time," and the man had snapped, "Shut up." Had he reason for not wanting to be photographed?

"Hi, Cindy? I'm waiting!"

In response to Tom Slade's call she dressed hurriedly and slipped the cord of the camera over her head.

"Forgotten we're going places, Cinderella?" he reminded as she appeared in the doorway.

"No, Tom." She glanced toward the pavilion. The man and the girl in the red swim suit had gone.

# SIX

THEY STOPPED at The Castle while she changed to an
aqua linen shirtwaist frock and fastened a pink rose at
the opening of the Eton collar. Later, seated in Tom
Slade's Town and Country convertible, she had the curious feeling that Time had given the day a shake and her
life had fallen into an entirely different pattern as the
colored fragments shift in a kaleidoscope.

"Had your hair cut," Slade observed. "It's terrific,
lovely. Whither? You know the high spots here. We'll
make a day of it. O.K.?"

"Double O.K. Are you staying at the Inn?"

"Uh-huh. Arrived this morning early."

"Let's stop there and inquire if a man named Bill
Damon, Colonel Bill Damon, is registered. You can tell
the clerk you are expecting a friend and are interested
to know if he has arrived."

"Why the fictional approach? Do you still doubt that
the guy on the beach is the person he claims to be?"

"I just want to know if he is really Bill Damon, here
to represent Kenniston Stewart."

"You don't need anyone to represent Kenniston Stewart. I'm here."

"I know you are here and I'm worried. Something
tells me you had better keep out of the limelight. Page
Counselor Armstrong for confirmation of that opinion.
To return to the man we left behind us. You sold me on
the idea that he might be other than he claims when
you said: 'I'll bet he's a guy horning in for a take when

38

the oil property is sold, like one of those five-per-centers being front-paged.'" She had a close-up of the man's steady eyes, his suggestion of invincibility. "He gives me a shivery sense of ruthlessness, but much as I dislike him, I believe he is honest."

"But, not so sure that you don't want to check on him, are you? Here we are at the Inn. Snappy outfit with prices in character. I've never seen such corking flower borders."

"We do those things well in the State of Maine."

He whistled softly.

"And here comes a sliver of pulchritude who fits into the picture," he declared as a girl in white linen blouse and shorts, tennis racquet under her left arm, ran down the broad steps. Her short hair was definitely red, not auburn. Her eyes were definitely green, not hazel. She stopped beside the convertible with a dramatic start of surprise.

"Cindy Clinton, as I'm alive!" Her eyes lingered for a split second on the man at the wheel before they flashed back to the girl beside him.

"Or is it Cinderella Stewart now? Is this the absent groom returned to claim his bride at long last?"

The mocking voice sent hot color to Cindy's hair. Cat! Pride conquered anger.

"Wrong number, Lyd." Her voice was miraculously gay considering the tumult within. "May I present Thomas Slade, attorney, from the great open spaces. Tom, Lydia Fane, the runner-up for the State of Maine Tennis Championship last year."

Slade, who had stepped from the car, gently pressed the hand Miss Fane eagerly extended.

"I can't see you as a runner-up," he declared smoothly. "You look like champ material to me—in every way."

"Tom is staying here at the Inn." Cindy was giving the girl a chance to think up a reply worthy of the saccharine tribute. "His tennis is something to write home about, too."

"Really?" The green of Lydia Fane's eyes deepened. "There are so few men here you'll be mobbed, Mr.——"

"Hasn't my pal Bill Damon checked in yet?" Tom Slade's surprised question cut into the prophecy.

"Do you know him? Sure he is here. We are all crazy about him in spite of the fact that so far he doesn't know we are on earth. Hands off, *Mrs.* Stewart," the green eyes flashed to Cindy. "I saw him first. And his car—this is a nice deluxe station-wagon type, isn't it?— but his is one of those new club coupés, long and dark green and sensational. The garage man told me it has a hundred and five horsepower engine. Mr. Slade, we'll plan some tennis. I'm late, I'll be seeing you. By!"

She dashed along the drive and opened the door of a light gray sedan. Tom Slade waited until her car had coasted out of sight before he started his.

"Huh! The fair Lydia certainly punctured my belief that I was buying something snappy when I bought this car," he griped.

"You did. It's a beauty and the latest and smartest model I've seen this summer. Don't mind Lyd Fane. She always leaves a thorn pricking in one's heart."

"I knew that when she took the first crack at you. What did you think of my cagey inquiry about my pal—what's his name?"

"Bill Damon. It was a masterpiece of subtlety. Now that I know he is the person he claims to be let's forget him and get on with our day. In spite of your recognition of her claws, you fell flat on your face for the lovely Lydia, didn't you?"

"She asked for it. I'll bet her tennis doesn't touch yours. Something tells me that life here will have its points while I wait for you to be free. Relax. I won't say any more. Just want you to realize why I am here, that no green-eyed Circe can come between us. Where shall we lunch? Remember I am from the interior, and make it lobster. Sea air has made me ravenous. After that we'll paint the Maine shore red and I mean red."

After lunch at the Lobster Pound they stopped at the Country Club to watch the tennis. Cindy went into the house to make out a guest card for Tom Slade. When she returned he was surrounded by the female of the species dating him for games.

In a car which was the last word in smartness, performance and speed, they skimmed along black roads bordered in places by thickets of sumac and sassafras; the pale gold and purple of goldenrod and asters; past cultivated fields where sleek, well-fed black and white cows placidly chewed their cuds; by neglected fields coming up in broom sedge grass. From a towering pine the noisy "Caw! Caw!" of a crow convention rent the air. Past rocky shores, echoing with the thunder of white-capped breakers, beyond which stretched an illimitable expanse of sapphire blue and dark green ocean. A briny breeze stirred Cindy's short hair and tugged at Slade's luridly hand-painted tie.

He talked of his ambition politically, of his hopes and plans for the future, of her part in them. She interrupted:

"Not now, Tom, don't talk about me now. I asked you not to come here till the annulment of that crazy marriage had been granted. Your presence may start unpleasant conjecture. I don't want that. If you stay there is to be no mention of love or marriage between us."

"O.K., that's so like you. You won't drink or smoke or play cards for even a penny a corner, but you're the girl I want. I'll be cagey and concentrate on the dames at the Inn, only don't run away with the idea I've gone cold on you. Are you afraid that guy Damon—the snappy Lydia nailed his identity for fair, I guess there's no doubt he is here to represent the absent groom—will report to Stewart if we are seen together a lot and tie up the release?"

"*No.* Ken Stewart wants his freedom. During the years since the marriage by contract I have given no one a chance to gossip about me—you know I wouldn't go out with you unless others were in the party."

"Do I know it? You bet I do. In spite of the chaperons we had a lot of fun. Remember the roller-skate parties? The prizes we copped for our act?"

"I do. There is a rink a few miles from here, highly respectable, in fact verging on top-drawer. I've been planning to go there some day. My skates are in the turret room at The Castle."

"Remembering the fun we had, I brought mine on the chance there would be a place to use them. We'll smash a few more records with our turns and whirls."

"Meanwhile, play with the attractive girls at the Inn, give them the time of their lives."

"Suppose I fall for one of them?"

"All right with me. Better now than later."

"Jupiter, you're a hard-boiled critter, Cindy."

The bracelet man had said that, only he had called her a female, not a critter.

"I don't see why? Because I intend to have my next marriage—if there is one—of the 'till death do us part' kind?"

"That makes it unanimous."

They dined and danced. Stopped for a late snack. It was midnight when Cindy softly closed the front door of The Castle behind her. She listened till the purr of Tom Slade's convertible faded in the distance, then turned the shaded lamp in the hall to low and crossed to the stairs. Foot on the bottom step she stopped.

Why go up now? She wouldn't sleep if she went to bed. Her mind was in a hectic tangle, mussed like the drawer of her dresser when she had searched it in a hurry. More sensible to curl up on the chaise longue in the patio while she tried to restore order to the impressions of the last twelve hours.

She tiptoed through the hall. Sarah Ann Parker was the original watchdog. She slept with one eye and both ears open.

Perfect night, so enchanting it made one homesick—for what? she asked herself as she snuggled among soft green cushions and stretched at length on the chaise longue. "What a day," she said aloud. "I haven't stopped a minute. I'm dead to the world. Part of it is because shame at my treatment of Bill Damon after he saved my life has been gnawing at my conscience."

Fragrantly warm air rustled the balsams. A three-quarters moon, already taking on a tinge of autumn ruddiness and attended by a brilliant lady-in-waiting star, grinned down at her with a what-you-going-to-do-about-it smirk.

"Oh!"

The descent of a warm body on her knees jolted the exclamation through her lips. The black Persian cat circled several times before settling down in a purring lump on Cindy's aqua linen lap.

"Make yourself at home, Darius," she whispered as she scratched the top of the satin-smooth head. "At what point in my tabulation of the events of this epoch-making day had I arrived when you switched the dial?"

The cat tucked nose under velvet paws, blinked topaz eyes at the face above and closed them. His rhythmic purr accompanied the monotonous chirp of crickets in the flower border, the scratchy call of a katydid and the insistent far-off shrill of a tree toad. Shine and blink, shine and blink, myriad fireflies flitted about the patio and snapped their lights on and off.

Head against the downy cushions, eyes closed, Cindy heard again that shouted "Come back!"; lived over the moments under water till the crazy motorboat had passed high above their heads; the following session on the beach. Who was the man? Why wonder? Hadn't Lydia Fane declared that Bill Damon was registered at the Inn?

Just a minute, gal. Did he ever tell *you* he was the man of whom Ken Stewart had written to Armstrong? The question brought her sitting up straight. He said that I refused to speak with Bill Damon when he phoned, that answers that doubt, doesn't it? Maddening that my lawyer is away. Another week to wait. Will he try to see me meanwhile, or was he too annoyed by my doubt of him to care if he ever saw me again?

"Cindy, you here?"

The hoarse whisper brought her to her feet and the sleeping cat with a thump to the flagged floor of the patio.

"Good heavens, Sary Parker. You might as well kill me as scare me to death. What's happened?"

"Sssh-h-!"

The warning hiss came from the figure enveloped in a

dark bathrobe. Sarah Ann Parker laid a work-worn re-
straining hand on the girl's bare arm.

"Speak low, Cindy. We may not be the only folks
watching."

"Watching *what?*" Chills feathered along Cindy's
veins. She was indignantly aware that the huskiness of
her voice was going the housekeeper's one better.

"Want tó know somethin'? That big yacht I told you
about is in again. I was lookin' out my bedroom window—couldn't get to sleep till you came in—an' I saw
two lights flash. Suppose that Mrs. Sally Drew's goin' on
the water this time of night? Don't seem respectable."

"Sally." The name reverberated with startling clarity
along the corridors of memory. "You know Sally," the
bracelet man had said. Later he had claimed that the
name had been an improvisation. Had it been or was
there such a person in his life? Perhaps he knew this
Sally Drew who made mysterious excursions at midnight, perhaps—he was really here to see her.

"My sakes, Cindy, why'd you gasp as if someone had
knocked the breath out of you?"

"Why not? You've got me all excited about your mystery hunch, though common sense tells me that dozens
of boats come into this harbor and at midnight, too.
Why shouldn't Mrs. Drew go for a sail?" She glanced at
the illuminated dial of her wrist watch. "It is half after
the witching hour of midnight. A yacht and a beau to
twang a guitar is the perfect answer to this moonlight.
Wish someone would invite me."

"You're pokin' fun at me, Cinderella. I feel it in my
bones 'tain't as simple as that. Want to know somethin'?
There's a terrible lot of skulduggery goin' on and it
ain't all bein' pulled off in the cities, either. I read in
the paper that they're findin' that some of the folks
that 'pear mighty respectable are mixed up with crimi-
nals dealin' in stolen—"

On the screen of Cindy's memory flashed a close-up
with sound effects of a man in a blatant checked suit
ogling a girl in red. He looked as if he might deal in
stolen goods and he didn't look mighty respectable,
either.

"Listen!" Sarah Ann Parker's shrill whisper shattered the vision and iced Cindy's blood already chilled by memory. "Somethin' at our landin'. Too late for company to be callin'. Smugglers?"

She held her breath. The sound was that of a boat bumping against the wood. Silence again, broken only by the monotonous chant of crickets, and the weak chirp of a bird settling more securely in its nest.

"Did you hear it, Cindy?"

She nodded in response to the whisper, and pulled off Sarah Ann's enveloping bathrobe.

"Give me this. Smugglers! That's a laugh. Your imagination has dropped you back more than a hundred years, Sary. I'll find out who it is, what goes. Hustle into the house. That nightie is shockingly thin for a public appearance."

"I'm not in my—"

She eluded the housekeeper's indignant grab. Swathed in the dark garment she stepped from the patio, sped along the green borders of the flower beds to avoid the crunchy pebbles of the path, crossed the putting green.

Now she could see the rocky point jutting into the sea, twin to the one on which The Castle had been built. Moonlight picked out the spreading California-type house and spotlighted a pier from which a long, fleecy wake made a path toward the dark horizon. Had a boat returned to the yacht? She stood in the shadow of a tree near shore.

Sary was right. A boat was at the oceanside landing of The Castle. Muffled voices. She held her breath to listen.

"They've made the getaway safely. Now we can go. Our job is done for the present. No one awake here—luckily for them." The low voice was followed by the muffled sound of oars.

Cindy drew the dark robe closer about her. Its warmth didn't decrease her shiver. What did "luckily for them" mean? Who were "them"? The residents of The Castle?

# SEVEN

THERE WAS an electric fan in action in the old-fashioned room in the small white office on the lawn of the imposing yellow colonial house, White Pillars. A breeze stealing through an open window lightly stirred papers spread on the broad, orderly desk. A ray of sunlight sifting in added a touch of gold.

Seth Armstrong in open-neck white shirt tipped back at a reckless angle in his swivel chair, fitted the fingertips of his plump waxen hands, and regarded with pale eyes between half-closed lids the bronzed face of the man seated opposite.

"Sorry I had to keep you waiting a week, Colonel Damon, but I wanted to check on the oil holdings, leases and patents myself. That's the way I do business, firsthand information. Your explanation of your presence in our village is confirmed by a letter I received from Kenniston Stewart. Now that I meet you I suspect that your service record is sensational."

"No more so than that of dozens of men who gave all they had and didn't come through. My part in the holocaust is ancient history. Now I wish to live and work in the present. I am out of active service, though on call if needed. Please drop 'Colonel,' Bill Damon to you. I am eager to get Ken Stewart's affairs washed up that I may get on with my own life. I have a book to write and a partnership as the patent man in an engineering firm waiting for me."

"No reason why they can't be washed up speedily." Armstrong tapped a legal-looking sheet spread on the

46

desk. "Your power of attorney is in order. Stewart's signature agrees with those on letters I have received from him. You also have checked on the leases and registration of the patents in use at the oil holdings on the field and in Washington and report them to be unimpeachable—a rumor got around to the contrary, circulated, I have reason to suspect, by would-be purchasers—which means that the transfer can go through without a hitch."

"That's good news."

"Only one person can hold it up. Mrs. Stewart. Have you met her?"

"Twice."

"By your smile I deduce it was a pleasant meeting. I am surprised. I was with her in the garden patio when the housekeeper delivered your telephone message. I heard her declare she would not see you. What happened?"

He told of the runaway motorboat; of his talk with the girl on the beach; of her indignation when she discovered his identity; of the advent of Tom Slade. Seth Armstrong inflated and deflated his cheeks as he listened for all the world like a man blowing up balloons for a lot of kids.

"He's assistant to the Western lawyer who put across the written-contract marriage, isn't he?" he inquired thoughtfully. "What did you think of him, Col—Damon?"

"I had no time in which to form an opinion, he flashed on and off the scene so fast. I haven't seen either of them since that day. Knowing that I couldn't confer with you for a week, I spent the time in New York, I had important business there. Cindy Clinton—as you see, I have picked up the name her friends use—had previously assured me that Slade is tall and terribly good-looking. I'm willing to take her word for it. Is he the man she is planning to marry when the annulment goes through?"

"If he is she hasn't told me. There is talk to the effect that Hal Harding, a playboy who owns The Hundreds, a spectacular estate here, is determined to make her the third Mrs. Harding. It's gossip, take it for what it's worth. I'd say the Western lawyer has more on the ball. How do you feel about holding off that annulment till after the deeds of sale of the oil holdings have been signed? It will make only a few days difference, I had a conference with Judge Shelton about it this morning. I think it should wait."

"I agree with you. Optimism is expressed over the near term outlook for the oil industry. I have been informed that so far as one can see production of crude oil will be permitted to rise over the next several months at least. The buyers are eager to acquire the property, which is in the middle of hundreds of acres on which they own mineral rights. I understand that neither Ken nor the girl he married wants to shoulder the responsibility of the business. The holdings are small as oil holdings go, but good. It is their chance to get out from under with a sizable profit. The lawyer of the buyers waved two checks in the seven-figure bracket practically in my face if I would put my John Hancock on the deed of sale while I was on location, they would obtain hers later. I refused on the ground that Mrs. Stewart and I would sign at the same time."

"Would you get a bigger price if you played hard to get?"

"Undoubtedly. General market conditions permitting, oil shares are likely to be in better investment demand over the next few months than they have over the last several, but, I have my orders to sell. Will you use your influence with her to get her to sign?"

"It won't be difficult when I explain that the sale first will mean only a short delay to her freedom. Now if you have time I'll check with you on the financial report."

The touch of gold on the desk vanished, the room grew shadowy in the corners as the two men discussed and compared facts and figures. Seth Armstrong snapped on the desk light. He glared at the door in response to a knock.

"Who is it?" he growled.

"It's Ally, Seth. You asked me to bring the tea tray at four-thirty. Hurry! It's heavy. Open the door!"

Armstrong snatched up his coat from a chair.

"Just a minute. It's my sister, Mrs. Barclay, Colonel. Let her in while I get this on. She detests—"

"I'll drop the pesky thing if you don't—" The tall white-haired woman in a thin soft green frock opened dark eyes wide and stared at the man who flung open the door. He seized the huge china-laden silver tray which tilted dangerously.

"I don't wonder you are startled, Madam, to see a stranger when you expected your brother to take over. I'm Bill Damon pinch-hitting for the Counselor at the moment. Where shall I deposit this?"

She put her hand to her throat as if to loosen tension.

"On the desk," her voice was husky. "There appears to be plenty of room. You shouldn't spring a surprise like that, Colonel—Damon. I almost dropped the tray when I saw your face instead of my brother's. Seth, I was an aide in a field hospital when your present guest was brought in with the ugliest wound of the engagement."

"How about the cup of tea you brought along, Mrs. Barclay? Do I smell cinnamon toast? The Counselor and I have been figuring till we are on the verge of a nervous breakdown for want of nourishment."

"Right." She seated herself in the chair he had occupied at the desk. "Seth, come out of the coma into which my recognition of your guest—or is he a client?—appears to have plunged you. Sit down, both of you. How do you like your tea, Colonel?"

He drew up a chair at an end of the desk, Armstrong tilted back in the swivel chair opposite his sister.

"Strong. I need a stimulant after your surprise appearance. To reminisce for a split second, Counselor, your sister was shipped to England with me and helped me fight back to life in the hospital."

"It seems as if it happened yesterday, and it was the last month of the war. Time no longer marches on. It is geared to modern tempo. It flies. Here's your tea, Seth."

Armstrong took a mighty swallow from the cup his sister passed to him and swore inarticulately.

"Why didn't you warn me that stuff would scald, Ally?" he demanded.

"Don't tell me that the superefficient secretary of
yours, about whom you brag, serves it cold," she coun-
tered. "Aunt Minerva still makes the most heavenly
toast out of captivity—she won't allow my maids to do
it—it's so luscious and cinnamony and sugary. Try it,
Colonel. You don't look as if you needed to count calo-
ries."

"Now that we are through with the prologue, let the
play go on. Did you come to this town to meet Damon,
Ally?" Seth Armstrong demanded.

"Me? I never was so surprised in my life as when I
recognized the man who opened the door as a onetime
patient. I had no idea he was in this country. I haven't
seen him since the fighting war ended. The one time I
heard of him he had been sent on a dangerous mission."

"That mission was supposed to be secret."

"One of those secrets that were circulated to hide the
truth? Now that surprise has given way to curiosity, why
are you in this small town—Bill Damon?"

"I'll tell you why." Seth Armstrong deposited cup and
saucer on the desk and answered the question. "Remember Cinderella Clinton, Ally?"

"Do you mean little Cindy Clinton, that adorable
youngster with a tousle of goldy-brown curls? Of course
I remember her. Aunt Min has kept me posted on
village gossip. Wasn't there a story going the rounds that
she made a phony marriage?"

"Nothing phony about it. Legal to the last dot of an *i*.
It is about to be dissolved. The Colonel is here to
represent the absent husband."

"Dissolved. Another marriage gone wrong. Can't you
save it, Colonel?"

"No. I am under orders from the husband to conform
to the lady's wishes and the lady says, 'Off with his
head.' That leaves me no alternative." He rose.

"As we have finished our business, Counselor, I'll take
off. Won't you dine at the Inn with me some evening,
Mrs. Barclay? I'd like to check with you on news of men
we both knew."

"I'd love it. On the chance of appearing to gulp your

invitation, I suggest that if you are not tied up we make it tonight. Every other evening this week is taken."

"Perfect. I will come here for you at seven."

"No, thank you. I want to make a short call on the way."

"I'll be waiting for you at the Inn. The earlier we dine, the better the dinner, I have discovered. That being settled, all right if I drop in with Mrs. Stewart tomorrow morning to sign the deeds of sale, Counselor?"

"Yes, if she will come. The buyers are so eager they have sent checks to the bank here to be turned over as soon as you both sign. If she protests tell her that the other matter, which appears to mean life or death to her, will be held up till the sale goes through. I'm glad you are here to twist the thumbscrews, Damon. I'm soft. Good luck to you."

"Something tells me I will need your good wishes. Until seven, Mrs. Barclay."

At five minutes before the hour he perched on the rail of the Inn porch looking toward the beach with its lacy capped waves. Was it only a week ago he had rescued Cindy Clinton from that onrushing boat? The memory of her danger set his hair prickling at the roots. It had been a close call.

The stone house on the dark, rugged promontory that jutted into the ocean was The Castle. The estate had the advantage of bordering also on the channel and the harbor which at the moment was presenting a scene of breath-taking beauty.

The fiery ball of a setting sun flooded the sky with color. Lights were twinkling on in houses. The horizon, against which a bridge was etched in black, was crimson; shades of red rayed upward; planes of pink melted into fields of vivid green which faded into soft yellow at the upper edge which in turn fused into violet where it met and lost itself in the blue sky. The still water in the harbor reflected each colorful shade and tint, each boat large and small at anchor. Mast tops were tipped with crimson and every bit of brass or chromium on board became a little leaping flame as the boats swung lazily in

the outgoing tide. A few rosy cloud fluffs moved slowly
across the darkening sky as if to give one brilliant star
the right of way. The beauty tightened his throat,
twisted his heart, set him wondering if his plan for the
future was—

"Dreaming, Colonel Damon?"

His self-questioning shattered like a thin glass
dropped to the floor, he could almost hear the tinkle.
The challenging query brought him to his feet. He had
a dim recollection that the Inn hostess had presented
him to this redheaded girl in a frock as green as her
eyes, with a neckline which must be what was currently
known as "plunge." She was remarkably beautiful and
knew it, he concluded.

"Not dreaming. Feasting on that amazing show of
color in and over the harbor."

She glanced at the western sky.

"It is nice." Her eyes came back to him. "The reflection even reaches this porch. It is turning your white
dinner jacket pink. I am Lydia Fane, in case you are
scurrying madly in your memory for my name. Don't
apologize. You were introduced to a half dozen of us at
once the day you arrived. It would take a master mind
to identify each girl."

"Why conclude that I am not master minded, Miss
Fane?"

"Then you can smile? That's a break. You have appeared so grave and stern since your arrival we've hardly dared look at you, much less speak. That word
'arrive' reminds me, your friend was looking for you a
week ago, said he expected to find you here. Apparently
he had just come."

"One week ago? My friend?"

"You have an adorable scowl." Miss Fane was not
inclined to subtlety of approach. "He stopped here with
Cindy Clinton—my mistake, Stewart—to ask if you had
registered."

"Now I get you. You mean Tom Slade. Great guy.
Smart as they come. With whom did you say he came?"

"With the village Cinderella. You'll meet up with her
and her pseudo romance before you've been here long.

Meanwhile—I was tapped to invite you to join us at Canasta this evening."

"Mighty good of you to include me, I like the game, but I can't make it. I am expecting a friend to dine with me, and here she is," he added as a light beige roadster stopped at the drive and a beautifully coifed white head appeared at the car window. "If you will excuse me—"

He was at the roadster door held open by a chauffeur as Alida Barclay stepped out.

"Here I am, Colonel Damon. Scott, come for me at—"

"I'll drive you home, Mrs. Barclay, when you are ready to go."

"That will be perfect, Colonel. You needn't come back, Scott," she said to the chauffeur. He touched his cap and slid behind the wheel.

She was the most distinguished looking woman present, he thought as he followed her from the dining room. The sweeping black satin skirt, the regal collar of the long-sleeved jacket of superb white lace over the low-cut bodice, the long pendant earrings and necklace of pearls, her brilliant dark eyes, her short, silky white hair, suggested a portrait by a master artist of an earlier age.

"What would you like to do? Smoke, of course, I remember that, listen to music, play cards, tune in on video?" he asked.

"I want to talk, you may remember also that that was one of my favorite diversions. Let's find a secluded corner on the ocean side from which we can see the moon rise out of the water. I'll pick up my wrap."

Her trailing black satin cape lined with scarlet made a dramatic background for the black and white of her costume as they crossed the brilliantly lighted lobby.

They were the only occupants on the porch from which could be seen an illimitable stretch of ocean. A faint light where sky and water met heralded the rising moon. Gold stars freckled the indigo dome. The soft breeze that stirred Alida Barclay's white hair had filched scent from a bed of petunias in its travels. From the house drifted the music of violin, viola, cello and piano.

"Listen. They are playing Tschaikowsky's 'Sleeping Beauty Waltz.' Exquisite, isn't it?"

"I don't wonder you whisper. Combined with the starlight it suggests enchantment, can't you hear adventure calling? You being you, I'll bet you can. Comfortable?" He held a lighter to her cigarette, then to his own. "I'm listening. Talk."

She laughed.

"Talk. Just like that." She glanced over her shoulder. "Sure we are alone?"

"Sure's shootin'. The blank wall of the house is directly behind us and the whole Atlantic Ocean is in front. Your question has set the air vibrating with mystery. Another secret mission?"

In the dim light he could see her affirmative nod.

"You haven't forgotten my one small success, I see. Intelligence has me listed. When the head of the Customs Department heard that I had a brother here, I was asked to help run down an elusive gang."

"In this small place?" His low voice was incredulous.

"Yes. Luck is on my side. Seth is at home which fact provided a valid reason for my visit. And I can see your presence here as a fortuitous arrangement devised by Fate. Remember the case we cracked together? My one and only?"

"I do. I am not on that kind of an assignment here, Mrs. Barclay."

"Mind telling your old pal why you are here—Ken Stewart?"

# EIGHT

"Mind!" As he echoed her word, he threw back his shoulders as if ridding them of a burden. "Good Lord, I'll be glad to have someone with whom I won't have to watch my step. Of all places in the world how did you happen to drop into this Maine coast village where for a few weeks I am trying to conceal my identity, Ally Barclay?"

"Thank goodness you've dropped that 'Mrs.' I told you, I am following a trail."

"I can't realize that you are still a government agent."

"Only in this one case. I have the time, and the higher-ups think I have ability. I'm thrilled to help. Someone must do the work for the country, besides I like it. It's interesting and exciting. After my war work I've found it tame to settle down to the life of a socialite. Why are you here under an assumed name? Are you on secret business or have you deserted from the service?"

He laughed.

"No. Officially discharged. I am due in Washington later, after I drop this alias, to receive a citation for 'exceptional service,' that's just to reassure you that you won't have to turn me in as a deserter. I am here to try to adjust—"

"Ken Stewart! A matrimonial tangle? I remember now. Seth said you were here to represent the absent husband in a marriage to be annulled."

"Sit tight. This will make the terrestrial globe whirl. I

am the absent husband—but the lady in the case doesn't know that."

"Whirl is too tame a word. I'm caught up in a twister. Quick, brief me on the situation. I'm sorry, perhaps you'd rather not talk about it."

"I'd like to talk about it, Ally—it may help assuage an unbearable feeling of guilt—after you cross your heart and swear that under no circumstances will you reveal a word of what I tell you."

"I swear." Diamonds on her fingers sparkled in the dim light as she made the sign above her heart. "Enter the moon to witness my promise."

Their eyes were on the red orb that inched its way from out the dark ocean as in a low voice he told of the reasons for the marriage by written contract; of his assignment to a job with Death forever stalking or riding at his side; of his determination as time went on and the two fathers died to keep out of the girl's way until she could claim separation as a cause to annul the marriage. She had been such a sport, she deserved her freedom and quick. To do it before then might wreck the plan it had been made to protect.

"Why reverse your decision by coming here?"

"Two months ago I received a letter giving me the devil for side-stepping responsibility and loading it on the shoulders of the girl who had married me to help save my property; that is the gist of the first part, the pen of the writer who signed P.A.S. had been dipped in acid. She or he wasn't afraid to name names, went on to say that Cinderella Clinton was being pursued by Hal Harding, a rich playboy who already had two ex-wives on his alimony list. If I didn't care that her health and spirit were being broken by business cares, I ought to be man enough, as her only protector left, to come back and talk turkey to her before she was eaten alive by a wolf. The argument was undebatable, my job there was practically finished. Here I am."

"Have you seen Cindy Clinton?"

"Yes."

"Did she appear as if spirit and health were being broken? If you can laugh like that in answer to the question I judge she isn't in grave danger. Did you recognize her when you met?"

"Not the first time. We were in that shop in the village run by—"

"Ella Crane, known to her intimates as the Public Address System. What a break—for Ella. Did she know who you were?"

"No. A girl standing beside me advised me about a bracelet I was buying to send to the wife of one of my outfit who was terribly homesick, thought it might cheer her. I mistook her for a teen-ager, her hair was tied at the neck by a broad ribbon, she wore pedal-pushers, a green and white striped blazer, her lovely brown eyes were young, mischievous. Why would I suspect she was Cinderella Clinton? The woman by that name who had sent me long, formal reports and monthly statements, which contained no personal touch except 'Best wishes' at the close, had taken definite shape in my imagination as a tall, spare individual, more machine than human, who didn't hesitate to contract a marriage for business reasons, who had about as much sensitivity as a female robot."

"Apparently she had enough of what you call sensitivity to care a lot for that father who was ready to throw her to the wolves."

"By wolf do you mean me?"

"Who else? Is she attractive?"

"Lovely. I'd say 'sunny' is the word to express her personality, plus depth of character. I know that last from her letters, also drive, and combativeness, I learned those traits the day we met the second time. She has a charming voice and a nice sense of humor." He laughed as he thought of the reference to the "Prince."

"The plot thickens. I *see*, said the blind man. I agree with the writer of that letter. It was your job to take the first plane back to relieve that poor girl of the business responsibility."

"You've got her wrong, Ally. No one could think of her as 'poor girl.' She has too much vitality, charm, poise." Thoughtfully he blew a few smoke rings.

"I'm sure I was right not to return. *Right?* I couldn't

have come home before. I had been assigned to an organization job in the airlift. Do you realize what Operation Vittles accomplished? I bet you don't. It made 275,000 flights and delivered a total of 2,230,000 tons of food, coal and often emergency supplies in Berlin for the city's civilians."

"I'd forgotten the Herculean task accomplished. How many of the citizens of the good old U. S. remember if they ever knew, do you suppose?"

"One in a million, perhaps. They ought to remember. Every mother's son of them should be made to realize that the cost was $500,000 a day and that seventy airmen lost their lives. General Clay had some of the best airmen in the British and American forces supporting him. Mine was a job of terrific responsibility, I made uncounted flights with my men."

"Responsibility. Your voice shows the strain as you tell of it. I wonder you are alive. I thought the blockade was formally lifted last July?"

"It was, but the airlift kept up delivery of supplies as insurance against more blockades. It's tapering off but the framework will remain. I wish I felt sure it won't be needed again. All the time I was haunted by a sense of guilt that I was allowing the girl who had married me to carry the load of the oil holdings. I spent hours considering the situation. I argued that if I could go back and we didn't live together, as of course we wouldn't have—she would have been outraged at the suggestion—the persons against whom the marriage had been planned as a defense might try to invalidate it."

"Isn't that argument still good? If you are so sure you were right why come now?"

"The 'playboy' menace bothered me. I could come now. I thought I explained that."

"Really you came because of a letter probably written by a village crackpot—initials don't save it from being anonymous—or maybe, by a girl who wants to be the playboy's number three wife herself."

"Could be. Don't think I didn't weigh both of those possibilities. Having made up my mind to come I moved with speed. My service record entitled me to extra consideration. I collected back pay. Flew to this country. Bought a car. Spent several weeks at the oil holdings under my own name; arranged the terms of sale; had a day in New York to stock up on civilian clothes and start inquiries about a certain person; arrived in this village after the third anniversary of the marriage had passed; that fact will give Cinderella Clinton an uncontestable case of desertion or separation, whichever it is."

"All this under the name of Bill Damon. How could you get away with it?"

"No, no, you misunderstand. I adopted the alias for this town only. I wrote to your brother that my friend Colonel Bill Damon would arrive as my deputy. My plan was running along on oiled wheels, till you appeared there had been no hitch."

"How ungallant to refer to me as a hitch." He smiled in sympathy with her gay laugh. "Seriously, Ken, I think you have started on a dead-end street. How are you getting on with Cindy Clinton?—my mistake, Stewart?"

"We had made a fair start on the friendship road when Slade appeared. Then something roused her antagonism again."

"Again?"

"Yes, she had resented the fact that Ken Stewart had sent me instead of coming himself to settle the business and other matters."

"Other matters refers to the annulment, I assume. How about this Hal Harding menace?"

"Do you know him?"

"Certainly I know him. He's a lot younger than I, but he was the rich little boy who went to prep school while the rest of the youngsters his age went to High. He came here summers and made love to each of the girls in turn. He's a charmer. What are you planning to do about him?"

"I haven't taken up that matter yet with the present object of his affections. Give me time. This is my third day here. I was away a week."

"Will you let her go?"

"Let who go?"

"Don't bite. You know perfectly well that I am referring to your wife."

"I haven't a wife, really. If you mean Cinderella Clinton, of course I shall let her go. *Let* her go? That's a joke, I couldn't hold her to that written contract if I wanted to, which I assure you I don't."

"Ken Stewart, you exasperate me. You were always the most unimpressionable man. You never went off your head as other patients did about the lovely aides in the English hospital. I was so much older than you that your indifference didn't touch me. I used to wonder if you had left a girl behind you."

He clasped his hands behind his head and tipped back the chair against the wall of the house.

"No, sometimes I wondered myself why I didn't fall for the lovelies. Must have been because all my jobs have been dangerous. Death kept his reminding hand on my shoulder, which fact made me realize that girls and women had no place in my life."

"Now that is over, no reason why you shouldn't go off the deep end and soon."

"Not until this annulment goes through. Technically I am a benedict."

"Suppose you fall in love with this girl, who I deduce from your description is adorable?"

"I face the possibility as one of the hazards of my present life, Mrs. Barclay."

"Gone dramatic on me, haven't you? I caught your grin, even in this dim light, it was in your voice, too. Watch your step, Bill Damon, pro tem, or you may wake up to the fact that you have lost something you would give your life to keep. Somebody said, sounds like the immortal William S., 'Who ever loved that loved not at first sight?' "

"It was Marlowe. Shakespeare quoted it in *As You Like It*. You see, I salvaged something from my college course."

He brought his chair down on all fours and leaned toward her.

"Ally, the followers of the Prophet have a proverb, 'Leave the future to Allah, and pitch a tent for today.'

My tent is pitched." He held a lighter to her cigarette then to his.

"Period. Let's drop my affairs and get on to yours. What secret mission brought you to this village? Why is my presence here, I quote, a fortuitous arrangement devised by Fate?"

She glanced over her shoulder, then up at the dark sky.

"The face of the Man in the Moon is so clear I feel as if he were bending an ear to listen."

"Forget him. No one can hear. Go on with your story."

"Remember the treasures we were shown in hidden temples and shrines when we worked together on that foreign assignment?"

"Do I? I strolled into a huge jeweler's shop while in New York. When I saw the outlay there I was reminded of the diamonds, emeralds, rubies and sapphires galore we saw set in the eyes and heads of idols, of the strings of pearls, the gold and carved ivory urns and vases. Go on."

"Many of those treasures are being secretly sent to the United States—by a complicated route to dodge customs —and the loot sold to finance rebel elements in a country overseas."

"The stuff is being smuggled in to this small seacoast town where each person appears to know his neighbor's business from A to Z? Incredible."

"Smuggled is the word. It fits in with the Pirate's Cove legend. Perhaps that very story suggested this shore as a landing place for the loot. A week ago I was alerted to watch for developments, but the receivers this end must have been tipped off. Nothing happened except that a yacht appeared off the twin points: two lights flashed from one of them. It was on and off so quickly that the exact source was doubtful. A speedboat streaked in the direction of the yacht which immediately came about and sailed away. Later I discovered that the one I saw is the property of the tenant of Rockledge, a rich business-woman not likely to be interested in stolen goods, so she's above suspicion. Now I have to start over on the jackpot question, who in this vicinity is on the receiving end?"

"In this vicinity? Sounds like something thought up by a mystery-story expert."

"Maybe it does but my informant isn't a mystery-story writer. He knows his job. Will you help me? Don't answer yet. It's only fair to tell you that an occupant of The Castle is under suspicion."

"The *Castle?* Do you mean Cinderella Clinton's Castle?"

"Sorry, but that was the tip. Willing to help?"

"Willing? Sure, I'm willing. I'll clear her home of suspicion if it's the last thing I do."

# NINE

"THAT's your second birdie, Cinderella. Call it a record for the day. It's too hot to putt even at 10 A.M.," Hal Harding declared. "I've got something to say to you. I came early to get ahead of the western guy with whom a little bird told me you've been spending most of your time the past week while I've been away. My speed runabout is at your landing. Come for a spin and cool off."

With her putter Cindy knocked the small white ball idly back and forth on the velvety green. Better let him talk. A showdown between them was overdue. It would be a relief to get it behind her.

"For the love of Mike, why are you staring at me as if you'd never seen me before? Cinderella Clinton Stewart, may I present Hal Harding? He's been dying to meet you."

She laughed and bobbed a little dancing-school curtsey.

"I have long anticipated this pleasure, Mr. Harding. You win, Hal, the sun is blazing. Too hot for the boat. I'll settle for the patio. It will be cool there. You may talk and I'll listen, after which perhaps you will let me speak my piece. Ooch, it's sizzling. I should have worn a hat. Hear that cicada. Is there a hotter sound in the world?" She stopped on the path. "I wonder if the yacht dropping anchor belongs to Mrs. Drew, the tenant at Rockledge? It's sensational."

"Sensational, you've said it. Whoever owns that boat owns a beaut inside and out. It measures 87′ × 17′ × 6′.

There are three staterooms with showers, large main salon with one end equipped for dining. Spacious aft deck. Twin 165 h.p. G.M. diesels, diesel generator. Boy, oh boy, it's the kind of craft I intend to own some day."

"That description sounds like a yacht broker's ad in capitals. How come you know so much about the boat?"

"I—I sailed on her once with a former owner."

"Is Mrs. Drew the owner now? Have you met her, Hal?"

"No. I don't want to. I hear she's downright ordinary. Steer clear of her, Cindy."

"She's my nearest neighbor. I intend to call." Sary's words echoed through her memory: "Every little while a big boat drops anchor off her shore, signals, I guess she goes off in it. Kind of mysterious. Gives me the hibby-jibbies."

"Don't get mixed up with her, sugar. It's a darn lot easier to keep out of being friendly than to get out after you're in," he warned.

One side of the patio was cool and shadowy. Diamond spray from the fountain shot high into the air and fell to the surface of the pool with a refreshing tinkle. Hal Harding pushed the chaise longue back into deeper shade.

"Sit here and be comfortable," he urged. "You are perched on the edge of that white chair as if poised for a take-off, Cindy. Curl up in this and relax."

"No. The cushions make it hot." She brushed the short curls back from her moist forehead. "The tips of the hollyhocks, phlox and delphiniums are drooping as if they couldn't hold up their heads a minute longer. You look maddeningly cool in that open neck white shirt and slacks. How do you do it?"

"Peel off your jacket and you'll be cool."

She started to pull off the bolero of her pale pink cotton frock to bare her shoulders and arms, thought better of it as she noted the appraisal in his blue eyes. Pity that a man so lavishly supplied with wealth, blond good looks and personal charm, gave one a feeling of distrust.

"Why are you giving me the once-over again, as if trying to pick out a suspect from a Rogue's Gallery?"

"A cat may look at a king, sirrah. Proceed with what you want to say, Hal. I have a date with Counselor Armstrong at eleven sharp." She glanced at her wrist watch. "Speed. Speed. We haven't much time."

"This is not a subject to be hurried." He drew a straight chair to face hers, straddled it and crossed his arms on the top.

"Like me, Cinderella?"

"With reservations."

"I know what that means without asking. You think me fickle. No use explaining the reasons for the bust-up of my two matrimonial ventures, you wouldn't understand."

"I have told you before, Hal, that I am not interested in the reasons."

"We'll drop that for the present. When will you know the date your annulment case will come before the Court?"

"I hope Mr. Armstrong will tell me this morning. He assured me that he had a decision in my favor nailed down, that it will be granted at once, that I will walk out of the courtroom a free woman. Even at the thought my spirit spreads its wings and soars. See it soar? See it soar?"

"I hear it flutter. Hooray! That night I'll give the party of the century at my place to celebrate."

"You will not. We've gone over this before. It isn't decent to make whoopee, I know your brand, over a thing like that. It is too much of a tragedy."

"Tragedy! Have you gone *screwball*? What's tragic about it? Why turn sob sister? You just shouted to the housetops, 'I'll walk out of that courtroom a FREE WOMAN!' "

"I didn't shout."

"Have it your way, sugar. I'm not interested in what you say, only in what you do. The minute you are free, you'll marry me. Right?"

She shook her head till every short gold-brown curl was in motion.

"No, Hal. I will not marry you. I hoped I had made you understand that." Here was the showdown. She must make her refusal so clear there would be no doubt that it was final. "And furthermore, if you give that party ostensibly for me, I won't come. I'll leave town."

"Why? *Why* won't you marry me? I'm crazy about you. My family is tops, and—"

"Where you came from doesn't mean so much to me as where you are going—and what you are is even more important."

"I suppse you mean by that, accomplishment. I don't need to work. I can give you everything you want, now."

"Not everything, Hal. I want a man who feels the responsibility of money and power. Wealth creates power, and to my mind responsibility. A man like you shouldn't go through life doing exactly as he wants regardless of the harmful example he is setting to others who admire him for what he has."

"I get you: my brother's keeper fixation, what?"

"Don't sneer. You claim you can give me anything I want. You can't. A sense of responsibility when there is wealth and power is the way I see life, and that's the way I intend to try to live it, live it with a man who sees it that way too. When I promise 'to love and to honor' I'll mean it with all my heart and soul and mind."

"Hold everything, Cinderella, you have it wrong. In the marriage service the words are 'to love and to cherish'—I ought to know."

His heartless chuckle increased her determination to make him understand.

"I still stick to 'to love and to honor'—accent on honor. If you honor a person you'd be bound to cherish him or her, wouldn't you?"

His laugh was a shout of derision.

"This is a scream. You orate about loving and honoring a husband after having married a man you'd never even *seen*."

Her face crimsoned.

"I understand, Hal, how that marriage must look to those who weren't in the know. I did what seemed to me right. Like Arabella Allen, in *Pickwick Papers*. If I didn't know then what I *did* want, I know now what I *don't* want."

"That means me, I suppose. Nice of you to compare me with Bob Sawyer. Boy, but you've mounted the rostrum this A.M. Jump down, Cindy. I don't care how you live your life if you live it with me. I'll make you happy as a queen. You intend to get rid of Kenniston Stewart P.D.Q., don't you?"

In the impelling need to make him understand she had bared thoughts she hadn't realized she had, they had formulated and risen to the top of her mind as she talked. He had about as much comprehension of what she meant as had that flash of gold in the pool. No use to be serious with him. She laughed.

"I'm not so sure that I intend to get rid of Ken Stewart. I'm beginning to wonder. A bird in the hand—you've heard that one. Perhaps I'm *not* gonna wash that man right out of my hair." She sang the paraphrase with a hope that she could end a situation now and forever which threatened to get out of hand.

"You *can't* have changed your mind?" The words were hoarse with incredulity. "You *can't* mean that you're going to stick to that written contract, go through with it? You've gone hay—"

"Sorry to interrupt at what appears to be a crucial moment," apologized a voice from the doorway behind them, "but Counselor Armstrong asked me to stop for you and bring you to his office—Mrs. Stewart."

Cindy wheeled. Bill Damon again. Looking as cool in white as if this weren't the hottest summer day for years. Had he heard her silly declaration about Ken Stewart? Could he hold up her case in court by repeating that gem of flippancy? Why would he want to? Wasn't he under orders to push the matter full speed ahead?

"If you have lost your voice, Cinderella, mine is still in working order." Harding's incisive words were tipped with vitriol. "Who are you in the doorway and what do you mean butting into a private conference?"

"Shall I present my credentials to the gentleman, Mrs. Stewart?" Bill Damon took a step down to the patio. "It will take time and we really shouldn't keep the Counselor waiting."

I could wring your neck, Mister, for the amusement in your voice and eyes, Cindy thought, before she explained:

"Colonel Damon is here to represent Kenniston Stewart, Hal. We are to sign deeds this morning for the sale of the oil property. The Court has spoken. I must go."

"You bet I'm not getting in wrong with the Court in this case by detaining you, I have too much at stake. We'll pick up this conversation again, sugar, in a place where we will be safe from *officious* interruption. Your argument floored me for an instant, but I'll have an answer. I'll be seeing you."

She watched him as he strode down the garden path, switching angrily at the rose border with his putter, watched him cross the green and disappear from sight. A motor hummed. His boat. The sound diminished in the distance. That was that. Now what?

"Who was the gentleman? You didn't introduce him," a voice reminded.

"I'm sorry, Colonel. He is Hal Harding. We had had a hot argument and I forgot my manners."

"Couldn't have been very hot. He called you 'sugar.' "

"I know he did." She brushed her hair back from her warm forehead. "Three times. I never heard him use the word that way before, that sort of greeting from him seems so out of character. I wonder where he got it."

"Words are as infectious as the common cold. Easy to pick up from a person one sees even occasionally. We should be on our way."

"It's too hot. I'm not going. Those deeds don't have to be signed today." To avoid his intent gray eyes she picked up shears from a gathering basket on the glass-top table and concentrated on cutting bachelor buttons until she had a sizable bunch. She carefully drew the stems through her belt.

"That's a corking color combination, the deep blue against the delicate pink of your frock. If you are not going would you mind sitting down? I can't until you do, and as you observed, this is a hot day."

"I can see no reason why you should stand or sit in my garden. You are at liberty to go." Her defiant eyes glanced quickly away from his which were alight with laughter.

"Come on, now, Cindy—"

"Don't speak to me as if I were a kid. You did that once before."

"O.K., Mrs. Stewart. You want to get the complications in your life straightened out so you can begin real living, don't you?" His authoritative voice sent little tingles along her nerves.

"Certainly I do." Allah be praised he hadn't heard that brainless, "Perhaps I'm not gonna wash that man right out of my hair."

"Then come on, pronto. Armstrong told me yesterday that the sale of the property must go through before he would finish the case of the annulment of the marriage contract with the Court. He and I checked the deeds of sale. As soon as we have signed, you for yourself, and I for Stewart, Armstrong will go along with us, present them at the local bank here, where cashier's checks for a million bucks, one for you and one for Stewart, will be exchanged for the deeds."

"A million for each of us? That's two million." Her eyes were wide with amazement. "Those people offered me two hundred and fifty thousand for the holdings. They claimed the registration of the deeds and patents was faulty and the presence of more oil a gamble. Cheats!"

"Had you given me the sliver of a chance to explain I would have told you the result of my investigation. The registration of the deeds and patents is as sound as the U. S. mint, otherwise why the two million offer? If you say the word, we'll hold out for more. We can get it."

"But that would delay everything else, wouldn't it?"

"If you mean the annulment, yes."

"Accept the offer. It won't be the first time freedom has been preferred to money."

"They thought they had an easy mark when they offered you a fraction of what the property is worth.

Stewart deserves to forfeit his share for dumping the responsibility on a girl."

"But, this girl didn't fall into the trap, I beg to remind you. I can afford to forget that now. A million dollars. What in the world will I do with it? All right, laugh. I mean what I say, why would I want all that money?"

"I laughed at the thought of you worrying about the amount. Your Uncle Sam has your welfare on his mind, he will see to it that you are not overburdened with moola, lady. He'll leave you a nice little nest egg to invest. Let's do it together, you for Cinderella Clinton, I for Ken Stewart."

"Do you mean *speculate?* Thanks, *no.* I've had enough of that in drilling for oil to last my lifetime."

"I said *'invest.'* There's a heap of difference."

"How can we? You'll be on your way, won't you, as soon as Ken Stewart's business is finished?"

"No. I'm planning to remain here until my book is written. After years spent in the midst of tragic devastation, I've fallen hard for the order, cleanliness and beauty of this village, the tree-shaded streets, the well-cared-for houses and lawns. I like the people, too. How about it? Shall we set the annulment ball rolling by signing those deeds?"

"Lead on, Sirrah. Don't mind my flippancy. The prospect of ending an intolerable situation, neither maid, wife nor widow—that gem of rhetoric was borrowed from a nineteenth-century novel title—has unfolded the wings of my spirit which has been grounded. The moment I am free I shall begin to live daringly. How are we going?"

"My car is outside."

Sarah confronted them in the long hall.

"Trader Armstrong just phoned, Cindy. Wanted to know why you wasn't in his office?"

"Give him a buzz, tell him I am on my way, Sary. Colonel Damon, this is my guardian angel. Sarah Ann Parker. Colonel Damon is here pinch-hitting for Kenniston Stewart, Sary." Why should the introduction send color to the woman's face as if she were having an acute attack of blood pressure?

"Pleased to meet you, sir. Stayin' long?"

"Until Stewart's business is finished. He felt guilty leaving so much for Mrs. Stewart to do and as I was coming to this country asked me to take over."

"Hmp. Want to know somethin'? Folks is sayin' 'bout time he come to his senses. You be back for lunch, child?"

"I will answer for her. Better not count on it. We have a lot of business to put through this morning."

"Got the door key in your bag, Cinderella? 'S'long as you won't be home, I'll lock up an' later drop in to Ella Crane's shop. Rena Foster told me she's got a television machine on trial. Good mornin', Mr. Damon."

As the long dark green car slid forward smoothly he inquired:

"What did you say her name was?"

"Sarah Ann Parker. She has been housekeeper at The Castle for years. She spends the winters in Sarasota that she may watch the practice of her favorite ball team. She's a dear."

"S for Sarah. A for Ann. P for Parker. Reverse the initials and you get P.A.S. You said she is your guardian angel. I have reason to believe you."

# TEN

"AMAZING how quickly the pattern of a life can change." Cindy reflected aloud, as an hour later they drove away from the local bank. "I give you the Cinderella story, From Rags to Riches. You as Kenniston Stewart's deputy, I for myself sign papers at Counselor Armstrong's office; he goes with us to the bank, turns over the deeds and receives two checks in return. I deposit mine to my account and here I am, no longer living on an income that had its ups and downs, with the emphasis on downs, but a comparatively rich woman, minus Federal, state and local taxes."

"And a happy one, I hope?"

"Not entirely till the Court grants me the right to resume my maiden name."

"Will you insist on that?"

"Of course. Why the surprise?"

"It jarred me for a moment, you are erasing Stewart so completely from your life. You are right. Where shall we lunch?"

"Do we have to lunch now?"

"Certainly not. What do you want to do?"

"Just beyond here is a bluff that overlooks the ocean. It is a popular spot but likely to be deserted at this time of day. I'd love to sit there for a while and adjust my mental balance. At the moment my mind feels like a great empty attic which has been swept clean of the accumulations of generations. The last three years have been so packed with problems." She brushed her hand across her eyes as if to clear them.

"I would ask myself, 'With twenty thousand ways to earn a living in the U.S. why did Dad have to fall for oil wells?' 'Is it wise to do this?' 'Am I selfish to refuse to contract a marriage?' Being shot to the top of the world when a well showed a streak of oil; plunged to the depths of discouragement when a rush of water followed."

"Did that happen often?"

"Often? Eight out of ten times. 'Will I be able to pay the taxes on The Castle this year?' 'Are the men who want to buy the oil holdings cheating me?' No sooner would I mail a monthly statement to Ken Stewart than it was time to prepare another. Why are you looking at me so hard?"

"Better take time off to breathe. Pretty excited, aren't you?"

"Positively balloonish. Those are only a few of my doubts. Lucky I took the course in accounting at college. It was something to which to hold tight. I had to work or I would have been dropped from the class. I was determined to be trained for a job in case the bottom fell out of the oil holdings completely. It can happen."

"It not only can, but does. Do we turn here?"

"Yes. Stop at the end of this dirt road. My apologies for sobbing out my troubles on your shoulder, figuratively speaking. The recital has deepened the lines across your forehead."

"That wasn't what did it, it was the thought that Ken Stewart should be here in my place, with your head really on his shoulder."

"What an awful thought. If it is all the same to you I'll pick the shoulder, there is another I would prefer. I am just beginning to realize that with all that money I can make some dreams come true. I'll endow a room at the Hospital in Father's and Mother's name; establish a trust fund to assure the minister of the church here a decent living salary; I'll pension Sary and—but why not a hospital wing, it's terribly needed. After that I will—"

"Hold everything. If you go on at this rate, that money will be spent before the check goes through the bank."

She laughed.

"I told you I'm floating on top of the world. Leave the car here. We follow that path. Quite a climb, but it's worth it."

On top of the bluff was a sandy patch in front of a giant boulder. Cindy dropped to the ground, pulled off the pink jacket, and leaned back against the rock.

"A breeze! Isn't this heavenly? For the first time today I am cool. Sit down. Share nature's perfect seat. O.K., if you'd rather perch on that boulder, you look mighty uncomfortable, if you ask me. Isn't the ocean beautiful? Shades of green and blue and purple swelling gently on and on until they meet the sky. The six identical sails on the horizon must mean a boat race. Now they are spreading out to windward, exciting to watch even at this distance, isn't it? I wonder if the yacht headed this way is the one that anchors off Rockledge shore so often?"

"It looks impressive."

"If it is the boat credited to Mrs. Drew it is. Hal gave me a summary of its outer measurements, interior and deck arrangements this morning. If you believe his fervid description it is sensational."

"How come that he knows so much about the yacht? Is he a friend of the owner?"

"Not this owner. He doesn't approve of her. Advised me not to call at Rockledge. He said he sailed on the boat when she belonged to a friend. I don't understand Hal this summer. He used to be gay and charming, ultrasophisticated, of course, but he had a way with him that made one forgive that. Now he appears to be at loggerheads with the world in general and this spot on the Maine coast in particular." She placed her hand over her mouth and stifled a yawn.

"I beg your pardon. I have the most curious feeling, as if my spirit really is soaring in space, as if I could close my eyes and sleep for an aeon or two now that the care of the oil property is off my mind. It won't be really, though, till I make out the tax returns on the sale, for myself and Ken—"

"Ken will take care of his own."

"That's a break, I'll tackle mine soon, hang a notice

on my workroom door, WOMAN AT WORK, and—"
She yawned again, this time she didn't try to stifle it.
Her eyes half closed. "I don't understand—"

"I do. Stand up, Cindy. *Quick.*" He caught her hands
and pulled her to her feet, held her tight in one arm as
her eyes closed. Her head fell against his shoulder.

He glanced at the path which led down to his car. She
had said this spot was a popular rendezvous. Suppose a
party were to come along now? Would they believe that
she had succumbed to mental exhaustion? Would she
believe his explanation that many a time he had seen a
man in his outfit released from hours of the strain of life
and death responsibility go to sleep on his feet? He
shook her gently.

"Cindy, wake up. Come on, darling, try to walk. I'll
take you home."

No response except her limp body sagging a little in
his arm. He must get her to The Castle. She might sleep
for hours. This was nature's reaction after the sudden
release from years of responsibility. Only one way out,
carry her to the car.

He picked her up in his arms and kicked the little
pink jacket she had discarded ahead as step by cautious
step he descended the path. Lucky she wasn't heavier.
Her weight pulled painfully on the muscles stiffened by
the wound on his shoulder.

"Cindy, try to put up your foot, darling," he pleaded
when he reached the car, but her only answer was to
settle her head more comfortably.

He lifted her and laid her on the back seat, pulled off
his white coat and tucked it under her head for a
pillow, covered her shoulders with the pink jacket.

"May the gods be with me," he pleaded as he sent the
car ahead, "don't let us meet anyone who knows us.
Lucky the top is up."

"Hi, Colonel Damon!"

It was the predatory Fane girl calling, holding up her
thumb as he passed the Country Club gate. The man
beside her—Good Lord, it was *Slade*—stepped into the
road as if confident he would stop, and called:

"Hey, take us—"

He pretended not to see or hear and drove on. That was a narrow escape. Had they seen Cindy they would have thought—Take it easy, they didn't see her, common sense reminded.

Seth Armstrong, seated in a car in front of the bank, called to him and waved a sheaf of papers.

"Stop! Take these for your files—" He ignored the hail and stepped up the engine.

His collar was wilted to a wet rag when he stopped the car at the entrance door of The Castle. Now he would have co-operation. Sarah Ann Parker would help him get Cindy to her room, then tuck her into bed where she belonged.

He sprinted up the steps and pressed the button concealed in the antique brass knocker. The bell resounded through the house. He pressed again. He must get Cindy into the house before anyone appeared. Was the Parker woman asleep? Damn! She had said she was going to the village to watch television! That tied that.

Now what? Only one answer. Get into the house. There was a key in the pink bag. Miss Parker had reminded Cindy of it when they came in from the patio. The patio! If he could get her there it would help. He charged down the steps and followed the drive around a corner. He could.

Back to the car. He glanced at the sleeping girl before he drove into the garage and shut off the engine. That path must lead—

"Hey, Cindy!"

The call came from the front of the house. A man's voice. Which one of her stag line? She had said there was a shoulder she would prefer to Ken Stewart's. Had she meant Tom Slade or that piker Harding? Perspiration trickled down his back. Now he knew how a murderer must feel when trying to get away with the corpus delicti.

"Cindy!" He could hear the ring of a bell in the house. "Hey, *Cindy!*" An instant of silence followed by a second shout, then the whirr of an engine, and the purr of a departing automobile.

He drew his hand across his damp forehead. Whew, it

was hot. He investigated the path. It led through the garden to the patio. He must get her there before another swain showed up. He'd better go to it, not stand here thinking about it.

It seemed an eternity before he laid the sleeping girl on the chaise longue and dropped her pink jacket and his white coat on a chair. He returned and carefully closed the door of the garage. That would shut his car away from inquiring eyes for the present.

He flexed his stiff shoulder, he sure had given it a workout. Looking down at her he had an instant of panic. She was so quiet. She looked like the little girl who had spoken to him in Ella Crane's shop. Ought he phone for a doctor? No. He couldn't be wrong. This was the sleep of mental exhaustion. He had seen it scores of times. She would awake refreshed. Her color was good. He laid his hand on her moist forehead, gently picked up her wrist with the other. Pulse was normal. It was sleep.

Wilting day. Unbearably humid. Curled leaves drooped. A spike of delphinium bent double for all the world like an old man carrying a heavy load. Nothing alive stirred. His mistake. A cicada was on the job. The shrill call fairly sizzled. Those pillows must be hot. He withdrew one and settled her head more comfortably, drew off white sandals from feet covered by sheer nylons. If he had water—

Water. He looked toward the door to the house. Of course it would be locked and counterlocked, hadn't Sarah Ann Parker said she would lock up? Water? What was coming from the fountain but water, gallons of it, tinkling back into the pool? Even the sight of it was cooling. He drew two handkerchiefs from the pocket of the white coat.

He wrung out one of the white linen squares in the cool spray, grinned as he realized that he had made the trip to the fountain and back tiptoe. Crime motif again. He bent over the chaise longue and gently bathed the girl's face, dried it with the other handkerchief. She didn't stir, her sleep was too deep, but she looked cooler.

He drew the wilted bachelor buttons from her belt

and laid the stems in water at the edge of the pool, then dropped into one of the green cushioned chairs, drew up another for his feet, jerked off his tie and unbuttoned the collar of his white shirt. That somewhat relieved his discomfort. He lighted a cigarette and watched a hummingbird poised above a giant dahlia filching honey from its blush-pink heart. With the exception of spray from the fountain the fanning wings were the only moving object visible. Even the shrill cicada had succumbed to the heat.

I'll relax for a few minutes, then I'll make a stab at breaking and entering. Another downward step on my career of crime. This is what it must mean to be a baby-sitter, he thought as his eyes lingered on the sleeping girl.

"Will you let her go?" Alida Barclay's question echoed in his memory. "Of course I shall let her go," he had answered. He hadn't told her of his mental reservation, that if Cindy showed even the hint of a desire to marry Harding, he would hold up the annulment. Neither had he confided that with his sense of responsibility toward her, which had been roused by the P.A.S. letter, he had used part of his first day in New York to start an investigation on the trail of the playboy.

Yesterday he had received a detailed account of the man's life to date. The most startling item was the statement that the two heavy alimonies he was paying made such inroads on his income that he had borrowed on his principal. Did need of money figure in his pursuit of Cinderella Clinton Stewart? Doubtless he had posted himself on the value of the oil holdings. "Sugar," he had called her. Cindy had been puzzled by his use of the word, had declared it out of character for him. Curious. It would be interesting to know where he had picked it up.

It was evident that she was not in love with him. It would be unnecessary to antagonize her by postponing her freedom on his account. That was a break. Ally Barclay had been right when she had prophesied that sooner or later he would wake up to the fact that he had lost something he would give his life to keep. That realization had been quicker than "sooner," it had struck like lightning the first time he had seen her.

Suppose I don't let her go? Suppose I induce Armstrong to hold up the annulment while I try to win her love, his thoughts trooped on. No. *No*. She has a right to freedom. I don't want the handicap of that contract marriage. Suppose she said "Yes"? I never would be sure her conscience hadn't dictated the answer. Ally is wrong.

Ally. With the name came the memory of her confidence last evening on the Inn porch. The smuggling yarn was unbelievable. Was she being fooled? He had worked with her before being assigned to the airlift—there had been espionage problems there, too. She was keen at her job or she wouldn't have been picked for this one.

"Willing to help?" she had asked. Willing to help with Cindy in possible danger? She couldn't know how willing. He would have the credentials he had used before O.K.'d, then somehow, somewhere he would pick up a loose end that would reveal the identity of the receiver of smuggled loot.

His eyes rested on the sleeping girl. He'd better quit planning the future and make a stab at getting into the house.

It was amazingly simple when he tried it. He braced his shoulder against the door in the ell for a mighty push. It opened so suddenly that he clutched the handle to keep from pitching forward.

"Is my face red," he said under his breath. "The darn thing wasn't locked."

He entered the kitchen darkened by half-drawn shades. Cool as a tomb. That last was a cheery comparison. An icebox suggested food. He glanced at the wall clock. Well past the lunch hour. He could toy with something to eat. He opened the door.

A whole chicken, roasted. Tomatoes, big, red, luscious *and* peeled. Looked like mayonnaise in a jar, must be bread somewhere, he had read that it kept fresher in a refrigerator. Right, there it was and sliced thin. He would make sandwiches. When they were finished he—

Confound that doorbell. Had everyone in town conspired to drop in at The Castle today?

He waited motionless until the second prolonged ring died away. He would make the sandwiches before he brought Cindy into this cool house. Moving her might waken her.

A few minutes later he glanced from the window, swore softly under his breath. Harding was crossing the patio. It must have been he who had rung the bell, had he left his car in the front drive? He was bending over the girl on the chaise. With the intent to kiss her?

Bill Damon opened and closed the door to the patio gently behind him.

"Don't waken her," he warned.

# ELEVEN

HARDING jumped as if the hand of the law had touched him on the shoulder, wheeled.

"Oh, it's you again." His angry eyes in a face drained of color met those of the man who had taken a few steps forward, dropped to the open collar of his shirt.

"Just what are you doing here, *en négligé*—and how?"

Keep your temper, the man looking back at him reminded himself. You've got to. He pulled a cigarette from the package in the pocket of his shirt and lighted it.

"Let's be civilized and not get into a row, Harding," he suggested in a low voice. "You know what I'm doing here. I'm representing Kenniston Stewart. Cindy told you this morning that she and I had deeds to sign, that we were selling the oil holdings."

"Did the sale go through? Two million was the price offered, I hear." The inquiry was spiked with eagerness.

"Yes. It went through. After we left the bank she became sleepy, suddenly, in a minute was as you see her now. You're an ex-Marine, I understand. You must have seen deep sleep follow prolonged mental strain."

Harding looked from the girl to the man facing him.

"What mental strain has she been under? She's the most alive, gayest girl in this town."

"I have been told that she has carried the entire responsibility of the oil property that belonged to her father and Stewart's; has been the court of last resort when there has been a difference of opinion among

81

department managers. This morning after she signed the deeds that disposed of the property she declared in a frightened voice that it seemed as if she were floating in space, then suddenly she was asleep. This excessive heat did its part in her collapse."

"That's a slick explanation."

"Maybe so, but a true one." He buttoned the collar of his shirt, and knotted his tie in place. He repressed, "What can you do about it?" which his mind suggested as an effective wind-up. Harding turned suddenly, bent over Cindy and stretched out his hand as if to touch her arm.

"Sugar," he said softly.

"I said, *don't waken her*. And I *mean* don't waken her."

At the low, tense warning Harding thrust the hand he had extended into the pocket of his white slacks and straightened belligerently.

"Who do you think you are, giving me orders?"

"I don't think, I know I am here to pinch-hit in a business deal for the man she married, authorized by him to act in all matters concerning her happiness and safety. I'm sure had he seen you bending over his wife a few moments ago he would have pinned your ears back, I'm not living up to orders not to do it for him."

"Is that so? Now we're getting somewhere." Harding took a menacing stride forward. The patio door slammed.

"What are you two men up to?" Sarah Ann Parker demanded. Her cheeks were as red as her checked dress. "I see you through the window drawn up like two pugs startin' to fight. You go 'long, both of you. Who's that on the chaise longy? 'Tain't *Cindy*. Cindy Clinton?" She pushed Harding aside with a force that rocked him on his feet. "What's happened to her?" Her breath caught in a sob. "She been run over."

"This guy Damon says she's asleep, Miss Parker. He gave me a song and dance about her being worn out by the cares of business. Phooey. Cinderella Clinton asleep at this time of day. Tell that to the Marines."

"He's right," the girl asserted as she slowly swung her

feet to the flagged patio. She stretched her arms. Stood
up. Swayed a little and steadied. "I was asleep, but I've
been awake with my eyes closed since you bent over me,
Hal. I thought for a minute you had the Sleeping Beauty story mixed with that of Cinderella who was *not*
awakened by a kiss. If the gentlemen will excuse us,
Sary, we'll go in where it is cooler."

Sarah Ann Parker picked up the white sandals and
pink jacket and followed her into the house. The patio
door banged.

"Something tells me you are not the person you claim
to be, Damon," Harding accused furiously. "There's a
report going the rounds that over 250,000 persons are
living under assumed names in this country, some of
them out-and-out swindlers, some of them posing as
glamorous personalities."

"Surely you don't count me in the glamorous class?"

"You won't feel so much like grinning when I get
through with you. There is a rumor that queer things
are being seen and heard in this neighborhood. From
this minute I make it my business to find out who you
are and why you are here."

"O.K. When you've found out report to me, I'd like
to get in on this mystery at which you're hinting. I'm a
mystery-yarn addict. Meanwhile—" he picked up his
white coat, opened the door to the house, closed it
behind him with a reverberating bang and shot the
safety bolt.

I've made an enemy of him, he thought as he watched
Harding stalk along the path, turn toward the front of
the house. Let him find out the truth. I can't double for
Ken Stewart much longer. I only hope he'll hold off
until after the annulment, when I'll tell Cindy myself.
Keen to know if the property was sold, wasn't he? Had
the price down pat. That ties in with the report that
he's desperately in need of money.

I don't like his hint as to a mystery. It may mean
danger for Alida Barclay. If she— He stopped to listen to
the sound of feet running down the stairs. Had Cindy—

He started for the hall. Sarah Ann Parker narrowly

missed a collision in the doorway. He caught her shoulder and drew her into the kitchen.

"What's happened?" he demanded. "Is she all right?"

"Sure," Miss Parker adjusted her spectacles which were hanging by the band. "All right, 'cept she's scared 'bout out of her wits. She said she was with you on the bluff, remembers feelin' terrible sleepy, the next thing she knew she was lyin' on the chaise longy and Hal Harding was bendin' over her. 'Fore she could make a move to push him away you spoke. She's frightened for fear she had an attack of am-am—you know the thing folks have when they forget where they are?"

"You mean amnesia. Nonsense." He explained what happened. "She has been carrying a big responsibility for years. When it was lifted nature took over and put her to sleep."

She nodded in sage agreement.

"Responsibility, you're right, an' she couldn't ever have felt young an' happy the way a girl her age should feel. Her father was a good man, but a fusser, an' one of the leaning kind. Everything had to be just as he wanted it or he'd raise a rumpus. Want to know somethin'? Just before Trader Armstrong come to see her the first time she was talkin' 'bout the business an' tellin' about a man named Atlas holdin' up the heavens on his shoulders an' then she says, 'I been holdin' up the oil business on mine. If ever I get rid of it I'll sleep for a week.'"

"You see, I was right in my diagnosis. I—" he stopped speaking as, after an experimental turn of the handle the door from the patio swung in cautiously. As if reconnoitering, a head appeared in the opening. Sarah Ann Parker caught his arm and administered a warning squeeze to command silence. The two stood motionless in the cool, darkened kitchen as a figure in a pink and white striped dress slipped in and soundlessly closed the door behind her. It was the girl in the red swim suit whose picture Cindy had snapped at the beach.

"My sakes, Rena, why you stealin' into this house as if you was afraid you'd be caught?"

Startled by Sarah Ann Parker's rasping query the girl dropped the basket she carried.

"Gosh, Miss Parker. You scared me out of a year's growth. I thought you'd gone to the—Coming in from the blazing sunlight I couldn't see anything in this dark kitchen."

"Hmp. So I gathered. What do you want?"

"Mrs. Drew has unexpected guests coming to dinner and she wondered if you could spare a dozen eggs. I couldn't get one in the village. The cook needs them." Her voice which had been shaky at first gained assurance.

"From the size of the basket you just picked up looks as if you expected to lug home a crate of them."

"It is big, I had a lot of things to buy. Can you spare the eggs?"

"I cannot."

"Nothing in my life, it's the cook's problem. It isn't part of my work to market. I was trying to help. Sorry I burst in on what looks to be a *secret* meeting." From under long black lashes she glanced at the man standing at the window hands thrust into the pockets of his coat.

"Don't be saucy, Rena Foster. The next time you come into my kitchen knock before you open the door."

"Sure, I will before I come into *your* kitchen. How long since you owned The Castle? I'll tell Mrs. Drew that you wouldn't accommodate her about the eggs."

The door slammed. Sarah watched from the window as she ran across the garden, the putting green toward the pier.

"Now, what do you make of that, Mr. Damon?"

"Is she in the habit of entering without knocking?"

"Yes, but she wasn't 'enterin',' she was stealin' in. Didn't you hear her begin, 'I thought you'd gone to the—' then she stopped short. 'Twas her that told me Ella Crane had a television set, an' she hasn't got one. Looks kinder like she was tryin' to get me out of the way so she could get in for somethin', don't it?"

"Who is the girl?"

"Rena Foster. She's what's called a parlormaid at Mrs. Drew's. Folks say she's runnin' round with a tough-lookin' man who's tryin' to get a job at one of the summer places."

A tough-looking man trying to get a job at one of the summer places. He mentally filed the description for further reference.

"Didn't you have a dozen eggs to loan, Miss Parker?"

"Sure, I had, you don't think I'd get caught with supplies so low I'd have to borrer, do you? I didn't like the way that girl came in, something sly about it. 'Twasn't eggs she was after."

"Any suspicion what she would come for? Ever heard that she is dishonest?"

"Nothin' that was proved. When she burst in I was just about to ask if you'd go up and tell Cindy what you told me, that it was natural for her to drop off to sleep. She's scared it may happen again when that divorce goes through."

"It won't, you may assure her of that. She has had no lunch. Tempt her to eat, then suggest that she drive to the Country Club and see her friends. It is too hot for tennis."

"It's too hot to live, if you ask me. You won't go up?"

"She doesn't need me. Tell her what I said."

"I will. Perhaps I can make her believe it, though she's terrible jittery." She dropped her spectacles by the band and drew her right hand across her wet eyes. "When I saw that child lyin' there so still, though I knew he had nothin' to do with it, I could have choked that Kenniston Stewart with my bare hands."

"Sarah Ann Parker, that goes for me too—and double. Better hustle up a lunch for Cindy. She'll be gay as a lark after she eats. So long."

"Queer things are being seen and heard in this neighborhood," Harding's voice echoed through his memory as he crossed the patio to his car. Sary was suspicious of the Foster girl's reason for surreptitiously entering the kitchen a few moments ago. "Folks say, she's runnin' round with a tough-lookin' man who's tryin' to get a job at one of the summer places." He had seen them together at the beach. The situation would stand looking into.

She was employed as parlormaid by the owner of the yacht which dropped anchor often off the Rockledge shore. Did these facts tie together? Had Ally Barclay missed a trick when she decided that "the rich business-woman," Mrs. Drew, was above suspicion?

# TWELVE

"GAME and set for us, Cinderella, I hope we can add 'match' tomorrow. We knocked Lydia Fane and that boy she is running round with out of the tournament. Not that he isn't tops. I bet he's champ material. He has a volley that will take him places. Jupiter, Maine sea breezes have burned my Western skin to a crisp." Tom Slade tenderly touched his bright scarlet cheek before he tucked his arm under hers. "Let's go somewhere for lunch."

"Not today. Thomas, you are everlastingly wanting to 'go' somewhere. Don't you ever sit still and reflect on world problems or the beauties of nature?"

"I'm reflecting on the beauty of you in that white tennis rig and light blue cardigan, this minute. Sure I reflect on world problems, how can one help it if one reads of the menace of the cold war and the unrest simmering beneath the thin shell of diplomacy? But not when I am on vacation visiting my girl. Don't stiffen. I'm done. What a day. All green and gold and blue and a breeze straight from the ocean. Sniff the salt."

"And is the coolness appreciated after the wilting heat of yesterday? The Stars and Stripes and the Club pennant are standing out straight."

"Did you get the oil deal tied up?"

"We did."

"Did it take you all day to do it? I called at The Castle soon after lunch, rang and rang. When I phoned in the evening that watchdog of yours said you'd had a hard day and had gone to bed."

"Sarah Ann Parker told you that? At about three I looked in at the Club—no one there, too hot—" evidently the news of her sleep-fest had not reached the air waves—"I went home and found Mrs. Barclay there, making a formal call, she is Counselor Armstrong's sister, in case you care, and accepted her invitation for buffet supper and an evening at Canasta with her brother and herself." Had Bill Damon prompted the invitation? The two exciting games had been just what she needed to restore her self-confidence. The sudden sleep had frightened her.

"Who made the fourth?"

"I object to the hint of suspicion in the question. Three can play. Of course you don't play partners, but it is lots of fun."

"Do you like Mrs. Barclay?"

"Very much. She is charming. A glowing sort of person, if you get what I mean."

"Sure I get what you mean, that's the sort of person you are. You give out something, friendliness and interest, that makes the other fellow respond with the best that's in him."

"Tom Slade. That is the loveliest thing ever said to me."

"Don't let it turn your head. Lyd Fane says she thinks the ruddy Armstrong has views about you."

"What does she mean, 'views'?"

"The next Mrs. Armstrong. Guess telling you that was a mistake. May get your hopes up."

"Now who is kidding? Thomas, when, if ever, I get out of the present matrimonial quicksands it will be many a day before I am drawn into one again."

"Is that so? Let's tune in on another station. I sure am sold on your Maine coast. When I have made an immortal reputation as a jurist and incidentally, my pile, I'll buy a place in this town and raise strawberries. I've never yet had my fill of big luscious ones. Would that suit you, Cinderella?"

"Like the girl in Mother Goose who sat on a cushion and sewed a fine seam, dined upon strawberries, sugar and cream? No thank you. The prospect leaves me cold."

"Wrong number. I'll try again. Darn it, here comes the Fane menace. Wonder if she's sore because we beat her?"

"No. Whatever Lyd's faults, she's a good sport. She's had a curious life, parents separated, each has had two additional marriages. She spent several years abroad, Ella Crane says 'with a fast set.' "

"She may have had a curious life, but she remains a pest," Slade muttered.

"You'll come to the Bal Masqué at the Inn next week Friday night, won't you, Tommy?" Lydia slipped her hand under his arm and raised appealing eyes to his. "Small name band but a good one. Be-bop, jazz and waltzes. No do-si-do. Five dollars per person, not couple—for the hospital. Be a dear and make him come, Cindy."

"Wrong slant, Lyd. Thomas Slade, Second, can't be told to do anything. Of course he will go under his own power."

"Sure of that?" By shifting his racquet Slade detached the clinging hand from his arm. "How do I know I'll have any partners? You gals all but mobbed that Damon fella when he came out to get into his car this A.M. You had no eyes for me sitting on the porch rail."

"Don't be touchy, Tommy. We are all crazy about you." Lydia cooed, "but there is an unwritten law that we can't cut in on another girl's beau." The expression in the green eyes as they flashed to hers brought color to Cindy's face. She means Tom is mine, she thought.

"To return to Bill Damon; did you see him beat Tod Currier a few minutes ago? Our returned hero will draw a crowd tomorrow when he appears for the finals. This morning we were trying to sell him on the Bal Masqué."

"What luck?" Cindy asked.

"He promised to take tickets. Whether he came would depend upon what he could think up for a costume. There is a rumor that he is at the Inn to be near his heartbeat."

Where did she pick up that gossip, Cindy wondered.

Should she tell her the real reason for his presence in this village, that he had come to clear up Kenniston Stewart's business, matrimonial and otherwise? Lydia would love to broadcast that morsel.

"The plot thickens," Tom Slade declared dramatically. "Which gal at the Inn is his heartbeat?" Above the light he was holding to a cigarette he winked at Cindy.

"It isn't one of us girls, worse luck. The other night Alida Barclay, Lady Barclay to you, was his guest at dinner. I'll hand it to her for having clothes sense. Fashion firsts from haircut to shoes. She looked as a Duchess should and rarely does. A little bird chirped that they sat in a shadowy corner of the porch for all hours, very near together, watching the moon."

"Which one of the Inn young *ladies* put on the espionage act? Too bad there weren't wires to tap."

"Cut the sarcasm, Tommy. We are *not* snooping. We sent several emissaries to invite them to join us at cards, but they were so absorbed in one another that no one dared break in."

"Mighty considerate of the messengers not to disturb love's young dream."

"*Young* dream?" Lydia's laugh was a shriek of derision. "Alida Barclay must be at least ten years older than Bill Damon."

"What's ten years when Love is at the helm?" Cindy was shocked at the edge in her own voice.

"If you ask me, dearie, ten years is twenty when it is on the woman's side. Aren't you two coming in for a cold drink?"

Lydia Fane's question flagged Cindy's train of thought to an abrupt stop.

"No," she said hastily. "I'm going home to change my tennis clothes for something chic and elegant, after which I shall call on Mrs. Sally Drew at Rockledge. I hear she complains that the cottagers have ignored her. Come with me?"

"I'm not a cottager, that lets me out. Someone ought to tell her that blonde bleach may be a lifesaver, but when it turns hair the color of the brass rings at a merry-go-round, it shoots her into a different class. I'd

go, though, if I thought her *'secretary'*—interrogation
point—would be among those present. I'm told he's
blond as a Viking, has a where-have-you-been-all-my-life
manner and lives on her yacht."

"Is the yacht that comes in so often really hers? I've
heard rumors to that effect but never have been sure."

"Page Ella Crane. My information came from her.
Bring down two birds with one stone, Cindy, sell her
tickets to the masquerade."

"Not a chance when I am making a first call."

"Suit yourself. I'll tackle the secretary. So like you to
hear and respond to the conscience-call of neighborly
duty. Lucky it isn't so insistent as the call of marriage
bells. Don't forget your names are drawn for the
masquerade—send checks to me. We'll be agog to see
who picks up your glass slipper at the stroke of twelve,
Cinderella. Wouldn't it be thrilling if the long-distance
husband appeared? Now *that's* an idea. By." She ran up
the Club House steps and vanished.

"If that gal belonged to me I'd wring her lovely neck
and wring it hard. Though she didn't mention it, I bet
she was getting back at us with her wisecracks for knocking her out of the tournament. Don't you mind her,
Cindy, you look as if she'd given you a jolting right to
the head."

"That suggestion of the return of the long-distance
husband made it whirl for a minute. I don't mind Lyd
Fane. I'm conditioned to her viperish tongue. Counselor
Armstrong phoned me just before I left home that my
annulment would come up for a hearing tomorrow.
Two cases that preceded it have gone off the list."

"Tomorrow? We have to play off the finals early in
the morning."

"My case is called for the afternoon. Just wait till I'm
a free woman. Watch me put on a running interference
with Lyd, just watch me."

"What do you mean, 'running interference'? Cut out
the Fane menace with Bill Damon? I've been foaming at
the mouth fearing you might go off your head about
him."

"I'm not going off my head about anyone. No romantic entanglement for yours truly, Thomas."

"Oh, yeah? I'll drive you to the Courthouse tomorrow."

"No, thank you. Counselor Armstrong invited me to go with him but I prefer to arrive under my own power, my jalopy to you, if it will hold together."

"Then I'll be outside waiting when you exit a free woman. We'll dine and dance somewhere to celebrate. It's a date."

"It's not a date, Tom. Don't meet me at the Courthouse. I shall stay at home tomorrow evening."

"For crying out loud! What's the idea? A period of mourning for Kenniston Stewart? At least you'll let me come to The Castle and hold your hand?"

"I'm disappointed in you, Thomas. I thought *you* would understand. You don't. You are as uncomprehending as Hal Harding."

"Did that playboy suggest whoopee?"

"He did. If you really want to help take me to call on Mrs. Sally Drew this afternoon in your snappy Town and Country convertible. My car is not only shabby, it is unreliable, and I'm saving what is left of its performance for the trip to the Courthouse tomorrow."

"Hang it, Cindy, I can't. They told me as we left the court that I am scheduled to play off my semifinals in the men's doubles this afternoon. Terribly sorry. Here comes Ken Stewart's stand-in. He'll take you. Hi, Damon!"

The man with the crimson cardigan thrown across the shoulders of his short-sleeved, open-neck white shirt waved his racquet in response to the hail and joined them.

"Did I hear my name? You and Slade played a corking game, Cindy."

"Thank the gentleman like a little lady, then speak your piece and say 'Please' prettily, Cinderella."

"She doesn't have to say 'Please' prettily. What can I do for you, Cindy?" Bill Damon's voice sounded grave in contrast to Slade's light banter.

"I have planned to call on Mrs. Sally Drew at

Rockledge this afternoon, gloves, visiting card and all the social frills. My jalopy is unreliable, of course I could go across the cove in my Evinrude, *The Mighty Mo*, but I'm trying to engage a chauffeur with a snappy car. Will you take me?"

"That's what I'm here for. What time shall I come for you?"

"Will four be convenient?"

"Four it is, on the minute. I'll be there."

Two hours later he stopped his car in front of the low spreading contemporary California-type house with its huge windows clear as crystal.

"The ocean view from here is tops," he approved.

"Not any better than from The Castle," Cindy reminded jealously.

"Righto. Would it be in poor taste for your chauffeur to tell you that you are a knockout in that white frock, matching gloves, and big velvet hat? What's the color?"

"Coral orange."

"It's perfect on you. Did you have the corsage of sweet peas dyed to match? What does it say on those cards in the silver case?"

"I'm making it formal today." She was annoyingly aware that her color deepened. "I can't have myself announced as Miss Clinton when that isn't my name yet. Counselor Armstrong phoned me that the annulment case will be called and settled tomorrow afternoon."

"He notified me also. What do we do next? Are we to sit here admiring the view—and you—or are you going in?"

She laughed.

"*In*, Colonel Damon."

He stood beside the car as she stepped to the porch.

"I'll wait till we find out if the lady is at home. If she is, I'll drive around and come back."

"Return in twenty minutes—please. Don't make it a second longer than that."

He touched his soft hat.

"In twenty minutes, Mrs. Stewart."

# THIRTEEN

"MRS. STEWART." Bill Damon had called her by that name before, but for some unexplained reason this time Cindy's heartbeat quickened. She lifted the shining brass knocker and let it drop. The sound echoed inside the house like the knell of doom. She straightened the coral orange velvet hat to the fashion-proper angle and looked up as the door was opened.

"Is Mrs. Drew at home?" At the moment she asked the question she recognized the maid in smart white uniform and scrap of cap as the girl in the red swim outfit who had been returning the glances of the man in the black and white checked suit with interest. She must be Rena Foster, whom Sarah Ann Parker had declared was a "flighty piece." Now her eyes were coldly defiant. Did she recognize the caller as the person who had snapped her picture?

"She is, Madam. Won't you come in?"

"Tell her that Mrs. Stewart from The Castle is calling."

She entered the house and followed the maid through a hall to the threshold of a room that blazed with color. With a murmured word the girl departed.

I've read that color and bright light kindle the flame of the human spirit, the spirit of the occupant of this house ought to glow like a thousand-watt incandescent bulb, she thought as she crossed the rugless floor polished to a mirror gloss. Her heels clicked sharply.

A woman in white from head to feet, standing close to

95

the bleached maple wall with one hand touching it as if experimentally, turned quickly.

"Cindy Clinton! You gave me the start of my life." Alida Barclay's voice was gay if a trifle breathless. "Aren't the walls of this room beautiful? So sensible not to clutter them with pictures, mirrors or hangings. I was wondering if this maple would be practicable to use in my living room in New York."

"I like the spaciousness and color," Cindy approved. "It must be the last word in mid-twentieth-century decoration to harmonize with the architecture of the house."

A low couch was cushioned in the soft pink of the blossoms of a huge geranium in an Oriental lacquer stand in a corner; its pillows were the lightest shade of the green of the leaves. A flat dark blue bowl on a broad desk of natural mahogany held one mammoth pale yellow dahlia. A bamboo chaise longue was cushioned in aqua; a mass of auratum lilies topped a low black and gold cabinet. Tables at the arm of inviting chairs holding choice figurines or bronzes were reflected in the polished floor like colorful islands in a still pool. A Ming vase lamp at each end of the couch threw a soft pink light. Through the windows of the glassed-in extension of the living room was visible a vast expanse of sky and ocean.

Alida Barclay laughed softly.

"You appear to be considering a place to sit, Cindy. It must take a person with the spring of a gazelle to get out of the low chairs gracefully. These furnishings are as contemporary as flying saucers and the reduction of excise taxes." She glanced at her wrist watch.

"I've been waiting ten minutes. My hostess left me to answer a long-distance call. I can't wait any longer. I'm giving a little dinner for Mrs. Drew. The only date on which we could agree is next Thursday, the evening before the Bal Masqué. Plan to come in your best bib and tucker—I understand the lady thinks we 'natives,' quote, are provincial—and bring that good-looking Slade slave of yours. I'll phone details. Explain to Mrs. Drew for me, will you?"

Alone in the vast room, Cindy felt like Robinson

Crusoe on a desert island with no man Friday in sight. But—here he comes, she thought, as a yellow-haired, dark-eyed woman in a smart beige frock entered followed by a tall fair-haired man. The secretary, "blond as a Viking," Cindy decided and disciplined the smile the echo of Lyd Fane's words had started.

"Mrs. Stewart, how *sweet* of you to come."

Thirty? Forty? The figures flashed through Cindy's mind as she laid hers in the hand blazing with rings outheld in welcome. Better settle for early thirty. The man behind her hostess stood as if waiting to be included in the group. His fair skin didn't look as if he spent much time on the water; his blue coat and white trousers were well cut.

"I'm in luck to find you at home, Mrs. Drew."

"I'm the person who is in luck, Mrs. Stewart." She glanced around the room. "What became of that *sweet* Mrs. Barclay? I had to leave to answer a long-distance call."

Cindy explained.

"I am consumed with mortification that it happened. Do sit down, Laurie, I had completely forgotten you. Mrs. Stewart, may I present Laurence Lloyd?"

"You've heard of the forgotten man, Mrs. Stewart. Behold him." His blue eyes smiled into hers. Now I know what Lyd meant by his where-have-you-been-all-my-life manner, she thought before he added, "Your fame and your romantic story have preceded you. I have been hoping that we might meet. Sally, are we supposed to stand the rest of the afternoon?"

"Remember, Laurie, you are employed here. You are *not* the host," Mrs. Drew reminded sharply.

That starts off the party with a snap, Cindy thought. He looks too big and husky to take that lying down. Is he afraid of her? He laughed. Apparently he wasn't.

"That puts me in my place and how."

"Stop your nonsense, Laurie. Do sit down, Mrs. Stewart. I have ordered tea."

Cindy selected the geranium-pink couch as the seat least likely to force her knees under her chin. I'll never be able to rise. Here's hoping I won't have occasion to spring lightly to my feet. I couldn't make it, she told herself as she settled deeper into the cushions. Mrs. Drew sank down gracefully beside her. The secretary selected a low chair. His long legs bent sharply at the knees reminded Cindy of a grasshopper's.

"As to being lucky to find me here," the hostess had returned to Cindy's greeting, "I'm rarely anywhere but at home." Her mouth took on a sorry-for-myself droop at the corners, her voice sagged. The person who said that color and bright light kindled the flame of the human spirit hasn't polled this spirit, Cindy concluded.

"The wilting weather of the past few days has made home seem the best," she contributed aloud and thought, Is that the top gem of conversation I can produce? She tried again.

"I can't feel sorry for you, Mrs. Drew, with that beautiful yacht in which to escape." I hope rumor is reliable in this case and that it is hers, she added to herself.

"Escape? What do you mean, *escape?*"

So what? You're frightened, lady. Was Sary right when she hinted there was a mystery connected with the coming and going of that boat? Had the woman a spotty past or a smudged present? Was she so shrewd as to be dangerous or so dull as to be dumb?

"Mrs. Stewart meant to escape the heat, of course, Sally."

Her master's voice, Cindy thought, as the woman's hands which had been fluttering steadied at Lloyd's reminder.

"Here comes our tea, at last," she announced.

He moved a low table in front of her and the maid placed on it a mammoth black lacquer tray with Oriental eggshell cups and saucers, and gleaming silver. Mrs. Drew made the usual inquiries about her guest's preference as to strength and trimmings. The maid passed hot mushroom *canapés* and one-bite frosted cakes which Cindy recognized as carbon copies of Sarah Ann Parker's master creations.

"So sorry about that *sweet* Mrs. Barclay." The hostess had returned to the subject of her recent caller. "She's charming. Do tell me a little about her. Just what is her position in this town?"

"Do you mean her family? It's tops. She was born here, makes her home in New York, I believe. At present she is visiting her brother who is one of the most distinguished lawyers to come out of the State of Maine."

"Her face worries me. I'm sure I have met her before. She—"

"That is because she looked like a fashion model, Sally," Lloyd interrupted. He had a curious habit of pinching the lobe of his left ear as he talked. Had he been afraid of what she might say? "You've seen her in duplicate in your favorite fashion magazines."

"It's more than that. I have a feeling I have run across her somewhere. I've been almost everywhere abroad except the Orient. Has Mrs. Barclay ever lived in Europe, Mrs. Stewart?"

"I don't know, Mrs. Drew. I haven't seen or heard of her for years before this summer." That didn't tell much. Cindy had a quick close-up of Alida Barclay's outstretched hand feeling the wall of this room.

Mrs. Drew recalled her attention with a rapid-fire series of questions about guests at the Inn; summer residents; was there a putting green? she adored putting; on and on. Trifles that meant nothing to her, Cindy answered, desperately making small talk. At the first break in the Information Please quiz, she picked up her long gloves, rose, she hoped gracefully, from the geranium-pink couch.

"The tea was delicious," she declared to her hostess, who had extricated herself from the deep cushions with feline ease and grace. "You said you loved to putt. I'll plan soon for you to try the green at The Castle. Good afternoon, Mr. Lloyd."

"Not yet. I'll speed the parting guest."

Bill Damon, hatless, was standing beside the convertible when they stepped to the porch. He looked up. There was an instant of what seemed to Cindy an electrically charged silence. Were the two men enemies? She hastened to break the spell.

"Mr. Lloyd, Colonel Damon." They bowed formally.

"I hope you'll come again and often—Mrs. Stewart," Lloyd said as he came down the one step as if to assist her into the car. Damon stepped between them.

"Do come and putt at The Castle sometime, Mr. Lloyd," she invited from her seat beside the wheel. "Bring Mrs. Drew. Good—" The car shot ahead and left the rest of the word floating in thin air.

"You didn't give me a chance to finish my pretty speech," Cindy reminded. "What was the matter? Didn't you like the blond Viking?"

"Like him? Who is he?"

"He is Mrs. Drew's secretary and lives on the yacht. Ella Crane announcing. I suspected by the way you two glared at one another that in a previous incarnation you had been mortal enemies."

"What did you say his name was? I didn't get it."

"Laurence Lloyd. His employer calls him 'Laurie.' "

"Never heard the name before, that explodes your previous-incarnation theory."

Cindy looked back at the spreading house.

"Rockledge is full of beautiful Oriental pieces. I wonder if they belong to the owner or the present tenant. I would hate to have the responsibility of them if they were not mine."

"Perhaps Mrs. Drew has lived in the Orient?"

"During the conversation she volunteered the information that she had been almost everywhere abroad except there."

"What led up to that statement?"

"Alida Barclay was calling when I arrived. After she left Mrs. Drew confided that Mrs. Barclay's face worried her, she was sure she had met her before."

"Was—did you say the name was Lloyd—present when she said that?"

"Yes. He suggested that Mrs. Drew probably had seen her in duplicate in fashion magazines, as she was the perfect model of a smartly dressed woman."

"An orchid for Alida Barclay, I'd say. Too bad she didn't hear it." He glanced at her hand. "What's the ring on your left third finger?"

"What would it be?"

"I thought you didn't wear a wedding ring."

"I wore it today to back up my name. I felt like a cheat each time Mrs. Drew called me Mrs. Stewart. I was horribly tempted to add, until tomorrow. If I hadn't worn the ring what would she have thought? That was a rhetorical question. You needn't answer." She moved the diamond circlet up and down, then added:

"It is beautiful, but a plain gold band, not too wide, is my idea of a wedding ring. Perhaps because for years I saw one like that on Mother's finger."

"You don't like anything that is in any way connected with Kenniston Stewart, do you?"

"Let me think. I like his name."

"You're terribly unfair to him, Cindy. He *couldn't* come—"

"If I am my feelings about him won't make any difference after today. I know I am unfair to him, and I burn with shame after I've criticized him, but you can't understand, I don't myself, the restless, contradictory emotions fighting for control of my mind. The constant awareness and menace of world conditions does its part toward the tumult, I suppose."

"Does that mean you doubt the wisdom of the annulment, Cinderella?"

"No. *No.* How can I doubt it? Kenniston Stewart is as keen for his freedom as I am, isn't he? How did we get switched to my problems. Let's tune in on another station. I was thinking the other day—you know my life story from the cradle on, I don't know who you are, where you came from, except that you are a pal of Ken Stewart's. You may be married. Your past is a blank to me."

"It isn't a blank to me, Cinderella. It has been redly and indelibly recorded on the screen of memory. When I'm through with Ken Stewart's commission, I'll give you a decade-by-decade account of my life, starting back with the career of my maternal great-grandfather, who made it possible for me to carry on my education without having to figure funds. I'll confide my ambition to be an honored citizen who counts in the welfare of this nation while I climb to the top of my profession." He laughed. "Think you can take it?"

"Yes. I like the word 'honored.' "

To love and to honor, the phrase which Hal had criticized, flashed through her mind. Bill Damon would have understood.

"Did—did Counselor Armstrong notify you that the annulment case was set for tomorrow afternoon?"

"Yes."

"Will you be there?"

"I? Certainly *not*. As soon as I've played off my doubles I have a business appointment in Portland."

Conversation lagged after that. Cindy was afraid to speak for fear her voice would show her disappointment. She had had the foolish hope that he would see her through the hearing. At the door of The Castle, he said, "Good luck tomorrow. Good-by, 'Mrs. Stewart-for-the-last-time.' "

As Cindy entered the hall a radioed voice was singing: "I want to go where you are—"

The song ceased abruptly. Sarah Ann Parker appeared at the door of the old kitchen.

"Isn't Mr. Damon comin' in to have dinner with you? Thought perhaps he would to talk over your case comin' up tomorrow. Is he plannin' to be there?"

"He isn't supposed to be present. This is an uncontested case, remember. I'd like my dinner in the patio, Sary."

She went slowly up the stairs with a curious let-down feeling. "Why shouldn't he go off on business tomorrow?" she demanded of the girl who faced her in the long mirror of her room. This annulment is nothing in his life. He didn't answer when I said, "You may be married." Probably he is. She pulled off the coral orange velvet hat, unfastened the corsage of matching sweet peas, and brushed her hand across her eyes to clear them of tears.

"I want to go where you are—"

The voice rose from below. Sarah had switched on the radio.

# FOURTEEN

THERE WAS a gray-haired man in a black robe seated at a desk in the County Courthouse. On the wall above his head spread the Stars and Stripes. The sight of the flag stiffened Cindy's knees. Time she stopped feeling as if she were committing a crime. Perhaps after today the turmoil of her spirit would settle down. Perhaps in time the written contract marriage would seem as remote as if it had happened in a dream. The Judge's shaggy brows drew together in an appraising frown as the keen eyes under them met hers. Armstrong beside her inflated and deflated his cheeks.

"Mrs. Cinderella Clinton Stewart, Your Honor. Judge Shelton, Mrs. Stewart."

The man at the desk rose, reached across to offer his hand and smiled.

"I don't need an introduction to little Cindy Clinton. I used to see you when I played chess with your father before he became a celebrated inventor and I hung out my shingle for the law. We thought we were world-beaters. Sit here." He indicated a chair beside the desk. "Ready, Counselor." His voice had changed from friendliness to gravity as befitted the business before him.

She watched Armstrong step forward and spread papers on the desk without really seeing him. For one instant the friendliness of His Honor tempted her to ask if he approved of this annulment. That was a cockeyed thought. What difference would his opinion make? Kenniston Stewart's life and hers were to be considered.

Wasn't the defendant—he wasn't a defendant, he was a non-contestant—clamoring for his freedom.

Another perfect day. A breeze drifting in through an open window brought the faint scent of autumn. Was that silly wasp crawling up the screen and sliding down trying to escape into the outside world? Did each living creature who came into this room in the Courthouse want out?

"Have you no respect for the inviolability of a contract?" Bill Damon had asked. Why hadn't he asked that question of his friend before he crossed the ocean with the declared intention of freeing him from that same contract? Now she was being irrational. Why should he try to influence either of the parties involved?

"You are quite sure you want this marriage by written contract annulled, Cinderella?"

The dark eyes peering at her over the rims of the Judge's spectacles were as grave as his voice. He was questioning her as he might a daughter; his was the role of a friendly adviser, not that of the strong arm of the law.

"Yes, Your Honor."

"I understand you never have seen Kenniston Stewart."

"That's right, sir."

More questions, more answers. Why did he repeat questions the answers to which he knew from her lawyer's presentation of the case? It seemed as if she had been sitting beside the desk for hours. The breeze had wandered away. The amethyst cotton frock with the stem of a blush-pink dahlia drawn through the belt began to feel wilted. At the last minute she had pulled on a soft hat for fear that if she appeared in the Judge's chambers without her head covered she might be fined for contempt of court.

"That's all, Cinderella Clinton." She rose as he came from behind the desk with hand extended.

"Is that really my name again?"

"It is. Counselor Armstrong will file all necessary papers and send duplicates to Kenniston Stewart. You are as free as if you never had signed that contract. Legally

your marriage is held not to have existed. Consider
yourself a single girl. You may marry again as soon as
you like."

"Marry! No. *No.* You understand, don't you, Judge
Shelton, that I didn't ask for this annulment because I
was in love with *anyone,* anyone on *earth.*"

"I understand, Cinderella. If I had had doubts the
blazing sincerity of your eyes and voice would have
convinced me. I had that in mind when I granted the
annulment quickly, that and the fact that you sought
your freedom in your *actual* domicile. So many seek a
court in another state to hasten a divorce in violation of
the laws of their own state. Each state retains the power
to regulate marriage and divorce. You were well advised."

She was thinking of his words as she stepped into her
ancient jalopy in the Courthouse parking space. Sounded like an oft-rehearsed little speech to be delivered
after each divorce.

Now what? Thank heaven there was no indication she
would be rendered *hors de combat* by sleep at this
milestone in her life as she had been when the responsibility of the oil holdings had been lifted from her shoulders. What a curious experience! Lucky she had been
with Bill Damon who understood. Sary had relayed his
explanation. It had been so believable that her fright
had been assuaged. He hadn't mentioned it yesterday
while they were together. Was it really business that had
called him to Portland this afternoon or had he wanted
to side-step the hearing?

One! Two! Three! Four!

A village clock intoned the hour. Only four o'clock.
How quickly the marriage had been terminated that
had taken such an interminable time and endless corre-
spondence to contract. "Legally your marriage is held
not to have existed. Consider yourself a single girl,"
Judge Shelton had said. Why think of the past? From
this minute she was free to go forward. Where?

Too early to go home. Sary would be lying in wait to
pounce with questions, to ply her with tea and toast as if
she needed solace after a harrowing experience. On the

contrary, it had been heart-warming, the Judge had been so friendly.

Why sit here deliberating? She would drive to the shop where she had left the films to be blown up. She hadn't dared leave them with Ella Crane, who would have third-degreed her to find out why she wanted them enlarged, who the man and girl were.

"Hey, Cindy! Is it all over? Are you free? Now we can go places."

Hal Harding's eager voice hailed her. Hal Harding's hand was on the windshield. Hal Harding's light blue eyes were sparkling with triumph.

"Not today. Move away, Hal. I *don't* want company." With a snort the jalopy leaped forward.

"You'll have company. I never give up w-h-a-t I w-a-n-t."

His shout of angry warning with its hint of threat drifted into a murmur as she gave the car all it had, which wasn't so much, until she reached the highway. She slowed down. Glanced out the rear window. He was not following. Perhaps he realized how ridiculous he appeared standing in the Courthouse parking lot shouting after a departing car.

An hour later she drove the jalopy into the garage at The Castle. It was a modern miracle that she had made the trip without a crack-up. All the way to the city and back she had relived the experiences of the last three years with Hal Harding's "You'll have company. I never give up what I want," an obbligato accompaniment. The annulment hearing had been like a hand writing *finis* at the bottom of a page. Now she would leave the past behind and begin a brand-new chapter.

She stole into the house, successfully dodged Sarah Ann Parker, showered, changed to a sleeveless aqua organdy and fastened a pink Perfection rose to her shoulder. But when she sat down at the glass table in the patio, where a crystal plate piled with rosy balls of iced watermelon awaited her, Sarah swooped like an owl which had been watching for its rabbit prey.

She continued to hover after she served a delicately roasted squab chicken, a flaky baked potato, outsize peas of a sweet and melting tenderness, a fluffy roll, and currant jelly red as a mammoth pigeon-blood ruby.

"Who was the Judge?" she inquired as she filled a hollow-stem glass with a fruit juice combination sparkling as champagne, cold as a mountain spring.

"Shelton? The Federal Judge? He's a wise man, an' an awful nice one. Want to know somethin'? He was terribly in love with Ally Armstrong when they was young. Suddenly she went off an' married Lord Barclay, folks never knew what happened. He's an old bach, has a fine family place—up Portland way." She added Roquefort cheese dressing to slices of chilled avocado and sections of pink grapefruit on pale green lettuce.

"He told you he played chess with your father? Sure he played with him. I remember him coming to this house.

"You seem surprised he was friendly. Why not? That's the way a Judge should be to folks who bring their troubles to court, not scare 'em to death.

"Did he lambast that Kenniston Stewart for not being here to appear before him?" The question accompanied the serving of an individual baked Alaska, its meringue a delicate brown above vanilla ice cream.

"He didn't? Want to know somethin'? If I'd been that judge I'd have said a scorching thing or two." And on and on until the ring of the telephone called her away.

One thing to plan to start a new life and another to accomplish the feat, Cindy decided later in the old kitchen with the pumpkin-yellow walls she used as a workroom. She drew ledger and account book from the drawer of a flat mahogany desk, the only modern piece of furniture among priceless antiques, and laid them on top.

Hands clasped behind her head she leaned back in the swivel chair. Nice room. The mulberry borders and black centers of the Canova platter, tea and dinner plates on the shelves of the open cupboard were in charming contrast to the walls. They made an effective bit of color.

Allah be praised, Sary wouldn't follow her here. The *Woman at Work* sign hung on the knob outside the door and even she, whom nothing fazed, would Stop! Look! Listen! when she saw that.

The sight of the books she had laid on the desk in preparation for the evening's work induced a slight attack of nausea. Was it possible that after the final tax return was finished she would be out of the oil business forever? Out of work, too. Then what would she do?

Something definite. Something worth while. I will decide what I want most, plan for it and go after it with all there is in me. Bill Damon has the right idea. I want to be an honored citizen who counts in the welfare of the nation. I harangued Hal Harding as to the responsibility of wealth. Now it is up to me to prove I can practice what I preach.

She glanced at the six silver tennis trophy cups on the high shelf above the old oven. She had worked to win those. She had been up against amateurs who later had ranked among the best players in the country. The dated, autographed golf balls in the glass case on the wall she had won putting.

Yesterday she had invited Mrs. Drew to use The Castle green. The more she had thought of the woman since the call the less she liked her. Something artificial about her, might be her hair, undoubtedly it had been bleached, perhaps once it had been the color of her almost black eyes. She was pretty—in a way—but prissy. The word described her manner perfectly.

Was she really the silent partner in a big cosmetic company? Did that explain her need of a "secretary"? Or was the man Laurence Lloyd there for a different reason? In spite of her snap at him she was a little afraid of him.

Why had Alida Barclay pressed her fingers against the wall in the Rockledge living room? She jumped when I entered as if she had been caught stealing sheep. Her explanation that she was considering having a wall in her New York apartment done in bleached maple was a phony. Mrs. Drew was so sure she had seen or met her before, uneasily sure. Why? Ally had planned a dinner for her. Would she entertain the woman if she thought she was an undesirable person in the community?

I'd better stop speculating about my neighbors and tackle the accounting, but the neighbors are a heap more interesting, she admitted. As she reached for the ledger she saw the large envelope which contained the blown-up film she had dropped to the desk when she came home. She drew out the print. Tipped back in the swivel chair and studied it.

Nice composition for an amateur. "Gal, you're good," she congratulated herself. The enlargement had been well done. The faces were recognizable, the girl was the maid who had served tea yesterday at Rockledge, her swim costume had come out a brilliant red. The green tie worn by the man and each black and white check of his suit stood out against the turquoise of the sky and the ultramarine ocean. A successful example of color photography even if she said it who shouldn't.

She held the print under the desk light. In spite of the low drawn hat brim each feature of his face was clear cut. Tough, as she had expected. He looked like a person who would ogle a strange girl at the beach. The bad-man tilt of his hat reminded her of someone, not Bogart—

Her heart took off to her throat and as suddenly grounded. It was like the hat of the person who had slipped out the rear door of the hall at The Castle the day she had met the bracelet man at Ella Crane's shop. She had thought him a product of imagination then, now she knew he had been real. Why had he been in her house? Why had he sneaked—

What was that? The print she held fell to the floor as she sprang to her feet. Something was scratching at the outside of the priceless old painted shade she had drawn over the open window so the light of the room would not disclose the fact that she was within. A signal? Who was it? Tom Slade wouldn't intrude after she had told him she wanted to be alone. The sound again. "You'll have company." Hal Harding's threat echoed through her memory. He was as unpredictable as he was persistent.

"I'll show him—and how," she declared under her

breath and snapped up the shade with a force that sent it quivering on its roller.

"Sarah Ann Parker wouldn't let me in," explained a low voice from the gloom outside. "I had to see you." A leg slid over the window sill. A man swung into the room. He reached to the tassel, pulled down the shade, and turned.

"I have an important message to deliver," declared Bill Damon.

# FIFTEEN

A MESSAGE? From whom? What did he mean? Apprehensive of a crisis she backed away.

"Of what are you afraid?" He was smiling as he laid a large round white paper-covered box on the desk. "I'm off to Washington tomorrow. Before I go I have a commission to carry out for Ken Stewart. I am considering the most tactful approach to the subject."

The desk stopped her retreat. A wave of color swept over her neck and face to her hair.

"He didn't dare tell you to—to—" Fury choked her voice.

"To kiss you good-by? What an imagination you have. Certainly not. Besides, when I kiss a girl I don't post a notice." The laughter in his eyes set even her ears burning.

"Sit down, please. How can I talk to you when you appear to be figuring the distance to the door? What's this on the floor?" He picked up the enlarged print.

She explained, added:

"Remember the morning we sat on the beach and I told you the tilt of the man's hat was familiar? You laughed and declared it was the Humphrey Bogart tilt to the fraction of an inch. I am sure now where I saw it."

"Where?"

She told of entering the hall the afternoon after she had met him in Ella Crane's shop, of seeing the silhouette of a man at the other end, of his quick exit.

"Sure you saw someone?"

"I am now, then I thought it was an imagination hangover from last summer when this place swarmed with motion-picture smugglers and their hidden treasure."

He studied the print.

"Sure this is the same guy?"

"I wouldn't go into court and swear it was he, with only the tilt of his hat as evidence, but the girl in the red swim suit who was with him at the beach was the maid who opened the door at Rockledge yesterday."

"That's interesting. She dropped in while I was talking to Sary in the kitchen the day we signed the oil property deeds. Came to borrow eggs, she said. May I take this for twenty-four hours?"

"Keep it. I don't want it."

"We have detoured from the assignment which brought me here," he reminded as he slipped the print into the pocket of his bluish-gray coat. "Is it all over but the shouting?"

"If you mean the annulment, it is," she succumbed to an impelling need to confide in someone, "but, curiously enough, I don't feel like shouting. I thought when I was free my spirit would soar on silver wings, instead of that, I can't seem to get it off the ground. Believe it or not, I feel as if I had lost something."

"It seems to me you had everything to gain. What had you to lose?"

"Perhaps it is the name. I always loved 'Mrs. Kenniston Stewart.' "

"*Cindy—*"

"I don't need your shocked voice to remind me that I'm a mass of contradiction. I don't understand myself."

"Cindy—" He cleared his voice. "Please sit down." As she sat on the very edge of the swivel chair he perched on a corner of the flat desk. He drew an oblong violet velvet case from an inside pocket of his coat.

"Ken hopes you will accept this as a slight token of appreciation of all you have done for him. Don't draw back and stare as if you thought the thing would explode. Open it. O.K., if you won't, I will." He pressed a spring. The cover of the case flew up. She clasped her hands tight in thrilled surprise.

"Oo-o-oh. How exquisite! How lustrous! The center pearls in the string are as big as the peas Sary served for dinner. The diamond clasp is superb. Are they—they can't be *real?*"

"Sure they are real. Matched Orientals. You don't think Stewart would offer you costume stuff after the way you have slaved for him, do you?"

"Mister, don't sneer at costume stuff, it costs money." She pushed away the hand that held the violet case. "Put them back in your pocket. I can't accept them. Have you forgotten that the marriage contract was annulled today?"

"Not for a minute. I waited till I was sure that had gone through before bringing the pearls so you wouldn't look upon them as a bribe."

"A bribe? For *what?* That's the funniest thing I ever heard. I repeat, I can't accept the gift."

"I don't get you. Why? First you sacrificed yourself in that marriage that the property might be held together; you have kept Stewart's accounts; collected and deposited his income; sent him monthly statements; fought with the potential buyers of the oil holdings. What do you think the bill of a lawyer or a trust company would amount to for that service for three years plus? He considered sending you a check, then felt he had sized you up well enough to be sure you would return it in shreds; he thought of a ring—"

"I don't want a ring from him. I have one which I intend to return. He doesn't owe me anything. He advanced the money from a fortune he had inherited from his mother that his father and mine might acquire the property. Dad had only his inventions to put into the deal. Thank goodness every cent of our share of the loan has been paid. Everything I did I considered payment for his financial help in the beginning."

"Even the marriage?"

"That too. Now he is getting all his principal back plus his freedom."

"He doesn't take that view of what you have done for

him. Accept the pearls and wear them. They are not a gift. They are inadequate payment for value received."

"Did Ken Stewart select them?"

"Sorry, he couldn't leave his job. He asked me to buy pearls in New York. Hope the fact that he didn't make the selection won't detract from your pleasure in wearing them. Put them on. If they are hideously unbecoming he wouldn't want you to accept them."

"*Unbecoming!* Did you ever know pearls to be unbecoming? Hate those beautiful things? *Mon brave*, you have missed your calling. You're subtle. You should have been an advocate. I'll wager you would win any case you argued. Hear that little crash? It was my resistance crumbling." She snapped on an overhead light. "Hold the case while I try them on."

Before a gilt-framed oval mirror between the windows she fastened the necklace. He laid the case on the desk before he came to stand behind her. She could see his reflection as he looked over her shoulder.

"They glow on you. I wonder if the Prince gave the first Cinderella a gift so enormously becoming."

"Undoubtedly. Doesn't the fairy story end 'and they lived happily ever after'? What woman could remain unhappy with pearls like these?"

"If only those pearls could insure your happiness forever," he said gruffly.

"Then I wouldn't be much of a person. I'd be a restless, spineless creature with my soul and heart and thinking processes underdeveloped, if there were any, something tells me."

She moved her head from side to side and watched the effect. Her face flushed under the tan as she met his eyes in the mirror.

"Like me—in them?"

"Love you—in them. You're terrific, lifted from your admirer Slade's vocabulary."

"Where would I wear a superb necklace like this? Certainly not here."

"You don't expect to live here always, do you?"

"I don't know where I will live. That's one of my problems."

"Why not drift for a while? You've had your nose to the grindstone so long, make a play at being a free agent. The necklace is fully insured. Wear it. Don't worry about the value."

"Deep in your heart do you think I should accept such a fabulous gift?"

"Deep in my heart I think you will be cruel if you don't. Stewart is trying to show appreciation of an incalculable help you have been to him for which a money payment would be totally inadequate. I think you will be most ungracious if you don't accept the gift in the spirit in which it is offered."

"Then I will take it and write him a fervent 'Thank you' when I send a report of this afternoon's Court proceedings and his ring."

"Turn the ring over to me. It should be boxed and insured. I can take that off your shoulders."

"Thank you." She unlocked a drawer in the desk and took out a white velvet case. "Here it is. Now the very last link in that marriage by contract is broken."

As he dropped the case into his pocket she tried to unclasp the necklace.

"Let me do that. Why take it off? I have been told that pearls should be worn night and day."

"You don't know the difficulties of living with Sarah Ann Parker." The touch of his fingers against her neck sent little tingles along her veins. He put the necklace in her hand. She returned to the desk and laid it tenderly in the violet case.

"I need time in which to arrange my explanation as to why they were given to me. Sary knows every article in my wardrobe, every piece of jewelry I own. When I write Kenniston Stewart I'll tell him he picked an irresistible advocate when he sent you. Why are you looking at me like that?"

"Like what?"

"As if you were about to spring? Don't you like the orchid I handed you?"

"Sure. I hope the next time I have a case to argue—which something tells me will be the supreme effort of my life—I will be as successful. I'll write Ken that his gift pleased you. I forgot." He handed her the white covered box.

"Somewhat of a drop from pearls, but I thought you might enjoy a few chocolates from the big city."

"Chocolates!" She ripped off the paper cover. "What a gorgeous box! Wonderful! I haven't had one from this super, super shop for years. You've come across in a big way. Must be five pounds. Have one."

He shook his head.

"I believe you are more pleased with the candy than with the pearls," he declared incredulously.

She laughed, as after careful inspection of the delectable assortment she selected a chocolate, and looked up at him from under the sweep of long lashes.

"A huge box of candy has a romantic appeal. Silly, isn't it? Besides, you thought of this yourself. You didn't ask anyone to do it for you. That's one reason I love it."

"Ken Stewart thought of the pearls himself," he reminded indignantly.

"Yes, but he didn't take the trouble to select them."

"Want to know something? I think you're darned unfair. Good evening. I'm off."

"Why the rush? Mad with me?"

"When you smile in that beguiling way I couldn't be. I haven't dined. While getting this important assignment off my mind I have been nobly concealing the pangs of starvation. Never try to detain a hungry man, Cinderella, his resistance is nil. Could be he might go a little mad and say something he shouldn't. If you don't mind I'll leave by the front door. I have a hunch that someone in a car without lights parked by the side of the road observed my clandestine entrance. We'll make my exit regular."

He paused on the threshold.

"Yesterday when you inquired as to my past, you said, 'You may be married.' I'm not. Good night."

Why had he suddenly remembered that he hadn't answered my question? she wondered. I'm glad he isn't married. Now I can go all out in liking him. I've had a curious feeling that I'd better watch my step. I forgot to ask him if he is invited to Alida Barclay's dinner for

Mrs. Drew. He didn't wait to give me a chance to say "Good night." The door closed with a bang. Nothing clandestine about that slam, it could be heard at the Inn. Is it he whistling with operatic fervor, "Some Enchanted Evening"?

She raised the shade and stood at the open window listening till the sound trailed off in the direction of the garage. Had he left his club coupé there? Lights sprang on across the road. A parked car? Had the entrance and exit of Bill Damon been watched? Who would do it? A vision of a man with a tilted hat brim caught at her breath.

# SIXTEEN

THE EIGHT tall vases of rose-pink glads, placed at an
equal distance against the glass walls of the large porch
which was an extension of the dining room at White
Pillars, made a dramatic setting for the oval table with
its choice lace, gleaming silver, gold-etched crystal, and
gilt candelabra holding high eight tapers the exact color
of the flowers in the background and the sweet peas in
the low golden bowl in the center. Through an open
window came a soft breeze, the heavy scent of stock and
the damp earth of a garden.

A dramatic setting for Mrs. Drew also, and she is
making the most of it, Cindy thought, as from under
long lashes she observed the woman seated at the right
of Seth Armstrong, who presided at one end of the
table. Her hair, which Lyd had dubbed "brassy," had
been toned to the shade of golden honey, clipped and
curved to the shape of the skull, then dipped at the sides
in a winged effect. Her "doe" eye make-up lifted at the
temples like the tip of a wing was nothing short of
seductive, it accentuated the brilliance of her dark eyes.
Her skin was smooth and colorless as a gardenia. The
brilliant coral pink of her bow-shaped mouth was em-
phasized by a black beauty patch near one corner of her
lips. Her white bodice glittering with opaline sequins—
what there was of it visible above the table—lavishly,
generously exposed neck, shoulders and arms, the left
one glittering with diamond bracelets. Long chandelier
pearl earrings which touched her shoulders were the

only other jewels except rings a trifle more glittering than her pointed coral-pink fingernails.

"Hey, come out of the silence, Cindy," softly admonished Tom Slade at her right. "You've been staring at the guest of honor as if you'd never seen a woman in evening dress before."

"Right on the nose, Thomas. I've never seen quite so much of one before. She is lovely. He hair-do is the most ravishing ever designed by the mind of man."

"I don't like it as well as yours. Tonight you are looking like a million, lovely." He turned to the woman in gun-metal satin seated at his right and Seth Armstrong's left, her thin neck fenced in by a high dog collar of diamonds.

"I beg pardon, did you speak to me, Madam?"

"I said, 'Hussy!' to anyone who would listen." She pointed the word at the woman across the table.

Tom Slade's color already brilliant from sun and wind took on an added red.

"Hold it, she'll hear you," he warned and turned to Cindy.

"Brief me, quick, or I'll go down for the third time. Who is the Queen Mary twin at my right?"

"Counselor Armstrong's Aunt Minerva, 'Min' to her friends. Talk with her. She's interesting. Knows the name of every senator and representative in Congress and from which state they hail. Writes letters to them when she disagrees with their policies. She's an investment wizard also. The lady has views."

"You're telling me. She's agin the Circe who at the moment is bent on the enslavement of her nephew. She—"

"Young man," a sharp voice at his right interrupted, stopping all other conversation at the table. "Pay proper respect to your elders. Stop talking to Cinderella Clinton."

"Cinderella Clinton!" Mrs. Drew exclaimed. All eyes followed hers to Cindy's flushing face. "Was Miss Armstrong referring to *you*, sugar? Was the maid stupid when she announced you as Mrs. Stewart at Rockledge the other day?"

How maddening, I can't tell her that my marriage was annulled the day after my call, can I? Why didn't someone say something.

"Mrs. Drew, I'm not an envious person," Bill Damon was smiling engagingly at the woman at his left, "but, if I were to envy anyone I would you. I think your yacht is the slickest craft that comes into this harbor. You must be an expert to pick such a boat."

"Do you really, Colonel?" Cindy was aware of the little sigh of relief that ran around the table as the guest of honor turned an expanse of beautiful naked back on her host and brought her whole battery of charm to bear on the man at her right. "Then perhaps you will sail with us sometime."

"I'm all for it."

"I was brought up to believe that a 'sometime' invitation amounted to a 'no-time' invitation. I intend to nail you down to a date later in the evening, Colonel."

"Hmp! I guess that did it." Minerva Armstrong's remark to Slade set tongues loose again. "Young man, someone mumbled your name, I didn't get it."

"Thomas Slade, Second."

"That sounds strong and reliable. Now, let Cindy talk to Judge Shelton, and pay attention to me."

"I'd love to, Aunt Minerva, you see someone mumbled your name also. I hear you're a stand-in for the Goddess of Wisdom. Bear with me if I seem shy. I'm just a little Western lad unused to the effete East and its manners. You terrify me with your diamonds and dignity."

"Which part of the West?" She chuckled. "Cowboy?"

Tom is safely off skiddy ground, Cindy thought and turned to answer a question of Judge Shelton at her left.

"I have not made plans for the winter, Your Honor. Just at present I'm drifting and loving it."

The word drifting reminded her of Bill Damon's advice. He was seated across the table from her. When he was not talking to the guest of honor at his left he appeared to be absorbed in conversation with Lydia Fane at his right. Her eyes were as brilliant as her emeralds; the off the shoulder line of her green frock was perhaps an inch higher than Mrs. Drew's. She almost not quite snubbed Hal Harding who was sulking at her right. He was left high and deserted as a beached boat on a desert island when Ally Barclay at his other side was being monopolized by Judge Shelton.

Delicious dinner, expert service, Cindy thought and wondered if the two wisteria-silk-uniformed maids were those Sary said had been brought from New York. A beautiful party, as far as color went, she qualified. The lovely glads in the background, Mrs. Drew in sparkling white—if the scrap of costume showing denoted the remainder; Lyd in brilliant green; Ally Barclay in luscious mauve; myself in bouffant nylon net the exact shade of the glads; Aunt Min the minor chord in gray; the men in white dinner jackets, and—

"We'll have coffee in the living room." The voice of the hostess derailed her train of thought. "Judge Shelton has to leave. Cinderella, will you pour for me while I speed the parting guest?"

Later Tom Slade came to the table at which Cindy was seated and took a slow, appraising look around the large room. He whistled softly.

"The person who planned this decoration is an artist. The effect of French eighteenth-century paper panels set in blue-green walls, silk hangings to match, is something to write home about. Where do you suppose they picked up all these fine old pieces of French furniture? If the rug I'm standing on isn't a priceless Aubusson, I'll eat my hat."

"Spare your hat, Mr. Slade, it is." Seth Armstrong confirmed his judgment. He held out a cup. "Coffee for Mrs. Drew, Cinderella." As Tom Slade departed with a cup and saucer in each hand, he added, "I was sorry that our guest commented about your change of name. I have straightened it out with her."

"Thank you, Counselor. It took my breath for a minute. She came to The Castle last week for tea, I thought she knew then. Fortunately Colonel Damon rushed into the breach."

"Bill Damon coming up." He set a cup on the tray in front of her as Seth Armstrong turned away from the

table. "Black. This coffee is for Miss Fane, I'm taking it
to her after which I'm coming back to tell you how lovely
you are in that misty pink." As he crossed the room Hal
Harding took his place.

"One cup. Black. Why did you call on the Drew menace after I advised you not to, Cindy?"

"I told you I intended to be neighborly. You said you
had not met her. Now that you have, is she so terrible?
You'll have to admit she's a snappy dresser."

"She's cheap. I wish you'd give her the cold shoulder.
Damon had the nerve to invite himself aboard her
yacht."

"He dashed in to avert an explanation which would
have been embarrassing. As I remember it, she invited
him for a sail." She looked up with a smile. "*More*
coffee, Colonel?"

"I resent that 'more.' The first cup was for Miss Fane.
She told me you were getting a second for her, Harding.
Better take it. The Counselor said that if there were no
objections he would tune in on the broadcast 'Missing
Persons.' He explained that he is on the trail of a man
who has skipped out with an important will and had
asked the station to broadcast facts in the case."

"Sometimes I think that wills make more trouble than
they prevent," Harding growled and departed with two
cups.

"A large part of his fortune was tied up in a trust
fund," Cindy interpreted.

"So I have heard." Damon dropped two cubes of
sugar into the small cup. "Miss me while I was away?"

She was tempted to tell the truth and answer, "Terribly," but his nearness and the light in his eyes as he
looked down into hers set her pulses tapping a warning,
"Go slow." She laughed.

"Miss you? Yes and no. I didn't have much chance to
miss anyone. We had a lot of rain which turned the
putting contest I planned for Mrs. Drew into a tea. Then
I had my accounting to finish. As if that were not
sufficient to keep me busy I had an acute attack of
put-my-house-in-order, and cleared out slews of useless
things."

"You haven't mentioned being with Slade during my absence. That put-my-house-in-order attack doesn't mean that you are getting ready to go West with him, I hope."

Did the grave question mean that he would care if she did? She rested her elbow on the lace-covered table, cupped her chin in hand and looked up at him.

"Now that's an idea." The laughter of happiness brightened her eyes, rippled her voice. "Perhaps I'd better mention it to Tom."

"You know you have the power to torment me and are reveling in it, aren't you, Cinderella? Watch your step. I'm not playing. Why didn't you wear your pearls?"

It took her an instant to rally to his quick change of subject.

"I couldn't stand up under what I knew would be Lyd Fane's barrage of questions as to where they came from. I'm getting soft. I can't take it."

"We shall have to come out with the truth about them later. They would have been perfect with the pink frock. I like the long stem and leaves of the rose tucked under the shoulder strap. I've noticed that you never wear rings. I know why you didn't wear one. Don't you like them?"

"Mad about them, big, sensational choice ones. I haven't any. All the family jewels were sunk in oil wells."

"Those infernal oil wells. How they twisted your life."

"My life isn't twisted," she denied indignantly. "I'm on my toes with the thrill of being alive, free, I mean unencumbered by business cares. I'm fairly tingling with Monte Cristo's 'The world is mine' spirit. Don't you catch the vibrations?"

"I do. Something else, too. You are an exciting person, Cindy. May I take you home tonight? I have a story to tell you and—here's where I stoop to bribery—a present for you."

"Another?"

"The pearls were from Ken Stewart."

"I wasn't referring to *those*, I meant the chocolates. I

love them. Sary and I have been on a candy binge. I
adore presents but I can't fall for the bribe. And while
we are on the subject, I don't have to be *bribed* to go
with you *anywhere*." There was too much emotion behind that statement. Sounded as if she were throwing
herself into his arms. She laughed. "There's a whole
bunch of orchids for you, Sirrah."

"Think I don't realize that?" He cleared his gruff
voice. "Why can't you fall for the bribe?"

"I came with Tom. I can't let him down. Didn't you
bring Lydia?"

"At Mrs. Barclay's request. She has turned me down
for Harding. By the way, is he on calling terms with
Mrs. Drew?"

"No. He hadn't met her before this evening."

"Sure of that?"

"The morning you and he met for the first time and
almost came to blows in the patio he said he hadn't.
Why?"

"Just wondering. They both spend so much time on
the water seems as if they would have a lot in common.
I remembered that you told me he gave you a detailed
description of her yacht."

"But I explained then that he hadn't sailed on it since
she owned it."

"I remember that also. Here comes the broadcast. Our
host is sitting on the edge of his chair." He stepped back
to stand in front of the fireplace banked with ferns, set
the cup and saucer on the marble mantel and lighted a
cigarette.

From her seat at the coffee table Cindy could see the
occupants of the room in the gilt-framed pier mirror
between the open windows where blue-green hangings
swayed lightly in the sea breeze. It reflected Mrs. Drew
in sparkling white seated on a Louis XV couch below a
portrait of a lady in the costume of his court, languidly
twirling a lace fan with mother-of-pearl sticks; it gave
back Tom Slade beside her; the bulky host in a low
chair near, leaning a little forward inflating and
deflating his cheeks as he listened; Lyd Fane, a brilliant
splash of green on a twin couch, Hal Harding holding a

light to her cigarette; the back of a tall, spare figure as Minerva Armstrong crossed the threshold to the hall; Ally Barclay in her lovely mauve frock on a low *fauteuil* beside the door.

Cindy had been so absorbed in the *mise en scène* that she missed the opening of the broadcast. She was looking at Bill Damon's mirrored reflection when she saw his brows draw together, saw him lean a little forward as if intent on what a voice was saying. She listened.

"He had been AWOL for three years. Tired of dodging gave himself up at army headquarters. Explained that he deserted because he couldn't stand being bossed by a woman, a WAC Captain."

Cindy heard Bill Damon's soft chuckle. I'll bet no woman could boss him, she thought as she looked up at him standing straight and tall before the mantel from which vantage he could see each person in the room, for all the world like a general reviewing passing troops.

"The next case also has an army background," the announcer went on, "though this time we are looking for a missing person. A Captain of Infantry recently returned to Washington after several years service in the Orient has reported the loss of his wife."

A sound drew Cindy's eyes to the mirror. It reflected Hal Harding's quick catch of Lyd Fane's cup as it tilted dangerously; gave back the spots of rouge on her white face as he set the saucer on a stand and whispered to her. Seth Armstrong glanced over his shoulder, muttered a low, annoyed "Ssshh." At the sound Mrs. Drew looked up at Tom Slade, smiled, shrugged and with elaborate care closed the large lace fan she had been wielding.

I hope I didn't miss the crux of the story, Cindy thought as she caught up with the voice:

"Three years ago the wife sailed for this country to establish a home as the Captain expected to be sent back soon. She took furnishings and some valuable objects of art and jewels they had collected. He has received no word of her since. Orders were changed and he was kept abroad. Agents here have searched for her. No clue. She was an expert bridge player and had planned to teach the game and earn money for their home. He still hopes to hear of a slender, dark-haired, extremely pretty woman, who because of amnesia doesn't know who or where she is, whose nickname was Patty."

At the word amnesia Cindy looked up with startled eyes at Bill Damon, who was looking at her. He smiled and shook his head, as if he knew that for a frightened moment she had wondered if amnesia had caused that strange sleep the morning the oil property had been transferred. Seth Armstrong snapped off the radio.

"Thanks for listening," he said.

"Did you get what you wanted, Counselor?" his sister inquired.

"No."

"Then we will start our contract."

Lydia Fane sprang to her feet.

"I'm all for it. Those missing persons reports give me the willies. Thank goodness my hair is red, my eyes are green, I'm a rookie at bridge. I'll never be mistaken for the slender, dark-haired, extremely pretty woman who doesn't know where she is. No one will tap me on the shoulder and growl, 'Patty, you're wanted.'"

There was a hint of hysteria in her voice. Cindy remembered that her face had whitened, she had almost dropped the cup and saucer she was holding when the announcer had spoken of the returned Captain of Infantry who had lost his wife. Lydia had lived abroad. Could it be possible—

"Do we cut for partners, Colonel?" Sally Drew's wistful voice broke in on her reflections. "Heaven help the person who draws me. He'll slay me. I haven't played much bridge, and I have been told by an unfeeling critic that I haven't card sense. Now, who dares take me on?"

"I'm your man, Mrs. Drew. I'm distinctly in your class. We'll play together, then the pot can't call the kettle black."

"Before we begin let's make that sailing date. How about Monday, Colonel? You and Mrs. Barclay and the Counselor. We'll dine on board first."

"Sounds out of this world to me, Mrs. Drew. Here come our host and hostess to take us on. You can invite them now."

# SEVENTEEN

CINDERELLA stopped in the doorway of the white kitchen. Darius, the black Persian, rubbed his sleek body back and forth against her skirt to the accompaniment of a loud and rhythmic purr.

"I'm going to the turret room, Sary."

Sarah Ann Parker drew a delicately browned pie from the oven and set it on a trivet on the enamel table. Juice bubbled from the opening in the top crust and spread the delectable smell of baked apples, cinnamon and sugar. She sniffed.

"Smells good, don't it? The Duchess apples, on the tree your father planted years ago, are just ready to use. No flavor like 'em. What you goin' to the turret room for?"

"To select a costume for the Bal Masqué at the Inn tonight."

"What's that?"

"A masquerade party."

"Then why didn't you say so in plain English?"

"Don't scowl, Sary. Remember one smile in the morning is worth two in the afternoon. Now there's a line. It's original, woman."

"Hmp!" In spite of her disdainful sniff Sarah Ann Parker drew her right hand across her forehead as if to smooth out the frown. "You're right on your toes this mornin', Cindy. Thought the other night at dinner after you came home from Court you was going to cry instead of being happy you were Cinderella Clinton again. You've been kinder sober all this week, never knew

128

rainy weather to depress you before. Guess you had a
good time at Ally Barclay's last evenin'. You're so perky
now. Was the dinner nice?"

"Nice! It was dee-licious, delectable. The *filet mignon*
was done to perfection, and I haven't seen mushrooms
under glass bells since before the war. The mere memory of them makes my mouth water." She clasped her
hands on her breast and rolled her eyes in ecstasy.
"They were out of this world."

"Quit your play-acting, Cindy, and get down to earth.
Was the New York cookin' any better than mine?"

"No cooking could be better than yours, Sarah Ann
Parker. Cross my heart an' hope to die."

"I guess you're kind of prejudiced, Cindy." Sary at-
tempted unsuccessfully to discipline a pleased grin. "I
guess pickin' apples in the sun was what made me scowl.
What you countin' on to wear at the party tonight?
Seems to me you're pretty late getting a costume together."

"I have two ready to slip into. I went to several
masquerades while I was in the West. The costumes I
wore are in a chest in the turret room. I hope the moths
haven't feasted on them."

"Moths in clothes I have the care of? I'd die of shame.
Want to know somethin'? Last time I went through the
trunks up there I come across that skating costume of
your great-grandmother Clinton's. Full bright red skirt
with black velvet bands, an' big pockets just like women
are wearin' today, and the cutest panties. White fur
jacket; cap, muff to match, even the skates are there.
Looks just like new. Remember it?"

"I do. It's a collector's item."

"I don't approve of masquerades an' such goin's on,
Cindy, they can lead to a lot of deviltry."

"And a lot of fun, Sary. At midnight everyone un-
masks, and ten to one the man you are with isn't the
person you thought or hoped he was."

"I still don't believe in it. Get a lot of folks together
with their faces covered up an' how do you know who
you're dancin' with? A crook might slip in and hold you

up. I'll be anxious about you every minute you're gone."

"That's a foolish fear, Sary. The committee which is selling tickets at five dollars per will do a little screening, I hope. Lyd Fane put on a great selling campaign at Ally Barclay's dinner last night. Mrs. Sally Drew took five tickets, Judge Shelton five."

"That would be *fifty* dollars!"

"For the hospital, remember. What time lunch?"

" 'Bout an hour. Got a surprise for you. Something you like. Better put an apron over that light green linen dress. May be dusty in the turret room."

"Dusty in a house you have the care of? You're fishing for another compliment, woman. No, you can't come with me, Darius. I don't want you."

"That cat loves you, Cindy, but he's layin' it on extra thick tryin' to make me jealous because he knows he's in disgrace with me."

"Why, Sary?"

"This morning when I opened the pat-i-o door, there were three field mice laid out nice as could be on the flaggin', an' that cat stood looking up at me with a robin danglin' from his mouth. I spanked him good."

"Darius the Persian king laying gifts at the feet of his queen. I hope he won't express his love for me that way. I'm off. If I don't appear within an hour send up a rescue party. I may have cracked my head against a beam and been knocked senseless. After which cheery suggestion I will depart."

A few minutes later she read the tag on a chest pushed back under a window and dropped to her knees in front of it. Before she raised the cover she glanced out at the illimitable stretch of ocean—had pirates sailed that sea, had they been in this very room, she asked herself.

Nice old place. Clean as a whistle. Each box and chest and trunk labeled. What fun she and a little girl named Grace Temple had had playing with the big dollhouse in the corner. She never had dared come up here alone. She remembered how she had hurriedly shot the bolt on the outside of the door at the foot of the stairs when she heard weird creaks behind it as if someone were stealing softly down. She had been brought up on the story of the smugglers and their shuffling steps.

Gay boxes held hats in which she and her small friends trailing their mothers' long skirts had fared forth to call on the neighbors. An old-fashioned dressmaker form in front of the narrow door that opened on the secret stairs had an uncanny resemblance to a human watching her. Framed pictures, a motley score, were turned faces to the wall; the head and foot boards of a spool bed leaned companionably close to a dark chintz-covered wing chair. Vases in infinite variety, plates, colorful dozens of them, vegetable dishes of her great-grandmother's set of Canova were loaded on an oak dining table. The girl in green linen with a pink rose at her collar gave her a start. Silly. It was her own reflection in the long gilt-framed pier mirror.

Things. Things. *Things.* Too bad her put-my-house-in-order attack hadn't started on this accumulation. She would tackle it next. She was the last of her family, there were no relatives to whom it would mean anything, but it ought to be of use to someone.

I won't give away these costumes, she decided as she lifted the cover of the cedar chest. They represent too much fun and the fun one has had can't be snitched away, she philosophized as she held up a ragged dark blue denim work dress. She shook it and between the pendant rags glittered a frock of silver sequins. She remembered the night she had worn it, how at the stroke of twelve she had caught the tags of two zippers and with the prayer they would not fail her had dropped the dark blue garment to the floor. The lightning change from rags to elegance had been a sensational success.

How about wearing it tonight? No. Tom Slade had seen her in it, and Lyd Fane had wisecracked about shedding a glass slipper at midnight, apparently she was expecting a Cinderella costume; also she had suggested that Ken Stewart might appear. Better push that thought out of her mind and quick.

She drew out a fringed Indian costume, richly beaded.

Pocahontas. No one had recognized her the night she wore it. This would be perfect. A white box held a wig and hairpins with which to adjust it. One red and one dark blue quill were thrust into the black hair at the left of the middle part; two waist-length braids were tied at the ends with red and blue ribbons. She looped a half dozen strings of gay beads over her arm.

"Seems to be something missing," she mused aloud. "I remember. There were two broad copper bracelets not of the Pocahontas period, but effective. I'll hunt in the chest for those."

She hung the dress on the old-fashioned form to take out the wrinkles and perched the wig with its quills and long braids on top.

On her knees in front of the chest she burrowed for the bracelets. Funny. They must be here. Darn! Would she have to take out everything? What in the world— something that felt like a bag. When she packed the chest she hadn't put in a bag—or had she? She had had so much on her mind at the time she might have forgotten. She wouldn't swear now that she hadn't.

She'd swear she hadn't packed this one, she told herself as with an effort she pulled up a grayish-white cotton bag so full of something that there had been little room for the stout twine tied round and round at the neck. Looked like a five-pound salt bag washed clean of printing.

She sat on the floor, dropped it into her lap and regarded it curiously. Was it something the movie people had planted here last summer and forgotten? They had photographed the turret room. It was humpy as if filled with stones or pebbles. Icy fingers closed about her heart, chills feathered along her nerves. What was in it?

"Don't sit here staring at the thing, open it," she prodded herself.

Her fingers worked at the hard knot till they were numb. At the imminent peril of loosening a tooth she tugged with her teeth till she could have cried from frustration. It *must* be opened. She wouldn't take it out of this room till she knew what was in it. If only she had a hairpin. The wig!

She laid the bag aside and tiptoed across to the dress-maker frame. Eureka! four hairpins and not the useless invisible ones either, they were of stout old-fashioned black wire.

Back beside the chest, seated on the floor, legs out-stretched, she attacked the knot. Had she started it? A little. Another pry. That loosened it. One more—it—it was giving—that last poke did it. She pulled off the twine acquiring a few rough splinters in her fingers as it came. The bag spread open quickly as if glad of the release.

She looked into the gaping opening. Rubbed her left hand over her eyes. Looked again. This must be a dream. Those just couldn't be jewels winking and spar-kling up at her. Had sudden sleep overcome her again? Mentally she backtracked: I stopped at the kitchen door—told Sary I was coming up here—I know that was real—I couldn't dream the delectable smell of that fresh-ly baked apple pie. I came up the turret stairs. Opened the chest—there's Pocahontas, complete with wig and beads on the dressmaker form—perhaps this will tell the story. She placed a finger between her teeth and extract-ed a twine splinter. Glory be, that hurt. Now I know I'm awake, with a cache of jewels, real or fake?

She emptied the contents of the bag into her lap. A few brooches tumbled out, three sensational bracelets came after, too many rings to count, all set with dia-monds plus emeralds or rubies or sapphires, followed by a veritable cascade of unset precious stones.

She stared at them incredulously. This wasn't motion-picture stuff. The jewels were real as rain. Remindful of the value of fingerprints, with the bent hairpin she hooked up a ring with one huge diamond. Curious setting. For a guess it was Oriental and very old. Were these stolen jewels? Where had they come from? By whom had they been hidden in the chest?

Memory flashed a close-up. The tenuous shadow she had seen in the hall, the man with the turned-down hat brim? Could be. He wouldn't leave them here indefinite-ly. He would come back. Should she hide them or—

"Cin—dy!" Sarah Ann Parker's voice, Sarah Ann Park-er opening the door at the foot of the stairs.

"Cindy, why don't you come down? Want I should come up and help you find things?"

"No, *no*, Sary." She scrambled the jewels back into the bag. "I'm coming. I'm just closing the—the trunk." She had almost said chest, which might reveal later where she had found the bag.

"Did you find what you wanted, Cindy?"

"I did. Everything. I'm bringing the things down to my room. Wait till you see me tonight—I'll knock your eyes out. Run along and serve lunch. I'm *starving*."

"Want to know somethin', Cinderella Clinton? You're always starving. I don't know how you keep thin as a willer wand. You come along now, quick."

Cindy twisted the twine round the neck of the bag and considered. Should she leave it here and set a trap for the person who had hidden it or take it to her room and hide it? Better take it and make sure it wasn't retrieved by the thief.

She closed the chest and with the bag gripped in her left hand stood up. Oooch, her knees were stiff. What had rolled across the floor and under the spool bed? Her heart stopped, thundered on. One of the jewels from her lap?

Can't stop to hunt for it. If I stay here longer Sary will be on my trail. How shall I get this hefty thing down? I might meet her in the hall. My wardrobe case. I'll tuck the jewels under Pocahontas.

She opened the blue leather case marked C.C.S. and filled it. She looked back before she left the turret room in the hope of seeing the glitter of the missing jewel. With the sustaining thought that if it wasn't visible to her no one else would see it she went down the stairs with the blue wardrobe case bumping against every step.

Now what, she asked herself when she reached her room. I'll leave this just as it is until after lunch. No one can possibly get in while Sary and I are downstairs.

Some one had come in, she discovered as she opened the door to the patio. Bill Damon laughed as he rose. Had Sary expected him? There was an extra place set.

"I dropped in to return the enlarged snapshot I borrowed. I've been on and off long distance to Washington the entire morning," he explained. "Miss Parker invited me to stay for lobster salad—plus apple pie. I might have resisted the first, but not the last. I don't like your attitude of incredulous surprise, Miss Clinton. You make me feel like an intruder."

"Intruder. I would rather see you at this moment than any other person in the world." The fervor of her declaration startled her and sent a dark wave of color under his bronze.

"That's a greeting one doesn't get every day." He cleared his husky voice. "I'd like an explanation of it after lunch. I can't believe I owe it to my fatal charm."

"You'll get the explanation if I can wait that long."

"Sit here." He drew out her chair. "Stop shivering. What an excitable child you are."

"Are you referring to the dynamics of my emotional conflicts? I cribbed that from a psychiatrist's report." Her light voice was a triumph of will over seething excitement.

"I am glad to hear the laughter in your voice. You frightened me for a moment."

"How did you come out at contract with the fascinating Sally Drew last evening?" she asked in the hope of quieting her tingling nerves by switching her thoughts from the jewels. "Did she call you 'sugar'?"

"No. I heard her call *you* sugar. You said that Harding used that endearing word instead of your name several times. I wonder if he picked it up from her?"

"No, because that morning in the patio he declared he never had met the woman, didn't want to, objected when I said I planned to call on her. Tell me about the game."

"She was absorbed in her hand. Every few minutes her lips would move as if she were repeating rules recently learned. I hadn't supposed that an intelligent woman—and something tells me she is intelligent—could be so dumb."

"I heard you tell her you weren't good. I don't believe that."

"Goodness, like happiness, is a relative term, Cinderella. I was trying to give the lady courage, also to help my host and hostess. They are experts. Ally planned that we were to play with them. If Mrs. Drew were as new at the game as she claimed, no card sense, she said—I thought that the Armstrongs' evening would be ruined if one of them drew her as a partner. Miss Parker approaches with rolls that look light enough to have snowed down."

It seemed to Cindy that aeons passed before Sarah Ann Parker, who talked volubly while she served luncheon, mainly about the casualties of her favorite ball team, closed the patio door behind her.

"What's on your mind, Cindy? You've been so tense I was afraid Miss Parker would begin to cross-examine you."

"Can what I say be overheard here?" She looked behind her at the house, then across the putting green to the vast expanse of ocean.

"Let's go to the seat on the point. No one can overhear there."

"No. No, I don't dare be so far away for fear—"

"Suppose we talk in your workroom? With the door closed—"

"No, I couldn't see the front stairs. Don't look at me as if you suspected I am losing my mind. Wait till you hear—"

"Take it easy, darling."

"Don't call me darling as if you thought me an invalid or an incompetent."

"That wasn't the idea back of the word but we'll take up that also some other time. I'll sit at the table, smoke and keep my eyes on the house. You face me and watch that no one approaches from the garage or putting green. Let's go."

To the accompaniment of the hum of bees dipping into the hearts of the colorful blossoms in the flower borders and the tinkle of the fountain spray dropping back into the pool, she told of her reason for the trip to the turret room, started to tell of taking out the Pocahontas costume, stopped abruptly.

"Why the period?"

"I almost told what I plan to wear to the masquerade

tonight. It would have spoiled the fun. I'm sure no one will recognize me till we unmask."

"Want to bet on that?"

"I would be willing to. Let's go back to my STORY in capital letters."

She talked in a low voice without interruption from him. When she finished she clasped her hands tightly on the table and leaned forward.

"What shall I do?" she whispered.

"You left the bag of jewels in your room?"

"Yes."

He paced back and forth across the patio, smoking, thinking. He stopped beside her chair. She rose and laid her hand on his arm.

"What shall I do?" she repeated.

"Put the bag back where you found it."

"Put it back? Suppose—suppose the person from whom it was stolen—it must have been stolen, there's no other explanation—were to trace it to the turret room? I would be accused of stealing it."

"I'll look out for that. Go up now, quickly, and put the salt bag—if it is a salt bag—of jewels exactly where you found it and replace every article as it was when you opened the chest."

"If I do that I won't have anything to wear at the masquerade. What difference does that make? I shan't go. I won't leave the house until the mystery of that bag has been solved."

"You must go. You may give away the whole shootin'-match if you don't. You can think up something. There must be other clothes in the turret room you can wear. Repack the chest as it was, that's vital. Step on it, Cindy. While you are upstairs I'll engage Miss Parker in a base-ball argument that will keep her occupied, I promise."

"I don't understand why you want the jewels hidden again. I haven't had much experience in crime, but I think we should turn them over to the police."

"Then eight chances out of ten we'd never find out who put them in that chest."

"Do you think we will now?" She came close to whisper.

"I'm sure we will." He bent his head and lightly kissed her parted lips. Straightened quickly.

"You shouldn't tempt me, Miss Clinton. Hustle. Get the jewels back where you found them before anyone comes. Trust me, will you?"

"*Trust* you? Didn't I tell you I'd rather see you than anyone else in the world? That's my exit line. I'm going."

"I'm sure we will," Cindy repeated his words as she ran up the turret stairs. I have a feeling that Bill Damon suspects who hid them. How could he? He doesn't know anyone in this place. He appeared cool as a glacier, but—she brushed her right hand across her lips—I'll bet underneath he was so excited he didn't realize he kissed me.

# EIGHTEEN

HE WAITED till Cindy had had time to reach the turret room, then entered the kitchen. Sarah Ann Parker was at the open icebox.

"That Colonel Damon is an awful nice person, Cindy. Kind of exciting like a movie actor," she said without turning. "He has Hal Harding licked to a finish. I wish he was Ken Stewart."

"He is, Sary."

She whirled at the low assurance. The plate she held fell with a crash. She adjusted her spectacles hanging by the band and peered at him through the thick lenses.

"If that's the truth what's the idea comin' here under a false name?" she demanded caustically. "Surprised you didn't wear a fake beard."

He gave her a tabloid version of his explanation to Alida Barclay. As she listened she became intent on collecting the casualty at her feet.

"You wrote that letter to me, didn't you, Sarah Ann Parker, alias P.A.S.?" he accused.

She deposited the pieces of broken plate and its contents in the sink, pulled out a chair at a white enamel table which held a basket overflowing with green peas, and sank into it with a sigh.

"You've kinder taken the stiffenin' out of my knees. I did write that letter. I sneaked the address from the envelope of one to you Cindy left to be mailed. Want to know somethin', I'd do it again if I thought it would help keep her safe from that Hal Harding. This is the second summer he's been courtin' her. Besides havin'

two wives already he's supportin', folks think he's sidin'
with those men bein' tried for treason. I laid awake lots
of nights before I sent it wonderin' if I was takin' a
chance at upsetting her life by doing it."

"It's a ticklish business to play Fate, Sary."

"That's what I kept tellin' myself, I'd think, suppose
Kenniston Stewart came back because I sent that letter;
suppose he turned out to be a no-gooder who would
pester her by remindin' her she was married to him. I
was scared for fear I'd be like the woman Cindy told me
'bout one time, Pan someone, who opened a box she
found on the seashore and let a whole flock of troubles
out on the world. I sweat blood over that letter before I
posted it. You've been playin' possum so long how come
you're out with the truth now?"

"Out with it *only* to you. I need your help."

"Not consid'rin' moving in here, are you? Haven't forgotten that that marriage don't exist any more, have
you?"

"No. *No*. Sit down again. Where did you pick up that
crazy idea? I need someone in this house whom I can
trust."

"What's goin' on in this house?" Her eyes were startled, her voice was shrill.

"Ssh-sh. Not so loud. Can you keep a secret?"

"I'm not Ella Crane who blabs everything she knows
and a lot she doesn't. You'd be surprised if you knew the
suspicions she's started about you an' why you're here."

"What has she said?"

"Now I've heard your story, what she's been broadcasting's nothing like the truth. I think Lyd Fane's been
connivin' with her. She said when you were in her
shop you spoke of a Sally an' she's kinder tying you up
with the blonde who's leased Rockledge at Pirate's
Cove."

"Now I've heard everything. I met the woman for the
first time at the Armstrong dinner last evening."

"Ella don't need facts to go on. *She's* got imagination.
Lots of folks like that. Want to know somethin'? I
suspected who you were the day you phoned an' said
Bill Damon wanted to speak to Mrs. Stewart. Can't say

I'd been so smart if I hadn't written that letter. The mornin' you came to take Cindy to Trader Armstrong's office I was sure—then I was all at sea again when you let that annulment go through. Didn't seem as if a man after seeing Cindy would let her go. I'm sorry, I guess the way your jaw set I've blundered past a 'Keep Off' sign."

"Let's get back to open road. You're not such a gay deceiver as you think, I've had my suspicions that you knew who I am."

"Aren't you goin' to tell Cindy?"

"I had planned to tell her last evening, but the right moment didn't come. She's bound to resent the deception at first. I'll make an opportunity after we unmask tonight. You won't betray me?"

"Not me. I interfered in her life and yours for the last time when I wrote that letter."

"Your promise takes a weight from my mind. We must talk and talk fast. Watch the garden and garage and I'll keep my eyes on the hall door. I don't want Cindy to hear."

"Terrible in love with her, aren't you?"

He ignored the emotional unsteadiness of her voice.

"That road is posted 'No thoroughfare,' too."

"You're right. I don't mean to be nosy, but I've been so scared she'd take up with that Hal Harding. She never let on but I could see she was dreadful hurt that Kenniston Stewart wasn't interested enough in the girl he'd married to at least come and take a look at her, an' when a girl's pride is hurt there's no accountin' for what silly thing she'll do. Hal has had most every woman in town in love with him off an' on. I don't mean anything sinful, but they kinder lost their heads 'bout him. I'll admit that when he smiles at me an' says, 'How are you, Sary Ann Parker, how's the light of my life today?' I know perfectly well it's just his foolin', but I feel a kinder glow."

"Thanks for the tip, Sary." He laughed. "Now I know how to win friends and make love to a woman. Listen carefully, Cindy's safety and yours are threatened."

"Sakes alive, your voice gives me the merry-pranks up an' down my spine. What's threatenin' us?"

He told of the jewels Cindy had found in the chest in which her fancy dress costumes were stored. Sarah Ann Parker listened breathlessly. When he finished her eyes bulged with unbelief, her cheeks burned red as her cotton dress.

"I went through each trunk and chest in the turret room this spring when I opened The Castle. That bag wasn't there then. How could a person get in an' hide somethin' in this house without me knowin' it?"

"You don't spend every moment of your life here, do you?"

" 'Course not, but I lock up tight as a drum when I go out."

He remembered the patio door which had opened so easily into the kitchen the day he had brought Cindy home, started to refer to it, abandoned the reminder as not being germane to the subject under discussion.

"Do many strangers come to the house?"

"My sakes alive, there are always folks drivin' up an' askin' to see the secret staircase—"

"I've heard of the secret staircase. Where is it?"

"The cupboard side of the fireplace in the old kitchen swings out an' there's a long flight of steps."

"Where do they lead?"

"To the turret room. Story is that when smugglers owned this place they hid up there. There was no other way to get there then. The first Clinton who owned the place had the present stairs built."

"Do many people know about the secret staircase? That's a senseless question. Ella Crane told me about it."

"An' what Ella Crane knows, the whole world knows. That maid, Rena Foster, who works for Mrs. Sally Drew, come over to see it soon after the family moved in, said she'd heard of it all her life—she's a village girl—I let her go up the secret stairs, her eyes were big as saucers—" Sarah Ann Parker's face paled. She gasped.

"You saw her, she's the one who sneaked into this kitchen askin' for eggs, the day Cindy fell asleep. She's always runnin' across for recipes or crochet patterns. You don't suppose—"

"We won't suppose anything, we must plan, before Cindy comes."

"She won't be along yet. You told her to repack the chest as she found it. That will take time. Aren't you goin' to tell her what you're plannin' to do?"

"Later. You're breathless. Don't be frightened, Sary."

"Frightened? Me? I'm not frightened, I'm tickled pink. It's exciting. Always wished I could go to Hollywood an' act in one of those mystery movies, think I'd be good. Now I've got a chance at the real thing. A bag of jewels hidden in the turret. Can you beat that for a whodunit? What do we do next?"

"Listen carefully. If anyone comes to the patio begin to shell those peas."

With his eyes on the door which opened on the hall he told of a tentative plan which would afford present protection against the person or persons who were responsible for hiding the jewels. Sarah Ann Parker's nods of understanding, her muted "Yes"—"Yes"—"Yes"—in answer to his questions accompanied his low voice.

"You can see, can't you, Sary, that if the bag is removed from the chest the news is bound to leak and there wouldn't be five chances in ten that the person who hid it there would be caught."

"Sure, I see." She drew a long breath. "That eases the strain. I've been tense as a fiddlestring while I listened to what sounds more like a mellerdrama than anything that could happen in this village. Course the bag should be left where 'twas hid. I guess between us we're smart enough to catch the fella."

"Smart is as smart does. Don't budge from this house tonight—you won't be alone, I promise. Tell Cindy she must go to the ball, she declared she would remain on guard here, tell her you know what has happened. Everyone in town who can't be inside will be on the verandas of the Inn watching the masquerade through the windows. The person who hid the bag in the turret might consider this an opportunity to retrieve it, though something tells me it will stay there for a time unless the thief is tipped off that it has been found. Don't let her stay at home. Here she com—" He finished the word outside the patio door.

I don't want the local police in on this yet, he thought, as he started his car he had left outside the garage. We'll give them the credit but the fewer who know about this at present the better. The hidden jewels tie in with the tip given Ally Barclay to watch The Castle. Who cached them there to divert suspicion from himself or the smugglers? It's up to me to find out.

At the same moment Cindy appeared in the doorway of the kitchen. "Whose car did I hear?" she inquired. "Where is Bill Damon?"

"That was him just goin'."

"Going? *Going!* Didn't he leave a message for me? Not a word about what I am to—"

"You needn't cut off what you was goin' to say, child. He told me what you found in the old chest along with your costumes."

"He did? Perhaps he told you what I am to do about it? Then again, perhaps he thinks *I'm* not capable of doing anything."

"Quiet down, Cindy. It don't suit you to be sarcastic. Trust him. He's got everything under control."

"He has? Just like that. The masquerade is *out*. I won't leave this house till those jewels are turned over to the police. I know he doesn't think they should be, but I do. And after all, they are hidden in *my* house."

"Stop gettin' so het up, Cindy. Sure you'll go to the masquerade tonight. Mr. Damon said 'twas most important that you and I carry on as usual, as if we didn't know nothin', or whoever had landed that stuff there would be hep—that was his word—that we'd found it."

"Do you think I'll leave you here alone tonight, Sary? Not a chance."

"I won't be alone. I've been waitin' till you stopped boilin' to tell you I had a phone from my brother askin' if he could come an' stay here for a few days. Would you mind?"

"Mind? Of course I wouldn't mind. Is it Joe, the

brother who lives at Grand Manan? I think it's wonderful. You haven't seen him for years, have you?"

"No. He hasn't been very neighborly." She sniffed. "I wonder what's bringing him now? I'll bet he wants to borrow money."

"Sarah Ann Parker, you hard-boiled wretch. Why wouldn't he come just to see you? He named his first daughter for you, didn't he?"

"Yes, he did, an' he always sends me greetin' cards Christmas an' Easter. It was mean of me to suspect he had a motive for comin' other than puttin' across a lobster deal." She lowered her voice. "Could you get all the things back in the chest just as you found them, Cindy?"

"Slick as a bug in a rug. I brought Great-Grandmother's skating costume, plus the skates, down to my room in case I went to the masquerade. I had to reinter Pocahontas. I intended to convince Colonel Damon that the loot should be out of the house as quickly as I could get the police here. But, I haven't the courage to buck his decision."

"You better not. That man knows where he's goin'. What good will the skates do you with the costume? Not floodin' the Inn floor with ice, are they, but such crazy things are bein' done now I wouldn't put it past the summer folks."

"The skates are for atmosphere, Sary. Flooding the floor with ice? That gives me an idea. I'll take—"

"Now who's at the front door? Ringin' an' ringin' 's though he thought we was all dead or sleeping."

"Perhaps it is your brother or—I know. It's Tom Slade. In the excitement of finding those jewels I forgot we had a tennis date. Coming. Coming," she called as she raced through the hall. She flung open the front door.

"Enter, Thomas. You're the perfect answer to this maiden's prayer."

She regretted her fervent welcome as additional color swept to his already brightly sunburned face and his eyes darkened. *This is the second man I've greeted today as if he were a long-lost brother. I hope it isn't getting* to be a habit. He caught her hands in a grip which hurt.

"Is this what freedom does to you? Mean that as it sounds, Cindy?"

She shook her head.

"No, Tom. I'm sorry. I just had an inspiration for a razzle-dazzle entrance at the masquerade tonight and when you appeared you completed the picture. That's all."

"It's something to fit into a picture of which you're a part, lovely. It might have been Harding or the Damon guy who was elected. How about it, is the tennis game on or off?"

"Off, while we plan a gigantic act, Thomas. Come to the patio while I tell you how we can rock the very walls of the Inn this evening. We'll have to work like crazy to put it across. Are you with me?"

"I'm sold without knowing what I'm buying. On to the patio. Let's stop at the kitchen and ask Sary to rustle a couple of her tall, sparkling soda lemonades. Your excitement denotes a sizzling proposition. We'll need something iced to keep down our temperature."

# NINETEEN

"WHERE'D you and that Mr. Slade run off to this afternoon?" Sarah Ann Parker inquired of Cindy seated at the glass table in the patio. Candles in tall hurricane lamps gave out a soft yellow light in the rosy dusk. She served a crystal cup heaped with fresh raspberry sherbet and set down a plate of wafer-thin cookies. "When I brought the soda lemonades you were gone."

"I had a world-shaking idea for the masquerade this evening and we rushed off to get a little practice."

"What sort of practice? Want to know somethin', you looked tired to death when you got home. You didn't stop to change that green linen dress, just had time to wash up for dinner."

"I'll be fresh as a daisy after a little rest and a shower. I have loads of time before the party. Did your brother come?"

"Sure. He got here 'bout half an hour before you. He seemed awful glad to see me, made me kind of ashamed I'd suspected he'd come to borrow money. He's in the kitchen."

"I'll stop and speak to him. Did Colonel Damon phone?"

"Yes." Sarah Ann Parker matched Cindy's whisper. "He asked for you. When I told him you'd gone off with Mr. Slade, he said. 'Tell her to be *sure*,' that's the way he said it, '*sure* to go to the masquerade.' You'd better do as he says, Cindy."

"I will."

She sat for a few moments after Sarah Ann Parker

had closed the patio door behind her, thinking of the bag in the turret room, of her unsuccessful search for the jewel that had rolled from her lap, of Bill Damon's insistence that she was not to call the police at present, that she must go to the dance. If the person who had hidden the jewels came for them tonight it was his responsibility—it was hers to see that the thief was caught. Tom Slade would have been surprised if he had known the scheme she had been concocting while apparently absorbed in what he and she were doing.

Gorgeous evening. As she rose from the table she looked up at the blue sky dotted with swansdown fluffs of clouds tinted pink by the afterglow of the sunset beyond the harbor. "Wonderful world!" she said aloud. She stopped to pick a brilliant red rose for her white fur skating cap. Shook her head. Not so good. It would give me away. My friends know that I always wear a flower, fresh or artificial, it's what the fashion editors call my "signature." I'd better go in and get started on my crime-detector plan.

She stopped at the kitchen door.

"I am glad you could come for a visit with your sister, Mr. Parker," she welcomed cordially.

The heavy-set man with a glistening bald spot entirely surrounded by a crew-cut of bristling iron-gray hair rose awkwardly. Had his mannerly response to her greeting been prompted by a kick from Sarah Ann Parker who faced him across the food-laden table at the window? He shuffled his feet. Thrust one hand into his red and black plaid lumber-jacket pocket, took it out, repeated the process with his other. Coughed.

"Thank you, Miss Cinderella. It sure is a treat to get to the mainland. Right kind of you to let me come."

He speaks like a Canadian. Gives each *r* all it has, she thought.

"It is a pleasure to have you here. Stay with us as long as you can." She ignored the violent shake of Sarah Ann Parker's head. "It must be a treat for you two to be together. Come up when I ring, please, Sary, I may need your help. By the way, in case you should miss them, I'm taking three of my silver cups from the old kitchen.

The tennis committee of the Country Club is putting on a members' Trophy Exhibit." She nodded to the man who stood as if in embarrassed silence shuffling his feet.

"Have fun in our wild town if you can find it, Mr. Parker."

"Thank you, Miss Cinderella, but I'm not much of a night owl. At home I go to bed soon's the chores are done. I hope *you* have fun. Sarah Ann told me you are going to a party."

"I am." She laughed. "With bells on, figuratively speaking. Good night. I'll ring when I need you, Sary."

She stepped into the old kitchen, closed the door, drew the painted window shades and snapped on the light in the glass lamp which once had been used for oil. The pumpkin-yellow walls glowed in the light, copper saucepans shimmered like red gold. She caught a side of the cupboard and drew it forward with such care that not even one piece of the mulberry and black Canova on the shelves jiggled.

Had the person who had hidden the bag of jewels in the chest used the steep, narrow stairs behind it to reach the turret room? They looked spooky. Creeping up was indicated. She would have to mount that way when she planted her trap. So what? A private eye didn't stop for trifles when he started out to get his man, did he? And I intend to get mine or perish in the attempt, she told herself and wondered that she could chuckle over an imagined victory which might prove a tragic reality. Better tackle her plan and not stand here thinking about it.

With three silver trophy cups and one outsize copper frying pan in her arms she crept up the steep narrow stairway examining each step ahead as she went. Not a trace of dust, not a betraying footprint. The person who had hidden the jewels hadn't gone up or down this way.

On the second step from the top she placed the copper frying pan. Plenty large to accommodate a hasty foot. She swallowed a chuckle as she visualized results. Danger only for the thief. No one else would use these stairs. She backed down cautiously and at strategic intervals parked the silver cups. They would provide an additional alarm if or as the intruder descended. For clamor they would have a police siren licked to a finish.

Back in the kitchen she carefully swung the cupboard into place. Rearranged the remaining silver cups on the shelf above the old oven. Her explanation about the Trophy Exhibition would cancel Sarah's curiosity anent the vacant spaces.

An hour later she stood before the long mirror in her brilliantly lighted room analytically observing the girl who faced her. A soft briny breeze stirred the dainty muslin curtains between the long sea-green hangings at the two open windows. From the patio rose the strong scent of marigolds, the tinkle of the fountain, the monotonous chirp of crickets and a repetitive "Katy-did! Katy didn't!"

"Sakes alive, Cindy!" Sarah Ann Parker followed her exclamation into the room. "You gave me a start. Thought your great-grandmother had come to life. You was so long ringing I was 'bout ready to run up an' see what had happened when the bell sounded. Step away from that lookin' glass so I can see the whole of you." She walked around her.

"Want to know somethin', that full red cashmere skirt with the black velvet bands round it an' the big pockets each side looks just like a picture in the magazines you're always bringin' home. I guess the style has come round again. Wearin' the panties that go with it?"

Cindy lifted the hem of the skirt that came to the tops of her white skating boots.

"Ain't they the cutest things? Red like the skirt with narrow white lace ruffles where they bind your knees. Let's see if they show when you dance, Cindy. Whirl—good."

She whirled—good—again and again. Sarah Ann Parker nodded approval.

"They do. Awful cunning. You look like a little girl. How'd you happen to have the high boots? They are too big to be your grandmother's I packed away with those clothes."

"I'll say they are. I managed to squeeze my foot into one of hers, but I couldn't fasten it. This is an old pair.

I'm taking red slippers to wear after we unmask. Something tells me that when I dance in this fur jacket I will melt away in the arms of my partner."

"What you got under it?"

"Just a thin white silk blouse." Cindy turned back the collar of the coat to demonstrate.

"Where'd you get that string of wax beads?" Sarah Ann Parker adjusted her spectacles and peered. "I've never seen it before."

"One of the shops in the city had a sale of synthetic pearls, wonderful imitations at two ninety-eight plus tax."

*I didn't say I bought a string,* she assuaged an uneasy conscience. *I haven't found the right time to tell her that Ken Stewart sent me the necklace. I couldn't resist wearing the lovely things. I should have worn them to the dinner last night. I can't hide them forever. I'm banking on the fact that Lyd Fane will be too busy M.C.'ing the ball to notice them.*

"Two ninety-eight? Sakes alive, if they're handsome as those I'll buy some for my brother's girls for Christmas. Who is taking you to the party?"

"Tom Slade."

"I wish 'twas that Colonel Damon."

"You're completely sold on Bill Damon, aren't you? Doesn't take a mind reader to discover that he is teacher's pet in your kitchen, and speaking of kitchens, where's your brother?"

"He helped me with the dishes then went outside to smoke. I'll put him in the first-floor bedroom in the ell. Is that all right?"

"Of course it is all right, Sary. Give him a good time and plenty to eat. Make him realize you are glad he came. I thought you weren't very cordial."

"I guess I was cordial enough. Don't want to overdo it or he might make visitin' us a habit. Gave me a shock when he said he didn't know how long the lobster deal would keep him here. We don't have to cross that bridge till we come to it, though. Put on the mask and let's see how you look." She tucked a short golden-brown curl under the white fur cap.

"I'd never know you, Cindy, with that thing 'cross your eyes. Here's the muff on the bed. Now you're complete. Goin' to carry your great-grandmother's skates jingling from your arm like that? Does sort of make the picture perfect. Bright as silver, aren't they? I polished them the last time I went through that trunk lookin' for moths. There's the doorbell. Must be your beau. Goin' to let him see your costume? Thought it had to be kept secret."

"Usually it is, but he and I are putting on an act." She tucked the white satin eye-mask into a pocket of the fur jacket. "Hold my topcoat, please, Sary. The red skirt doesn't show below it, I hope. I don't want anyone to get a look at this costume before I reach the Inn."

Enveloped in a loose black-and-white checked raglan with huge pockets, the hood drawn over her head, she lingered on the threshold.

"Don't tell anyone, *anyone*, and that means especially Colonel Bill Damon, what I am wearing, Sarah Ann Parker. He was so cocksure he would recognize me. I want to fool him."

"Why would I tell and spoil your fun? I was young myself, once. Don't you stay too late. I'll be listenin' for you to come home."

"I shan't stay much after midnight. I want to get back. I feel uneasy about—you know what. They might come for *that* tonight."

"Forget it, Cindy, and have a good time. With my brother here do you think a person who wasn't wanted could get into this house? Joe is an ex-lightweight champion of his town. Go along, he and I will run this ranch. Your beau is ringing again. Get going, Cindy. Have fun, that's what you're always tellin' me."

"I'll have fun." An irresistible laugh rippled. "Something tells me I am about to spring a colossal sensation. The next time you see me, Sary Ann, I bet I will have made the front-page headlines. Wish me luck. I'm off."

# TWENTY

"DID YOU GET in touch with the leader of the band, Tom?" Cindy inquired eagerly as Slade's car slid into the highway.

"I did. After I crossed his palm with moola he was all smiles. He was sure his men wouldn't know 'The Merry-go-round Broke Down' which you and I decided would make a corking entrance tune, but declared they could go to town on 'The Beautiful Blue Danube.'"

"'The Blue Danube' is an oldie, but tops. It will suit us to a T. We practiced the waltz glide to that music at the rink this afternoon."

"I'll say we practiced, and—how."

"The costume you picked up for the masquerade is one hundred per cent perfect for our act."

"It is a neat number. We were so busy rehearsing I forgot to tell you that your guide, philosopher and friend was in the dry goods emporium while I was there. He didn't see me, though."

"And who is my guide, philosopher and friend?"

"Playing cagey, aren't you? Who but that guy Bill Damon?"

"Did he find a costume? What was it, Tom? Tell me. He was sure he would recognize me."

"Hey, get back on the beam, lovely. I don't know. You don't think I would give him away if I did, do you? He's a pain in the neck to me, you like him too much, but I've got to play fair."

"You always play fair, Thomas. You are the very nicest person I know."

"Are you playing fair when you declare in that passionately convincing voice that I am the nicest person you know? Forget it. I'm not beefing. I've settled down to a prolonged attack on what you think is your invincible heart. I'm one darn lucky guy to be putting on the act with you, but, I'm not kidding myself that I am *the* Prince—yet, Cinderella."

She couldn't declare that he was, better say nothing, let silence answer for her. She liked him immensely but never had felt the force of attraction that had drawn her to Bill Damon the afternoon in Ella's shop, which had increased in power ever since in spite of her indignation when she discovered he was Ken Stewart's deputy. She hadn't had the courage before to acknowledge it or probe into her heart.

"Perhaps Damon wasn't after a costume." Tom Slade's voice interrupted her self-examination. "He had a big man with him who looked like a movie plain-clothes guy."

A plain-clothes guy. Since she had stepped into Tom's car she hadn't given a thought to the mystery at The Castle. Had Bill Damon's insistence that she attend the masquerade been his way of getting her off the place while he installed a detective? Suppose the dick—if the man who had been in the shop with him were a dick—decided to investigate the secret staircase from the top?

"What's on the little mind, lovely? You muttered, 'Horrors!' as if something had frightened the daylights out of you."

"I thought—that roadster was heading straight for us."

"Oh, yeah? That isn't the truth and you know it."

She couldn't agree that it wasn't the truth, couldn't tell him that a vision of the plain-clothes man pitching down the secret staircase to the accompaniment of the clatter of copper frying pan and silver cups, had stopped her breath for a minute. Again silence appeared to be golden.

"Perfect night, isn't it, Thomas? There is still a tinge of rose color in the west from the sunset, and so many stars the sky appears gold-plated. Those must be the

Perseids darting through the skies trailing fiery stardust. It is the season for them."

"I can't concentrate on the stars, my thoughts are on my feet and what they will do to our act. Here we are. Every light in the Inn is on."

"I'm thrilled to the marrow. This masquerade was Lyd Fane's idea, I'll hand it to her for planning something exciting. Now that we are approaching the scene of our triumph—"

"Jupiter, I hope it will prove a triumph. I'm getting the jitters."

"Think defeat and you invite defeat, Brother Slade. Think success and you invite success. We'll be the sensation of the evening. One thing upon which we may count, there will be no audience participation in our act."

"You have something there, gal. Here we are at the rear door of the Inn. Our surreptitious entrance, our progress from this point on has been greased with folding money. Slip on your mask. I'll put on mine later. I've arranged to leave our coats in the dressing room off the stage of the ballroom."

"I'll take the car, Mr. Slade."

The sepulchral whisper oozed from the shadow of a shrub. It sent icy prickles slithering along Cindy's veins. Suppose the act laid an egg? Lyd Fane would be jubilant and Tom never would forgive her for making him ridiculous. She caught his arm.

"Suppose—suppose we're a flop, Thomas. Wouldn't we look silly—" A vision of what could happen choked off her whisper.

"Come on, not getting scared, are you? Think defeat and you invite defeat, Sister Clinton." He chuckled. "Atta gal. Step on it or we'll be seen. Sure you've brought your skates?"

She nodded. Her voice wouldn't come.

"Roger! When we get to the dressing room I'll put them on for you."

Minutes later—it seemed hours—boots on with roller skates attached she had brought concealed in her coat pockets—she stood hand in hand with Tom inside a door beside the stage which opened into the ballroom. The band was playing a polka. She tried to relax, glanced at her partner through the slits in her mask. He was trim and slender in a crimson jersey and black satin knee pants. Where had he found a costume so suitable? He looked like a French-Canadian ice skater.

The music muted to a wooing croon, softly seductive. Their cue—almost. She swallowed her heart which had zoomed to her throat.

"Tom! My knees have turned to jelly."

"This is the heck of a time to turn to jelly," he whispered hoarsely, and administered a shattering slap on her shoulder which rocked her on her skates. "Brace up."

"Ladies and gentlemen—" the voice of the band leader was sonorously impressive—"the management has provided a surprise for you. It presents the famous French-Canadian roller skate champions, *the de Barcos!*"

"Ready? Let's go."

An ear-splitting fanfare. A bar of "The Beautiful Blue Danube." The door before Cindy and Tom Slade opened as if by magic. "The de Barcos" skated into the hall in perfect timing.

A thunder of applause followed their entrance, died down till there was no sound but the nostalgic instrumentation of strings and brass, flutes and piccolos, a piano carrying the melody, the sound of rollers on the waxed floor.

Round the hall they went, arms crossed, hands together, separated, and united. Twice they executed waltz turns before they backed toward the exit. At the door Tom Slade lifted Cindy's hand to his lips. They made a sweeping obeisance and disappeared. A storm of applause, shouts of "Encore! Encore!" followed them.

"They want us back. Shall we go?"

"*No.*" Cindy refused breathlessly. "Why tempt Fate? We'll take a bow and fade away with laurel still crowning our brows.

"We put it across, Thomas," she exulted as in the dressing room he knelt to remove her skates. "I was

threatened with heart failure when you squeezed my
hand to signal the first waltz turn."

"Your heart condition wasn't a patch on mine. One
false step, one obstruction, even so much as a bobby pin
on that waxed floor and our act would have switched
into an uproarious slapstick comedy. I'll bet I aged ten
years in that trip around the hall." He pulled off her
skates and put on the high-heeled red satin slippers.

"There you are. All set? Slip out into the crowd
through this door. I'll make my entrance from the other
side of the stage. Leave the white fur coat here with
your raglan, you'll die in it when you dance. You were a
knockout, Cindy. You'll be bombarded with compli-
ments. Don't let them turn your head—away from me.
*En avant, Madame de Barco.*"

A tall chef in white from turban to gloves and shoes
was standing near the door as Cindy entered the hall.

*"Voulez-vous me faire le plaisir, Madame?"* The low
voice was unrecognizable.

*"Je suis enchantée, Monsieur,"* she whispered.

As he put his arm around her she glanced up. A small
blond mustache outlined his upper lip, the slits in the
black satin mask which covered his nose were so narrow
that only a glint showed through. The "secretary" at
Rockledge wore a mustache like that. Whoever he was
he waltzed like a dream to the music of "Stardust."
Halfway round the hall a monk tagged his shoulder
authoritatively. They stopped. Her partner raised her
gloved hand to his lips.

*"Je reviendrai, Madame,"* he murmured and was gone.
Her eyes followed him till he was lost in the maze of
dancers.

To the music of "St. Louis Blues" from peasant to
pirate she went. Men in the uniform of the army, air,
the marines cut in—she hadn't realized there were so
many ex-fighters in the town or among the summer
people, apparently there were guests from other places.
Each man complimented her on her performance, some
in whispers, some in a gutteral mutter, two in a high
falsetto, all voices too well disguised to be recognizable.

A woman in a costume made entirely of newssheets of

the county paper from low-cut bodice to plaited skirt, with black earrings matching necklace and bracelets, carried a bundle of papers under her right arm as she flitted from dancer to dancer apparently whispering news. A mysterious person. The tall chef appeared fascinated by her. Each time he danced with her a clown cut in.

Undine, in a wave-green sequinned confection dripping with seaweeds and strings of exquisite pink shells, was Lyd Fane, undoubtedly. No wonder she had suggested a Bal Masqué with that sensational costume up her sleeve. A catty thought, Cindy reproached herself, and turned her attention to what appeared to be a college president in black cap and gown who had cut in on a Red Cross ambulance driver. For a bulky person he was extremely light on his feet.

The clown touched his arm. It was the second time he had cut in on her dance. Red patches highlighted the cheekbones of his chalked face; an enormous mouth had been painted in the same brilliant color; a dab on the end of his nose and on his chin was black as the satin of his mask; his white peaked cap, the rest of his costume was the typical pantaloons and blouse of the circus. The glint of eyes between the slits in his mask sent icy prickles down her spine. Memory broadcast Sary's voice: "Get a lot of folks together with their faces covered up an' how do you know who you're dancing with? A crook might slip in an' hold you up."

Were his eyes fixed on her pearls or was it her hectic imagination working overtime? She gave a little sigh of relief when he was edged out by Prince Charming resplendent in sky-blue doublet and hose, a white satin cape swinging from one shoulder, and a beret with sweeping blue plume. He had cut in so often she was sure he was Hal Harding, the elaborate costume was right up his street.

A Marquise in pale pink satin, with three diamond stars sparkling on a black velvet band in her white hair, now dancing with the college president, was Mrs. Barclay, she was sure. She—

The tall chef laid a commanding hand on the shoul-

der of the Prince who muttered a protest which sounded
more like a threat but gave way. The musicians were
giving with saxophonic emphasis a Jerome Kern medley
when she saw the clown weaving in and out among the
dancers toward her.

"Quick. Let's dodge that clown coming this way," she
whispered at the risk of betraying her identity. "He has
cut in twice before. I—I don't like him."

A bell struck a resounding note. The music broke off
in the middle of "Smoke Gets in Your Eyes." The
dancers stopped. The lights went out.

"At the stroke of twelve unmask."

The band leader's voice reflected the tension that had
stiffened each person in the room.

*Two! Three! Four! Five!*

Cindy's nerves tingled as the bell tolled on.

*Eleven!*

"You are adorable in that skating costume—
Cinderella," whispered the chef.

Bill Damon, she had time to think before the bell
struck.

*Twelve!*

Lights up. Masks off. Excited laughter. Shouted names.
"I knew you all the time," in chorus. Cindy looked
up into the laughing eyes of the man beside her. No
mustache, only a faint red line where the falsie had
been pulled off. He held the high turban in his left
hand.

"I warned you I would recognize you," he reminded.

She had the curious feeling that another person, shadowy, unreal stood at his shoulder. She shook her head as
if to clear her eyes, brushed her hand across them. Had
excitement doubled her vision?

A bellhop in maroon livery with the yellow envelope
of a telegram in his hand appeared in the large doorway. He cleared his throat as if from nervousness. All
eyes turned toward him. Voices and laughter ceased.
The air was heavy with suspense, as if each person
present feared bad news. He entered the hall.

"Paging—Colonel Kenniston Stewart," he called.

"Paging Colonel Kenniston Stewart!"

# TWENTY-ONE

THE MAN beside Cindy gritted a furious expletive between his teeth. His hands clenched before he signaled
to the paging boy who ran across the room in answer,
his footsteps echoing in the still ballroom.

"I'll take it. I am Kenniston Stewart." He accepted
the yellow envelope and tore it open—glanced at the
enclosure, crushed it in his hands.

A seismic shock rippled through Cindy's body. She
remembered her inexplicable doubt that day on the
beach as to this man's identity.

"Are you Ken Stewart?" she whispered.

"Yes. Can you take it, Cinderella? You will when you
look at the faces of Harding and the Fane girl who
pulled this stunt. They are coming to gloat."

The trumpeter sounded the army mess call, "Come
and get it! Come and get it!" and the laughing, colorful
motley crowd, pirates and peasants, servicemen, dancing
girls and chevaliers, monks and nuns made a concerted
move toward the supper room.

The malicious triumph which glinted in the eyes of
Undine, in her wave-green costume, was duplicated in
the sardonic grin of the prince in his light blue doublet
and hose as they approached. Cindy considered the mer-
its of a mad dash to the exit and The Castle and
abandoned it. Why give that poisonous Lyd and Hal the
satisfaction of knowing she was panicked? From the
supper room drifted the music of an accordion playing
the melody of a Spanish fandango. Someone was adding
a castanet accompaniment. The ballroom was empty

except for the two men, the woman in green and the girl in her scarlet skating costume.

"What do you think of our H bomb, Cinderella?" Lydia mocked. She looked up and challenged, "You are Kenniston Stewart, aren't you? You won't deny it, will you?"

Cindy wondered that his laugh could be so light when the lines between his nose and mouth looked as if drawn in India ink.

"Deny it? My dear woman, why should I? You've only beaten me to the news by a few moments. I intended to cast off my alias when we went in to supper. It has served its purpose. I figured it would add one more dramatic touch to this gala evening."

"You planned to reveal your secret to the *ex*-Mrs. Stewart first, I assume?" Hal Harding jibed.

Cindy checked the spasmodic upward jerk of the arm of the chef by slipping her hand under it and holding tight. She produced what she hoped was a tormenting smile.

"Sorry to spoil the little joke, Hal, that you and Lyd have been working on for days I understand—even secrets get around—but 'the *ex*-Mrs. Stewart' has known the gentleman's identity since the day of his arrival." She looked up at the man beside her with a flicker of amused understanding, of mutual comprehension, then back with a smile and shrug of toleration to Harding and the girl.

"The way your reflexes take that statement is uproariously funny. Now that that's nicely settled, I suggest supper—and as if to pick up his cue here comes my skating partner to escort me to the buffet."

When Slade reached them she transferred her hand unhurriedly to his arm.

"I began to think you had forsaken me, Tommy, thought you never would come and I, literally starving." She took a step forward, turned, and looked over her shoulder.

"I'll be seeing you—Ken. To make this the perfect end of a perfect evening, you and I should be presented with an Oscar for our gay-deceiver act. By their expressions

I'll say we fooled 'em to the hilt. *En avant, Monsieur de Barco.*"

She shook Slade's arm as they crossed to the door.

"For Pete's sake, stop looking as if I had delivered a right to your jaw, Thomas. I—I—can't take—"

"Come out, Cindy. You mustn't cry here. What the devil is it all about?"

He pushed her ahead of him through a doorway, arm under hers, drew her to a shadowy corner at the end of the long porch. He pulled forward a wicker chair.

"Sit here, lovely."

"I—I—can't. I'd rather perch on the railing. I shan't cry—again." She brushed off two big tears that had spilled from her eyes to her cheeks. "I'm—I'm beginning to boil."

"Boil or cry, suit yourself so long as you tell me what it's all about." He leaned against an upright pillar facing her, watched her face as he shielded the light from a match he applied to a cigarette. "I came up in time to hear you call Bill Damon 'Ken.' That name must have packed a wallop. I've never seen a bronzed face turn so white as his. Take it from there, Cindy. You owe me that."

Through the open window drifted the mellow voice of the band leader singing to the accompaniment of a piano.

"Night and Day. Night and Day."

"The pink light on the horizon must be the battered old moon rising to see the dawn come up like thunder." She contributed the gem of observation in an attempt at casual conversation.

"I don't give a lead nickel at the present moment for the moon or the dawn, lovely. Play fair. Is the man who has been living at the Inn as Bill Damon, Kenniston Stewart?"

"That's his story."

"Cut out flippancy. Get down to cases." Never before had Tom Slade been curt with her. "Why did he crack through with the truth tonight? I slipped out while the clock was striking and missed the showdown. I had a hunch I'd better check on my car the boy drove off."

"Is it safe, Tom?"

"Sure. There have been so many automobile thefts on this shore during the last month I got the jitters. It is locked tight as I left it in the parking place in front of the Inn with dozens of models including two Town and Country convertibles like mine. I thought I had the one and only in this part of the country. I've given you time, Cindy, to pull yourself together, now I want the truth from A to Z about this Damon-Stewart mix-up."

"I don't know the truth. You'll have to page the dual-personality himself for that."

"Didn't he offer you an explanation?"

"I don't need one. Use your imagination, Thomas. He had to come to the United States to get his fortune out of the oil holdings. When he arrived in this town the marriage contract still was valid. Undoubtedly he figured that if I knew who he was I would burst into sobs on his shoulder and beg him not to desert me."

"You are unfair to him, Cinderella. Perhaps he came here to get to know you because of the business interests you and he had in common, to be friends with you. Be honest, he wouldn't have had the smidgin of a chance had he appeared as himself, Ken Stewart, would he? As to letting that annulment go through, I'm with him every step of the way. What man wants to hold a woman to a written-contract marriage?"

"Does that mean you couldn't love a girl who had made that sort of marriage, Tom?"

"I *do* love a girl who made that sort of marriage—but it wasn't to me."

Ken Stewart in white summer formals appeared suddenly from out the shadows.

"Beat it will you, Slade? Give me a chance to talk with her."

"You've had your chance, my God, what a chance it was. I—"

"*Don't* beat it, Tom." Cindy interrupted his bitter accusation. "I won't talk with him. I'll never speak to you again, Bill—Kenniston Stewart. You've made me ridiculous before—" She stopped to recover her voice. "I'm going—"

She deftly avoided the hands outstretched to stop her, raced along the porch, outdistancing pursuing feet, flew down the steps and along the broad drive banked solidly with automobiles on each side. Cinderella fleeing from the ball, she thought.

"Red shoes run faster," she remembered having read somewhere. Hers were fast as the wind.

She backed into the shadow of a black limousine and held her breath to listen. No sound save the ebb and flow of the tide on the beach in front of the Inn and the faint strains of "Old Man River" drifting through an open window. No footsteps approaching. The person who had followed her along the porch had given up the chase.

Now what? Time to think, she answered her own question. Shivered. The weather had put on a lightning-change act from the day's heat to cold so characteristic of the region. The white fur jacket was hanging in the stage dressing room with her raglan. Were her teeth chattering from cold or fury? The latter ought to make her hot, not cold.

If she could get inside the car against which she was huddling she could cover herself with a robe—if there were a robe—and watch for Tom from the window. Although the license plate wasn't visible the Town and Country convertible parked across the drive looked like his. No use to try to get into it, he had said it was locked. He would know she would be near and come looking for her. Better not dash over yet, she might be seen by Bill—Ken Stewart, he had said he wanted to talk with her and from past experience she had learned he was not to be diverted from what he set out to accomplish. Hadn't he persuaded her to accept the pearls from—himself? Just let her get home and they would go back to him so quick it would make his brain whirl.

She tried the handle of the rear door of the limousine. It turned. She reconnoitered. No one coming along the drive either way. She cautiously opened the door. A folded robe on the back seat. Br-r-r, that puff of icy breeze was straight from the ocean. Why stand here and freeze? Someone coming.

She stepped into the car with her right foot, drew up the other. The red satin slipper dropped. At the risk of pitching out on her head she leaned over to retrieve it. Someone coming down the porch steps. She flung herself back into the car. The red slipper was in the shadow. She would take a chance and leave it for the present.

Cautiously she closed the door, opened the window back of the driver's seat a crack, then pulled the soft dark blue plush robe across her shoulders. Heavenly warm. She knelt before the side window, raised it a bare inch, no danger now of being knocked out by carbon monoxide, no matter what else happened, and she could see and hail Tom when he came looking for her.

A stout figure plodded along the drive, the skirt of his black robe blowing in the breeze. The college president with whom she had danced twice had been Counselor Armstrong and she hadn't suspected it. She had seen him several times with the Marquise in the ravishing pink costume whom she had thought was Alida Barclay. The aging bellhop had flung his surprise grenade so soon after the unmasking that her mind had been in too great a tumult for her to check on the impression.

Tumult? Typhoon was the word. She had thought a century of thoughts from the moment Bill Damon had held out his hand for the telegram, his cool, "I'll take it," and her whispered, "Are you Ken Stewart?"

His "Yes, can you take it, Cinderella?" had been like a slim, shining knife blade thrust in her heart.

Why, why had he come to this village? Tom Slade's sympathetic explanation was phony. Why deceive her as to his identity? Stupid question. Only one answer. He was afraid that if he appeared as himself he might block the annulment. Block it? Ye gods! Had he thought for a minute she wanted to hold him to it?

I should have let him talk on the porch, she reflected. Then furiously, caustically told him what I thought of Kenniston Stewart, what I had been thinking through the years he sidestepped his responsibility. I wager that by the time I was through any idea he had that I wanted that written contract to stand would have been smashed and smashed hard. I missed the chance of my—

Who was opening the front door of the wheel side of this car? She tensed to watchfulness. It closed softly. She raised herself to her knees. Someone was on the front seat, someone with a peaked white cap—her heart flopped and righted—it was the clown who had cut in on her dance. He still wore the black satin mask on his chalked face. She must get out. A quick move of his head knocked off the peaked white cap and revealed black hair with one deep wave smooth as if it had been marcelled and lacquered.

The swoop of the car sent her back to the floor. Too late to escape. The driver was preparing to burn up the road. From what was he running away? Tom had said there had been many automobile thefts along the coast. Was this one?

Now what? Cautiously she raised her head till she could look from the side window. They were no longer on the Inn drive. The car was speeding. If she jumped she would break her neck or back. If she stayed here—that was the $64.00 question. A flash on the back window. A car following? Was another driver suspicious of the madly speeding limousine, which was giving an excellent imitation of a jet bomber on high? Whether it was or not the man at the wheel of this one feared it.

She drew the soft robe closer about her shoulders. She could pull it over her head if there were a crash and could a crash be avoided at this speed unless the thief or madman reached the safety of his hide-out first? a result which offered a more terrifying possibility than a broken neck. I'll settle for the latter, she told herself.

Another flash on the rear window. A warning siren. Were they being followed by a cruising car so early in the morning? She threw the robe from her shoulders and applied eyes and ears to the narrow opening of the side window. If another car approached she would scream her head off. The faint far whistle of a train. She looked at the illuminated dial of her wrist watch. A sense of impending tragedy set her heart pounding, blocked her breath. A freight train steamed through at this hour, she had heard it when she had a wakeful night.

Past a red light. The clown at the wheel must be desperate—or drunk. A car behind was getting closer. Crash! Had the pursuer gone off the road? A sob rose in her throat. That hope of rescue was gone. On they went. Past another stop light. The warning whistle echoed through the still morning air. Nearer this time. They were perilously close to the railroad. Had the driver heard? Should she warn him? Would he try to cross before the gates fell?

A shout! The gate keeper? The limousine bumped and swayed across the rails. The bell clanged furiously. They had made it. The gates fell. A train lumbered by. They were saved, but, also, the closing gates had stopped the automobiles behind them if one had been a police patrol as she had hoped.

The driver increased speed. A sharp turn on two wheels. Brakes screamed. Tires slid. Instinctively she pulled the robe over her head. It might save her neck— Was the car going over? She clutched at the seat, at the door handle to hold herself steady. It settled back with a mighty lurch that left her dazed.

Minutes passed before her mind came back from the threshold of unconsciousness. Voices outside. Loud voices. Rescue at last. She cautiously flexed her muscles. Nothing broken. The heavy robe had saved her. She pushed it back to get her breath. The door beside her was yanked open. Through a glare of light she caught the glitter of brass buttons. The police. She was safe.

The officer with an electric torch wobbling in his hand stood for several throbbing seconds, leaning forward, his eyes fixed on her. His gloating smile sent her heart to her throat. Who did he think she was?

# TWENTY-TWO

"I'LL CATCH HER. It's my job now," Slade flung over his shoulder as he started in pursuit of the girl racing along the porch.

Kenniston Stewart took an impetuous step forward. Stopped. Wiser for Slade to follow and take her to The Castle. For me to try to talk to her now would be about as safe as deactivating a contact mine, he told himself. She is too furious with Kenniston Stewart to listen to him.

He drew a long breath. It was a huge relief to throw off the Bill Damon alias. Voices and laughter drifted from the front of the Inn. The party was breaking up to the tune of "Good Night, Ladies." He glanced at his watch. Two o'clock.

Back and forth he paced like a bear in the confinement of a cage. Cinderella and he had provided plenty of food, a veritable banquet, of conversation for the masqueraders on their homeward way, he reflected, she with the superb exhibition of skating and he with the theatric disclosure of his identity. He'd hand it to the Fane girl and Harding for working up a clever denouement. When the boy appeared with the yellow envelope he had wondered who was slated for congratulations or bad news. Of course he need not have accepted it—but, for a split second he had thought it was a telegram from the War Department, he couldn't ignore it and deny his name.

He swore under his breath. If I could get my hands on Harding—Cindy thought I started to hit the heel in

168

the ballroom. Not there. The lift of my arm at his insinuating voice was an instinctive reflex action of the muscles.

"Ken? Ken, are you here?"

A woman materialized from the shadow, a woman in an enveloping black satin cape. The light from a passing automobile in the road below set three diamond stars sparkling in her white hair. She caught his arm.

"Ken, what happened?" she whispered.

"Haven't you heard, Ally? If not, you're the only person here tonight who hasn't."

"Ken, come over where I can sit on the railing. I'm suffering the tortures of the damned from narrow shoes." He steadied her as she mounted the rail. She kicked off two high-heeled silver slippers.

"The relief, the blessed relief." She flexed her toes in their sheer nylons. "Now, tell me what happened. First what was your costume? I didn't recognize you, though I had been sure I would."

"I borrowed an outfit from one of the chefs. Wore it over these clothes and shed it before I came out here."

"In the supper room I sensed an undercurrent of excitement, but no one would tell me what it was about. A group would stop buzzing when I joined it. What happened?"

"Sure you are warm enough? It has turned cold."

"Plenty warm." She drew the satin cape closer about her shoulders. "Go on."

"Weren't you in the ballroom when we unmasked?" Even in the dim light he could see the added brilliance of her eyes, her heightened color.

"No. If you must know the awful truth, Ken, at that climactic moment I was on the ocean side of the porch where you and I sat the other evening, listening to a proposal—of marriage, if you can believe it."

"I won't ask the question quivering on the tip of my tongue." How could he laugh when his life appeared to be torn up by the roots? "Does it mean that you are ready to give up adventure and, I quote, settle down to the tame life of a socialite?"

"Give up adventure? I would say I heard it calling.

Isn't marriage the greatest adventure extant? I will confide the romantic details to you later—after I have given my answer, which something tells me will be 'Yes.' I have always admired the profession of the law, and a Federal Judge ... Now, to return to the buzz-buzz. What happened?"

He leaned against a porch post facing her, feeling without seeing the beauty of the star-sprinkled sky, the riding lights on boats large and small as they swayed with the tide while he told of the entrance of the bellhop with the telegram.

"I have been waiting for just the right moment to tell all to Cinderella," he concluded. "I knew that her first reaction would be furious anger at the deception—I was sure I could meet that, we have become good friends, but to have the revelation break as it did before that crowd in the ballroom—"

"You didn't have to accept that telegram."

"I did. It might have been an order from the War Office. It was a blank sheet. Harding and the Fane girl were clever to address it to *Colonel* Kenniston Stewart. I could break their necks."

"I knew Lydia would resent your indifference to her lure. At our dinner for Mrs. Drew she had her charm running on all cylinders. You remained courteous but unimpressed. She's a 'Come hither-How dare you!' temptress, and bitterly resents defeat. How did Cindy take the revelation?"

"Like the sport she is. For an instant I thought she had turned to stone. Then she pulled herself out of stunned surprise and declared she had been party to the deception from the day of my arrival with such *savoir-faire,* such gay contempt aimed at Lydia Fane and Harding, that she almost convinced me she had shared my secret. I'm sure they felt their sensation bomb had proved a dud. If they didn't, their expressions belied them. They looked as if they couldn't believe their ears."

"It won't help for me to declare that the tent you pitched has collapsed on you, Ken."

"I refuse to admit that, Ally. I'll make Cindy listen to

me if I have to kidnap her. I told you before that I am sure I decided wisely when I came here incognito. This mix-up tonight hasn't changed that conviction."

"I hope you are right, but, women don't reason, they feel. It must have been a crushing blow to her pride to have the truth proclaimed where and when it was. Of course you are in love with your ex-wife."

*"Don't* call her that. Harding referred to her as the ex-Mrs. Stewart. I was horribly tempted to knock his teeth in, however convention held. Of course I am in love with her. I told you I came to this town because of a belated nudge from old man Responsibility. When I saw her that day in Ella Crane's shop and discovered who she was, I loved her tender mouth, her mischievous brown eyes. She was unbearably sweet, I felt as a man would who had suddenly discovered hidden treasure of untold beauty and value—which he knew was his— marked HANDS OFF. I determined that one day she would be my wife in reality." He tamped out his cigarette against the rail. "Think you can take more of this, Ally?"

"Go on, Ken. I want to hear all you will tell me. I am happy that you are willing to confide in me."

"My father used to write at length as to the fineness of Cinderella Clinton's character—he never mentioned her beauty or charm—of her devotion to her father. As I read those letters I would grin and think, 'Pop is remorseful that he has tied up my life in this zany marriage and is building up the girl to me.' When I saw Cinderella all he had written fused and fell behind her like a wonderful, colorful backdrop. I loved her. She was the woman I wanted."

"And you let that annulment go through. How could you?"

"When I was tempted to stop it I reminded myself that I had made a decision by the process of cold reason, that at present I was in too much of an emotional upheaval to trust my judgment. The day she went to court I played off my tennis finals, then faked a business appointment in Portland for fear my resolution would crack. However, I held fast to my determination to start with a clear slate with her."

"That same slate is slightly smooched, I'd say. Did Slade take her home?"

"I'm sure he did. She hadn't much of a start when he raced after her along the porch. He loves her. She is furiously angry with me. It is his chance to score. That isn't fair. Slade is a plus guy. I've bored you enough with my problems. Did you enjoy the ball?"

"Yes. Who was the girl or woman flitting from dancer to dancer, whispering news, on whom the chef cut in so often? I wasn't in the hall when the dancers unmasked."

"That was what the chef was trying to find out. Unfortunately at the moment of unmasking the onetime chef had been forced to reveal the fact that he had been leading a double life."

"Did you pick up any clues at our dinner last night?"

"Several, I think. I haven't fitted them into the pattern yet. I'll report to you when I have it worked out."

"I had a feeling that the news-carrier might be a person in whom we are interested. I noticed that a clown also was cutting in often on her dances."

"A *clown!*" Cindy had whispered. "Quick, let's dodge that clown coming this way. He has cut in twice before. I—I don't like him."

Had the man trailed her knowing she was from The Castle? Did he know of the jewels cached in the turret room? Had he followed her when she left the Inn? Suppose he had? So had Slade immediately.

"The clown also was shadowing Cindy," he explained. Perhaps Slade *hadn't* reached her first, perhaps—why stand here wondering? "I'm uneasy about her. I'm going to The Castle, Ally. Hang it, my car is in the shop."

"Take mine, Ken. Seth came with me but decided to walk to White Pillars, said he would sleep better. Drive me home, then use my roadster. Stop pacing like a prowling tiger. Undoubtedly by this time she is safe under Sarah Ann's watchful wing. Did you get your man installed at The Castle?"

"Yes. Let's get going. I'll snatch a topcoat on the way."

Seth Armstrong in a hectic plaid wool lounge robe which did not quite reach the bottom of the legs of his red and white striped pajamas, appeared on the porch as the roadster stopped in the drive in front of the white-columned yellow colonial house.

"That you, Ally?"

"Yes, Seth."

Ken Stewart held her long cape of black satin and bouffant pink skirt away from the wheel as she stepped from the car.

"What has happened? Why are you waiting up for me, Seth?"

"Have you seen Cindy Clinton? Oh, it's you, Colonel. I was glad the Damon alias cracked tonight. It had its dangers. When you told me of it the first time you came to my office I didn't believe you could get by for a day. Cinderella was too excited when the deeds to the oil property were signed to notice that the signature, 'Kenniston Stewart' under hers was not followed by 'Bill Damon, Attorney in fact.' "

"You were an enormous help in the deception, Counselor. I couldn't have carried on without you. Why are you asking about Cindy? What's happened?"

"I don't know that anything has happened." Seth Armstrong inflated and deflated his cheeks. "Five minutes ago Sarah Ann Parker telephoned that Cinderella had told her she would be home soon after midnight. She hadn't come. 'So many awful things in the papers,' she whimpered. She tried to contact you at the Inn, Colonel, but the desk reported you didn't answer the ring."

"I'll beat it to The Castle. I'll take your roadster, Ally."

"I'm sure you will find her safe—" The rest of the sentence dwindled in the distance as the car shot out of the drive.

Why did one always imagine the worst in a crisis? The wheels kept pace with his thoughts. The speedometer needle went to sixty, crept up to seventy miles an hour. The roadster hurtled past lightless houses. Gardens colorless but sweetly fragrant in the dusk of early morning.

Past a beach ghostly white under the starlight, mur-
murous with the swish of the tide. The harbor lights.
The Castle.

Sarah Ann Parker was at the open door in a dark blue
robe, when he stopped the roadster with a suddenness
that plowed up pebbles in the drive. He sprang out and
dashed up the steps.

"Have you brought her?" Her face was yellow-white
under the porch light.

"No. Come into the house, Sary." Arm under hers he
guided her through the hall into the old kitchen.

"Sit in the wing chair. Now, pull yourself together.
Why are you so terrified?" He glanced at the banjo
clock. "It is not quite three. That isn't late for a
masquerade." It is late, infernally late, he thought, but
why add to the woman's fear?

"Cindy said she'd be home soon after midnight,"
Sarah Ann Parker sat on the edge of the big chair and
wrung her bony hands. "She stood on the threshold of
her room laughing, you know the way her dimples prick
through, an' said:

"'Something tells me I am about to spring a colossal
sensation. The next time you see me, Sary Ann, I bet I
will have made front-page headlines.'

"I'm scared. I've been thinkin' she may have meant
she was elopin' with Hal Harding. I've been kinder
suspicious she liked him more than she let on an' he has
a persuasive way. Perhaps she's married him."

Could it be? The possibility stopped his heartbeat. If
Sarah were to be believed, Cindy had been cruelly hurt
by the indifference of Ken Stewart. She had been
shocked tonight by the brutal surprise of his presence.
She wouldn't, she couldn't marry Harding. Hadn't she
scorched him with contempt in the ballroom? Not more
than she scorched you later, memory reminded. Tom
Slade had followed her almost immediately, she
wouldn't have had time to see Harding.

The reminder sent blood coursing through his veins
again. Slade loved her too much to connive at a clandestine marriage. Which reasoning was good as far as it
went, but didn't answer the question, "Where is she?"

"There's the phone." Sarah Ann Parker started to her feet. "It's probably her tellin' us—" big tears rolled down her cheeks. "You take it, will you, Colonel Da—Stewart? If I try to speak I'll cry."

He was already lifting the receiver, tense with dread of what he might hear.

"Yes. This is The Castle. The county hospital?"

"Has she, is she—"

He shook off the clutch on his arm.

"Please, Sarah. Wait till I get the message." He spoke into the phone.

"Put him on. Kenniston Stewart speaking for Miss Parker. *Slade?* Where the devil are you? Is Cindy with you? What? Speak louder. You can't. O.K. Put on your nurse."

"Mr. Slade is trying to tell you—" A woman's voice— He could feel the color drain from his face, his blood turned to ice as he listened for what seemed years.

"That covers it." The voice went on. "Mr. Slade is hazy and feverish from shock. Slight concussion. No bones broken. He keeps muttering, 'Tell him to find her. Black limousine. Heading for Portland. Tell him I picked up her red slipper.' He keeps muttering, 'Cinderella's slipper.' I guess he must have heard Walt Disney has made a movie of that fairy story."

"Thank you, nurse. I'll report to the hospital the moment I find her."

He cradled the receiver, laid his hand on Sarah Ann's shoulder as he answered the question in her anguished eyes.

"Tom Slade followed Cindy when she left us. He remembered that her coats were in the stage dressing room, went for them for fear she would be cold. He was sure she would find his car and wait for him. When he reached the drive a big black limousine pulled out from a line of parked cars and shot away. Something about the take-off didn't look good to him and he ran to the space it had left, and saw—a red satin slipper."

"Stop an' get your breath, Bill—Ken Stewart. I got hold of myself now. What happened next?"

"He followed the black limousine in his convertible.

He was making sixty an hour with the racing car just ahead, when he heard a loud explosion. A tire, he thought, and the next he knew he was in a hospital trying desperately to make the nurses understand that he knew what he was saying, that he must get in touch with you."

"That's all he could tell about Cindy?"

"Yes. The nurse said that after he told her the story to pass on to me, he drifted into sleep he had fought off until he could tell what happened."

"Now, what do we do? We must do something."

He held his own agonizing anxiety in check to reassure her.

"I'm going after that black limousine, Sary. I'll phone the nearest police headquarters. First I must pick up an automatic—"

"A pistol? You don't have to go anywhere. Joe has one an—"

"*Joe!* Good Lord, I'd forgotten him. Rout him out. quick."

# TWENTY-THREE

Cindy had pulled herself to her knees. The triumphant glare in the policeman's eyes held her there. The insigne on his sleeve was that of a sergeant.

"Hey, see what I've found, fellas. Come here."

His shout brought several men from out the shadows to converge in the space in front of the limousine. He focused his flashlight again and addressed the group staring as if hypnotized at the girl framed by the open door of the car.

"Cheerio. Don't be downhearted. The guy we were after made his getaway. Headquarters told us he had a dame working with him and lookee, it's her. Get an eyeful of those pearls." He reached into the car and caught her arm.

"Come out."

She shook off his hand.

"Certainly I will come out, but *without* your assistance." She drew the dark blue rug over her shoulders and stepped to the ground with her slippered foot, followed by the other covered only by a sheer red stocking. Chin up she looked from one face to the other. Her eyes came back to the man who had broadcast the news of his find.

"What's it all about? I was in the back of the limousine—"

"Hiding, weren't you?"

"Stop interrupting me. I was in the back seat of the parked limousine when a clown slid into the front seat and—"

177

"Don't waste time lettin' the dame tell the story of her life," interrupted an authoritative voice from the background. "Bring her to headquarters, Sarge, then she can tell the chief all the fairy tales she wants."

"Yes, Captain." The sergeant who had so cockily proclaimed his find touched his cap respectfully before he seized Cindy's arm.

"Come along, you."

She administered a stinging slap on his cheek.

"Let me go. I shall not come-along-you—till I have spoken to your boss and told him who I am." Brave and ringing words, my proud beauty, but ten to one they land you in the hoosegow, she warned herself.

The sound of a starting car set her heart thumping. Had the "Captain," who supposedly had intelligence or he wouldn't be a captain, left her at the mercy of these men peering out of the shadows? They resembled nothing so much as a lot of movie gangsters. Her impulsive attack on the sergeant had been a mistake. The smothered guffaws from the onlookers hadn't helped her case.

"He's gone. You can't tell him. He'll be headin' a reception committee for you at headquarters. Come along, now."

Cindy glanced at her watch. Almost three o'clock. Sary expected her home soon after midnight. By this time she would begin to be anxious—she would phone someone, perhaps Bill Damon at the Inn—she didn't know he was Ken Stewart—or Tom Slade—Tom? He must have started looking for her—perhaps he had followed the speeding limousine in his convertible—perhaps the crash she had heard behind—

"Coming? Or will we have to carry you?" a rough voice demanded.

"You won't have to carry me. You may be surprised, but I'm coming. Listen, my cocky one. You have another surprise in store that will wipe that gloating grin off your face. Out of my way." I didn't know you had such defiance in you, gal, she told herself and flinched as her stockinged foot bore down heavily on a jagged fragment of rock.

Guarded by four men—only four—she had thought it

was a gang—she limped her way toward a police cruising car. Its headlights shot long yellow rays that were lost in the haze of distance. Spooky effect. She remembered the day in the patio when she had declared to Bill Damon— he was Bill Damon then—"The moment I am free I shall live daringly." Looked as if what she had intended for a joke were coming true.

Would he care if he knew she was caught in this mess? What difference did it make if he did or not? He was out of her life completely. In an effort to expunge him from her thoughts she looked up at the sky.

"I wonder which of those stars is broadcasting four-meter radio waves, Officer? I forgot, scientists declare that the stellar broadcasting stations that produce the waves are probably stars with surfaces too dim to be seen. Astronomy is a fascinating study, haven't you found it so?"

"Kiddin' me, aren't you? You know what you get for resisting arrest and assaulting a policeman?" Apparently the slap rankled. "You won't be so chatty when you reach headquarters."

"Your mistake, Sergeant. You will be surprised how much I will have to say. I hope you are not too fond of your job, that you have unemployment insurance. You may have to look for something else by which to bring home the bacon."

It was three-thirty by the huge clock on the wall above a long desk with five chairs behind it, when she entered police headquarters. A heavy white-haired man, occupying the center seat, curtly ordered her to sit on a bench facing it.

So this is what a police court is like, really, she thought. The movies I've seen didn't make it sordid or smelly enough. A male derelict, head down, shabby, pitiably thin, was being admonished and dismissed. His place was taken by a boy, who answered questions in a scared whisper before he was led away and a door clanged behind him.

"Me next," a woman with disheveled tarnished-gilt hair beside Cindy proclaimed shrilly. Her eyes were bleary, her make-up had been applied with a prodigal hand; her gay blue and red print dress glittered with cheap jewelry; she reeked of liquor.

"What you here for, dearie? In that red skirt, you look's if you'd been picked up at a gipsy camp."

Before Cindy could think of an answer to the hoarse whisper she rose and switched toward the desk.

"Here's your old friend, Judge," she said with such ingratiating humor that the man she addressed quickly covered a broadening grin with a red, hairy hand. It seemed as if the clock ticked away hours before the woman followed the boy. She turned, winked, and waved a friendly hand to the room at large before she made her unsteady exit.

"Next."

Did that mean her? Cindy looked around. It must. She was the only person present beside the policeman who had brought her here. The man at the desk leaned forward as if puzzled by her fantastic costume, as if trying to decide in which criminal pigeonhole she belonged. The dark plush robe trailed from her shoulders as she stepped forward. I must remember to return this to the owner, she thought irrelevantly.

"What's the charge?" the presiding official demanded.

"I'm interested to hear that myself, sir," Cindy answered defiantly unmindful of the fact that the question had not been addressed to her.

"Silence, Miss, till you're spoken to." The policeman beside her added the nudge of an elbow to the gruff reminder of his superior. "Go ahead, Sergeant."

"Yes, sir. We got a teletype that a black seven-passenger limousine, deluxe model, stolen from an Inn, was racing this way, had just missed bein' smashed by the early freight from Boston, that a Town and Country convertible, that's what they call them new models that look like a station wagon—"

"I know. You don't have to explain models to me. Go on, Sergeant."

"Which they think was chasin' the limousine, busted a tire and crashed."

"No. *No!*" Cindy's broken protest followed a vision of

Tom Slade, unconscious, perhaps dying by the side of the road.

"Silence! Go on, Sergeant."

"They told us they suspected the guy who was running away with the limousine was the brains of a gang which had stolen eight cars along this shore the last month, that they had thrown out roadblocks. We started after him in a cruiser."

"And *lost* him. Were you sitting on your hands?"

"*No*, sir." The sergeant's voice registered resentment at his superior's sarcasm. "When the limousine crashed into a roadblock he made his getaway. I don't know how he done it unless with mirrors, but," he cast a venomous glance at the girl beside him, "we got this dame hiding all wrapped up in a rug on the floor in back."

The dignitary behind the desk leaned forward. Cindy faced his scowling appraisal unflinchingly.

"What had the girl to do with the thief?"

"We were alerted he had a dame working with him. We figured she was the finger girl who located the unlocked limousine for him to snitch."

There was a sudden influx of men armed with notebooks and cameras. They looked as if they had been routed out to answer a hurry-up call and hadn't waited to shave or brush their hair. Only three? At first she had thought there were a dozen. Reporters! Had they been notified by phone of her arrest? Her heart went into a nose dive. She remembered her laughing boast to Sary:

"Something tells me I am about to spring a colossal sensation. The next time you see me I bet I will have made front-page headlines." I've made them, plus, she thought.

The man at the desk nodded to the group by the door before he commanded:

"Tell your story."

Cindy flinched at the report of the first flash bulb, held herself tense as three more followed.

"I refuse to answer, Captain—for fear what I say may tend to incriminate me." It was certainly educational to be a confirmed newspaper reader, she thought as the phrase, which had been used again and again by witnesses

at the trial of a man alleged to have conspired to make
United States defense secrets available to a foreign power,
surged to the top of her mind. "I shall not talk until I
can be represented by counsel."

"You'd better talk if you know what is good for you."

"That threat is a mistake, Chief."

Cindy's mind whirled and steadied. Bill Damon's
voice. She must think of him by his right name—Ken
Stewart in a well-worn aviator's greatcoat was standing
beside her. The relief. The unbelievable relief. This
time her knees had turned to water, not jelly. She
caught at his sleeve to steady herself. He stood frigid as
a deep-freeze and about as responsive to the clutch of
her hand on his arm.

"Who are you to come into this police court and tell
me what I can do?"

"Take a look at this, sir."

He stepped forward and laid an open billfold on the
desk. Bulbs flashed. The light revealed shadows like
smudges on his face; haggard lines between nose and
lips; little white patches in his dark hair at the temples,
as if someone with floury fingers had brushed it back.
He must have looked like this when fighting.

The official studied the identification offered. His
scowl changed to incredible surprise.

"Goramighty, it was you, Col—" He stopped at the
command of a raised hand. His face burned red. He
cleared his throat. "Sorry. I take it you're a friend of
this—this young lady. Will you advise her to tell how she
come to be picked up in that stolen limousine?"

Stewart slipped the billfold into his pocket and
stepped back from the desk.

"Go ahead, Miss Clinton," he said formally.

For a moment she thought her voice had dried in her
contracted throat. There was not a sound in the room
save the loud ticking of the clock. It must be old-
fashioned, she thought irrelevantly, modern clocks are
electrified, they don't tick.

"Take your time," Ken Stewart encouraged.

She told of the Bal Masqué, of running along the
Inn drive in search of a friend's convertible; of being

coatless and cold; of thinking she might find a rug in the black limousine beside which she was standing to put over her shoulders until her friend arrived.

"Why didn't you find your friend's car?"

"There were three in the drive like his, and he had told me his was locked."

She told of the clown's stealthy entrance into the limousine; her recognition of him; her attempt to escape as the car swooped into the drive.

"You are sure he was the man who cut in on your dances at the masquerade?"

"Yes, sir."

"Would you recognize him if you saw his picture?"

"No, sir, his clown make-up was perfect. The only thing I would recognize would be his slicked-back black hair and hundreds of men have hair like that."

She went on without further interruption to the moment when she had been roused from semiconsciousness by a glare of light, followed by a voice shouting:

"Hey! See what I've found, fellas. Come here."

As she talked she had been aware of the sound of scribbling pens and pencils; of an occasional off-stage phone ring; of the assenting nods of the presiding dignitary, of his twirling thumbs as he listened. He pulled a big book toward him.

"You have told a convincing story. Your name."

The pencils stopped scribbling. It seemed to Cindy as if the walls had closed in to listen. She looked up at Ken Stewart.

"Cinderella Clinton," she acknowledged in response to his affirmative nod. One of the reporters gave vent to a surprised whistle.

Now he will have something to write home about, she thought. He has me all tied up with that "marriage by proxy" which was publicized from coast to coast. Ken Stewart approached the desk.

"Doesn't that fill the bill for tonight, Chief? Miss Clinton was dragged here, suspected of being a person she must have convinced you she isn't, a mistake for which we will seek redress later. She is minus a shoe, is shaking with cold." His voice was as frigid as she felt.

"Certainly, certainly. Don't blame my men too much. They were working under orders. We've got to nab those auto thieves. They are thumbing their noses at us. You'll have to admit it isn't customary for a young lady like Miss Clinton to ride round the country rolled up in a rug in the back seat of a limousine. Case dismissed."

When they reached the roadster Ken Stewart pulled a coat from the front seat and held it.

"Put this on. Sarah gave it to me. Drop that rug."

"It should be returned to the owner."

"I'll attend to that. Sit in front. I have something to say to you." As she hesitated he added, "Not about what you think. Get in. Stick out your feet while I put on your shoes."

"How did you know I needed them?" she asked from the seat beside the wheel.

"We heard that Cinderella lost a slipper while racing away from the ball. There you are, shod again. All set? Let's go."

Dawn was breaking in a sky intensely blue, clear except for a low cloud bank on the eastern horizon. A rim of gold crowned its entire length. Above that a pink glow rose and slowly spread. One by one stars faded and disappeared. A lonely crow cawed in the distance. A frog croaked hoarsely from the faint glimmer of a pond. A breeze touched her hair lightly and sped on. Cindy put her hand to her head.

"I hadn't realized it was gone. Somewhere I lost my white cap," she explained, not that she cared, but to break a silence which was becoming unbearable.

"You wore it when you were on the porch with Slade and me."

The porch. Skiddy ground.

"How did you know where to find me?" she asked hurriedly.

"We had a phone message from Slade. That is what I have to tell you."

"Tom! I remember now. That sergeant said a convertible crashed. Was it his? He isn't dead? That isn't what you have to say to me, is it?" Her breath caught in a frightened sob.

"No. He isn't dead. He isn't seriously hurt. He was following a car in which he thought you had been kidnaped. A tire burst. He was going so fast that the convertible crashed off the road. When he roused from unconsciousness at the hospital he insisted upon getting in touch with Sarah Ann Parker. I happened to be at The Castle when the call came through. She was too frightened to speak. I took the message. The nurse relayed to me as he talked, he was too weak for his voice to carry."

Cindy listened breathlessly as he repeated Tom Slade's story. The sun rose from behind the cloud bank, a sudden dazzle of light, and touched the dark crouching tops of hills; cool, limpid surfaces of ponds shone like mirrors.

Shafts of sunrise sifting through the foliage of tall willows and stocky alders, sprinkled glinting pink sapphires on the purling water of a brook on its way to join a river. Glistening silver wires hummed as they swung from pole to pole. Heavy dew coating fields, trees and roadside shrubs sparkled like diamond dust. An oriole perched on his nest swinging from the tip of an oak branch poured out his heart in song.

"That is the story," he concluded.

"Tom smashed up and I responsible. I just can't bear it," Cindy declared brokenly.

"Don't blame yourself. The guy who stole the limousine is responsible." He slowed the roadster to look up at a sign. "This is the road."

"Not to The Castle. You've made the wrong turn."

"I'm not going to The Castle—yet. This is the road to the hospital."

"The hospital? You haven't deceived me? Tom isn't dy—"

"He is not dying. I told you he is not seriously injured, but he is so sure you are in danger, I thought if he could see you for a moment, hear your voice, his intolerable anxiety would be eased. Ready to be a good girl now and stop worrying?"

The tenderness of his voice sent a surge of tears to her

eyes. Maddening when she detested the man. She couldn't speak. She nodded.

"That being decided we'll go on. Don't stay but a moment. Remember that I am waiting for you."

In the corridor of the hospital redolent of disinfectant, she explained her presence to a white capped nurse.

"I am glad you have come, Miss Clinton. It has been difficult to keep Mr. Slade in bed, he has fought sleep, deliriously determined to start out to find you. He's quiet at present. He finally let us take a red satin slipper he had been clutching. This way. Don't stay but a few minutes. I will be outside the door."

Cindy cleared her eyes of tears as she looked down at the man in the narrow bed. She touched his hand which lay like a model in red-bronze against the white sheet. His eyes opened. A flash of recognition irradiated his face. His fingers closed over hers.

"You're safe, Cindy!"

"Safe and absolutely unhurt, Tom. I came so you would stop worrying about me and sleep."

"I found that—" he moved his head in the direction of a stand beside the bed. "See it? Cinderella's slipper— not glass—red satin. I'll fit it to her foot—you remember about the Prince—" His eyes closed.

The nurse touched her sleeve.

"He'll sleep now that he has seen you," she said softly. "You'd better slip away."

# TWENTY-FOUR

" 'FAITH, the substance of things hoped for,
  The evidence of things to come.' "
Sonorously the blond young clergyman in his black
robe announced his text from the high pulpit in the old
church. The same pulpit from which countless men of
God had proclaimed their belief in the invincibility of
the Divine Spirit in man for decade after decade as the
universe continued on its eternal rounds.

"Faith." Cindy repeated the word to herself and lost
the preacher's elaboration of the quotation and his ac-
knowledgment of its source. Faith. Without knowing
anything of his past she had had unbounded faith in the
man who had called himself Bill Damon and where had
it landed her? Certainly there was no evidence of things
she had hoped for from him. She had hoped, why not be
honest with herself and admit it, she had hoped he
would love her as she loved him. Now, in this aching
sense of loss she was paying the inevitable purchase
price of loving with heart and soul a man who didn't
love her, hadn't wanted her—she must keep reminding
herself—otherwise would he have allowed the annulment of the written contract marriage to go through
without a protest? Love, how it tore at one's heart.

That train of thought wouldn't get her anywhere, it
would land on a turntable and shoot her back where she
started. She looked at the world visible beyond the long
open window beside her. One could have faith in the
rotation of the seasons, they never disappointed. August

was showing definite signs of autumn; there was a new
tang in the air. The portion of the sky visible from her
seat in the old pew of the Clintons was cold and blue as
a lump of turquoise. Maples flaming. Weeds in the
garden were lagging. Baldwin apples in the orchard
beside the church were showing rosy cheeks; the weight
of luscious, juicy blackberries on the bushes along the
bank of the brook beneath the window bent till the tips
almost touched the rippling water. September on the
threshold. What would the month bring?

"Faith, your fortress against fear."

She shut out the confident voice from the pulpit and
allowed her thoughts to drift. That shivery, unbelievable experience in the police court yesterday morning
definitely belonged to August, that couldn't happen
again.

The weekly local newssheet had carried no account of
it. Had Ken Stewart been able to suppress the report?
He appeared to have unlimited influence. He had
shown his billfold to the Chief at police headquarters
and immediately the man's attitude had changed. Her
story had been listened to and believed.

Why live over that? Why anticipate September when
she had a chill uncertainty as to what trap tomorrow
might spring? Trouble was bound to break soon about
the jewels in the turret room. Was it only two days ago
she had discovered them? Was the theft of the limousine
tied in with the gang which had hidden the loot? She
had protested against leaving The Castle this morning
but Sary had said Joe would be there—

Joe! "Brother Joe" who came from Grand Manan on
a lobster deal. She had swallowed Sary's yarn hook, line
and sinker. Of course he was Bill Damon's—Ken Stewart's—man. Sary was missing her vocation. She should
be doing character parts on the stage. Hadn't Tom
Slade seen Bill Damon in a shop with "a heavy-built guy
who looked like a plain-clothes man"? A perfect description of Brother Joe. He rated an Oscar for acting. One
couldn't think of him as other than a lobster man from
Grand Manan.

Tom. Another problem, life seemed beset with them. When she had phoned the hospital this morning his nurse had reported that he would be discharged soon. She remembered the sharp stab of her conscience as she left his room. She didn't love Tom Slade, never could, she knew now, she should have told him before he came East this summer, but she had deceived herself with the thought that as she didn't love anyone else, he was so fine that perhaps when she was free—

Free. The word brought the fierce emotional storm she had been holding back down on her spirit like a collapsing house. Why hadn't she felt who Bill Damon was? That day at the beach the curious sense that he was not the person he claimed to be must have been instinct trying to get through a message to her brain.

Why, why hadn't Ken Stewart during that interminable drive home from the hospital seized the opportunity to excuse himself for the deception? Excuse himself? Not he. Hadn't he flung back at Lydia Fane in the voice of a man sure in his convictions, the voice of a fighter who would not admit defeat:

"Deny it? My dear woman, why should I? It is my name."

She had been braced to combat any defense he might offer as the reason for his alias, had fought an inexplicable power that was drawing her head to his shoulder, an aching desire to feel his arms about her, his lips on hers. She could have spared herself the strain. After inquiring as to Tom Slade's condition he had not spoken again until at the door of The Castle he had said:

"This is the second time I have rescued you, Cinderella. The third, if there is a third time, I shall consider findings keepings. Good night."

What had he meant by that?

The nudge of Sarah Ann Parker's sharp elbow brought her crashing back to the present.

"Sakes alive, Cindy, you asleep? Stand up. It's the closing hymn."

She rose quickly in response to the reminding whisper while the organ pealed a prelude.

"My Country 'tis of thee,
Sweet land of Liberty,
Of Thee I sing."

The volume of voices rose and swelled to the accompaniment of the organ till the magic and music of the song filled every inch and crevice of the old church and set the air outside the open window vibrating.

"Protect us by Thy might,
Great God our King."

As Cindy and she walked slowly down the center aisle Sarah Ann Parker indulged in a low-tone monologue, the black coque feather on her hat nodding with each emphatic word.

"That last hymn was rousin', Cinderella. Congregations will go to town on that if they never sing anything else. Funny how the preachers keep on proddin' folks to better living, more unselfish lives. With all the deviltry in the world you'd think they'd kinder lose faith in human nature, but they keep on believin' in it, keep on fishing for the divine spark in man and after hearin' that sermon I'm sold on the idea myself, I guess it's in all of us.

"There's that Mrs. Sally Drew from Rockledge dressed up to kill in aqua linen. She's bowin' and smirkin' right and left. Looks like being invited to the Armstrongs' to dinner kind of set her up. Alida Barclay near the big door is lookin' at you, Cindy, as if she wanted to catch your eye. She's stylish in that thin black rig but not so smart lookin' as you all in white. Mr. Damon has joined her. I thought he was the kind of man who would come to church. Want to know somethin'? I wouldn't be surprised if that turned out to be a match."

"You mean a marriage? Mrs. Barclay is years older than he."

"How do you know? Men keep awful young-looking these days."

She let that go. She did know Ken Stewart was thirty-two. She turned her back on the woman and man near the door and hailed Hal Harding who stood on the upper step outside.

"Hi, Hal. Waiting for me?" Her cordial laughing greeting widened his eyes in surprise, deepened the color of his face.

"Sure I am waiting for you, Cinderella. Didn't know if you would speak to me after we showed up your ex," he admitted as they went down the steps together.

"You and Lyd got off on the wrong foot. It was not much of a show-up when I knew who he was all the time."

"You really have nothing to forgive. The laugh is on us. We were knocked silly when he said he was Stewart. We planned for the boy to announce the name at midnight as a sort of Cinderella act, thinking to give you a start for a minute. Our joke was a boomerang. We had no idea that the name Bill Damon was an alias. Lyd put up a great bluff pretending she knew, but she was as flabbergasted as I."

"It was a mean trick, Hal."

"You are one hundred per cent right, sugar. I tried to find you in the supper room that night but you had disappeared. Now that we're pals again, come to a steak party tomorrow at my playhouse at sunset, will you? I will invite a few congenial spirits. Nix on your ex, though. We'll have a celebration. Don't stiffen. Nothing to do with your freedom. Just an early autumn binge, the days are getting too short for many more."

"I'll come."

"Hooray! Now I know we're pals. Thought I would count in the tenant at Rockledge. Have you met her?"

"You're slipping. Have you forgotten I was at the dinner the Armstrongs gave for her?"

"Sure you were. Boy, am I losing my memory? Here comes Lyd Fane." He waved to the girl approaching. "I wonder why she always wears green?"

"Thinks it matches her eyes, probably," she answered his impatient question. "I must hustle. I have to drive Sarah Ann Parker home. Her brother is staying with us. He's a lobster man from Grand Manan."

"Her *brother?*"

"What's so startling about that? Most women have a brother, haven't they?"

"I wasn't startled. I've thought of good old Sary as being the lone twig on the family tree. I'll call for you in the speed runabout tomorrow at four-thirty so we can get an early start on the fun."

"I'll be ready and waiting. I'm keen for a real party. Life has been deadly dull lately." Her response was unnecessarily loud, to make sure that Alida Barclay and Ken Stewart behind them didn't miss her enthusiastic reply.

That's a darned ungrateful remark, she told herself as she walked away. The gremlins will get you if you don't watch out, Cinderella Clinton. You discover hidden jewels; make a smash hit at the masquerade with your skating act; discover that the man you've gone all out for is a person you hate; and get kidnaped all within two days. You couldn't crowd much more into forty-eight hours.

Monday afternoon Cindy stopped at the door of the kitchen.

"Where you goin' now?" Sarah Ann Parker inquired.

"You know. I told you this morning that Hal Harding is giving a steak party at his playhouse this afternoon and that I wouldn't be here for dinner."

"Hmp! That's why you're wearin' that white silk shirtwaist dress an' the light blue cardigan with C.C.S. on the pocket at this time of day. Better tie the bright kerchief drawn through your belt over your hair. Don't stay late, child. After your experience Friday night I'm scared to have you off the place after dark. That reminds me," she drew a square of paper from the pocket of her red print dress. "Most forgot to give it to you. When I was putting your great-grandmother's skatin' costume back in the trunk this morning I found this in the pocket. Sealed so careful thought it might be a love letter. Time you was having them, child."

"A love letter?" Cindy ignored Sary's affectionate chuckle and turned over and over the folded paper

astened at one edge with Scotch tape. "You found this
in the pocket of that red skirt? My name isn't on it."

" 'Twas in the same pocket with your mask. Funny
you didn't know it was there. You were havin' such a
good time I guess you forgot someone gave it to you."

Had one of her unrecognized partners slipped it into
her pocket while they were dancing? Why not give it
to her? Queer. Perhaps it was tied up with the cache of
jewels in the turret room. The thought set her heart
drumming like a partridge on a log. Sary mustn't get an
inkling of that suspicion till she had found out what it
was. She tucked the folded paper into a pocket of her
light blue cardigan and laughed.

"I *was* having a good time and I *did* forget someone
gave it to me. Perhaps it is the question I was to ask at
an Information Please quiz that was to follow supper at
the masquerade. Something happened to wreck the
plan." You're getting to be a slick prevaricator, my girl,
she told herself before she added aloud, "I'm off."

"Does Mr. Damon know you're going?"

"He doesn't know I'm going and I hope I never see
him again. Make what you like out of that. Don't worry
about me, Sary. That stolen limousine adventure
couldn't happen twice in a lifetime. If it does—send
Brother Joe in search of me."

"What do you mean, saying 'Brother Joe' in that kind
of snippy voice? Not mad because he's here, are you?"

"Of course I'm not mad because he's here. There's the
speedboat siren. Hal is waiting for me."

"I should think he'd be polite an' come to the house
for you. Other folks goin' to be there?"

"Of course others will be there, Sary, and while we
are on the subject, I wish you would stop treating me
like a kid. You check every step I take."

"Sakes alive, Cindy, what's got into you? Haven't you
told me where you were going since you was a little girl?
Want to know somethin'? You've been cross as two sticks
ever since the masquerade. 'Tain't like you. I can't
figure out whether it's because you're worried about that
Slade fella or you've got a guilty conscience."

"Wouldn't you be on edge if you'd found a bag of

jewels hidden in your house and expected the police to
arrive any minute and accuse you of hiding stolen
goods?"

"Calm down, Cindy. Colonel Bill Damon—"

"Stop calling him that. You know perfectly well that
the person who claimed to be Bill Damon is Kenniston
Stewart. Good-by. Expect me when you see me and not a
minute before."

That burst of temperament set Sary's mouth ajar, she
thought as she crossed the patio. I'll bet she has known
who he is all the time. Why do I care that Ken Stewart
put on that "guide, philosopher and friend" act; that
Sary thinks there may be a "match" between him and
Ally Barclay? Plenty of other things to think about with
the paper which appeared so mysteriously in the pocket
of the red skating costume pricking in the pocket of my
cardigan this minute. I'd better get busy putting together the pieces of that puzzle.

Halfway across the putting green she stopped and
looked back at the house, before she pulled the folded
paper from her pocket. She ripped it open. Read the
clumsy printed message. Read it twice.

> "Keep away from the seat on the point.
> Stop flashing lights. DANGER."

# TWENTY-FIVE

"Keep away from the seat on the point.
Stop flashing lights. DANGER."

DANGER? To whom? What could it mean? She looked toward the stone seat beyond the putting green. Sary and she had been the only persons living at The Castle this summer. Joe was there now but it couldn't refer to him. He had arrived only a few hours before the Bal Masqué where apparently the warning had been slipped into her pocket. Had it been intended for someone else? That explanation was out. "Keep away from the seat on the point" must mean the seat she could see just ahead; there wasn't another like it on this shore.

"Stop flashing lights." The writer was on the wrong trail if he suspected an occupant of The Castle. Sary had said:

"You can see it plain from that seat on our point"— she had referred to the house across the cove, "I sit there a lot to watch what goes on. Every little while a big boat drops anchor off Rockledge shore and signals."

The suspicion that the message had been intended for Sary was ridiculous. Hadn't she rushed out of the house to report flashed lights the night a boat had bumped against the oceanside landing at The Castle? Later hadn't she herself heard a voice warn:

"They've made the getaway safely. Now we can go. Our job is done. No one awake here. Luckily for them."

She recalled the icy chills that had crept up her spine and slithered down. Even the memory set her a-shiver. Add to that the word DANGER and what had you?

Who had been in that boat? Who had slipped the note into her pocket at the masquerade? Was it a threat

195

or a friendly warning? She began to check partners by their costumes. It couldn't have been the chef or Prince Charming. The clown? She had distrusted him from the moment he first cut in on a dance. The suspicion that he would bear watching had steeled to conviction when he had slipped into the front seat of—

Hal was coming. Hurriedly she thrust the paper into the pocket of her cardigan.

"Have you turned into a pillar of salt, sugar?" he demanded. "You've been standing motionless in one spot for at least five minutes. Come on."

"I'm coming. I wouldn't turn into salt, Hal," she tied the light blue kerchief over her head as they walked side by side toward the pier. "I'm so sweet and charming I would turn into sugar. And that reminds me, why do you keep calling me by that saccharine name? If you hadn't declared you didn't know Mrs. Drew I would think you had picked it up from her. Didn't you hear her call me 'sugar' at the Armstrongs' dinner?"

"Perhaps she is Southern. I was playing round with a bunch of Virginians just before you came to town this summer. Must have picked up the word from them. It suits you."

"Maybe you think it does, but I don't like it. Don't do it again."

"I won't. Perhaps you'd rather I wouldn't talk to you at all."

"Good heavens, Hal, be your age. Don't sulk. Don't go adolescent on me and spoil our afternoon. Isn't that Rena Foster, the waitress at Rockledge, crossing the cove in a dory?" Not that she cared but in the hope of switching his mood which all signs indicated was set for "stormy."

"Yes. She came to tell me not to call for Mrs. Drew. I told you I intended to invite her to the steak party. She sent word she couldn't come as she had invited friends to dine with her aboard the yacht. All right with me. I asked her because you made such a point of being neighborly. I don't like her and I don't want you to become friends with her."

"Friends. No danger of that. She's all right enough

but not a person to whom I would confide the secrets of my heart."

"Has your heart secrets?"

"It has. What's a heart without secrets? Hasn't yours?"

"I wear mine on my sleeve proud to let the world know whom I love. It ought not to take long for you to figure out that one." They had reached the pier where the speed runabout tugged at a chain fastened to a ring. "Jump in. Grand afternoon, isn't it? I hope it brings me luck. Why are you waiting?"

She had hesitated because she hadn't liked his voice or his eyes when he had referred to his heart on his sleeve or his "I hope it brings me luck." Was she inviting trouble by going with him? Foolish. Other guests would be present.

She stepped on the brilliant red gunwale then down to a plastic-covered matching seat. Harding unfastened the painter and dropped behind the wheel beside her. He pushed a button. The runabout shot forward.

"Isn't this exciting!" Cindy declared breathlessly. "Like being on the front seat of an automobile. Lucky there is a glass windshield to keep off the spray we're kicking up. Hear it swis-s-h against the hull." She tightened the kerchief on her head.

"Lucky you aren't wearing a hat. It wouldn't stay on a minute."

"I haven't worn a hat this summer."

"Why snap at my conversational tidbit? The fact that you wear a hat or don't wear one is not of cosmic importance, is it? In the interests of this boat's color scheme you and I should be wearing red, Hal. Not that I don't admire your tone poem, snappy dark blue coat, light blue shirt and blue and beige striped tie, the outfit is immensely becoming to your blond good looks."

"Now, you're ribbing me. I don't mind. Glad to see you in such high spirits, sug- Cinderella."

"It is the exciting speed at which we are shooting over the water that makes me chatter."

High spirits. Lucky he wasn't a mind reader, lucky he couldn't divine the chaos of anger, hurt and love battling within her. Why think of that now when she was on a party? Hadn't she the mental strength to control her thoughts? "One good shove of the shoulder and God helping we'll get Britain out of this hole," she had heard a great statesman declare over the radio. Would one good shove of her shoulder oust Ken Stewart from her heart?

"A penny for your thoughts. A million of them if they are of me," Hal Harding demanded and promised in the same breath.

"A million pennies. Sounds like a magnificent offer. How many dollars would that be?" She pretended to count on her fingers. "Only a thousand. My inner thoughts are worth more than that, Mr. Harding." The motor hummed rhythmically. Creamy foam at the sides marked their swift progress. "This is the most thrilling sport in the world. I love it."

"Why don't you have a boat like this? I understand you have come into a fortune recently."

"You mean from the sale of the oil property? I suppose I could. I can't realize that I have money to spend on an extravagance. Before I buy a boat or a new car—the car is a must, at some not distant day the jalopy will lie down and die on me—I have other things I want to do."

"Such as—"

"I'm not talking about them till they are accomplished. What a gorgeous sunset. All the colors of the rainbow. Those fluffs of cloud make me think of irridescent galleons sailing majestically across the blue. I'm not crazy about that purple fog bank, though."

"That's nothing to worry about. It has been like that for several days."

"How fast are we going, Hal? The boat is skimming on top of the water like a jet plane through the sky. My eyelashes feel as if they were being pulled out by the roots."

"This motor has only a twenty-eight m.p.h. speed. Nothing spectacular. It's as large as a twenty-three-foot runabout can carry."

"I would hate to go faster. Perhaps I'm just a little outboard motor gal. I love scooting around in my dory

with the Evinrude." As the boat slid smoothly up to a
pier she pleaded:

"Hold it here a minute, Hal. I love the glimpse of
your house at the end of the avenue bordered by maples
bursting into flame at the tips. You should be very
proud of your home, Mister. The Hundreds is definitely
the show place of the county because of its history and
beauty."

"I've been trying to give it to you but you won't
listen." He stood on the pier and held out his hand.
"Come on." As she stepped out of the boat a man
approached and touched his cap.

"Want I should take her out to the mooring, Mr.
Harding?"

"Yes, Macey. Stick around to take care of other boats
as they come in."

"Yes, sir."

Cindy looked over her shoulder as they started along a
path.

"Am I the first arrival? Are both the outboard at the
pier and the second one at the mooring yours?"

"Yes. The one at the pier is for the use of Macey, the
boatman who lives in the village. Will you come into
the house? I have new record albums we could play
while we waited for the others."

"No. I've come for a steak party. Let's go to the playhouse."

I wish I hadn't arrived so much ahead of the other
guests, she thought, as they approached the pool. The
red-cushioned chairs ranged round it on the velvety
green lawn, the scattering of gay umbrellas gave her the
curious feeling that the party was over. There were no
signs of cooking supplies at the stone fireplace with its
iron grills. There should be a variety of long forks and
spoons and a pile of charcoal briquettes.

"I never give up what I want."

Hal Harding's angry shout with its suggestion of
threat in the Courthouse parking lot echoed through
her memory. His "I hope it brings me luck" followed.
Queer. Was instinct broadcasting a warning? Were
guests expected or had his mention of others invited

been a ruse to get her here alone? He had asked her time and again to come for tea. Fool suspicion. Unhampered as he was by ethical inhibitions he wasn't that kind of heel.

"Sit down, Cindy. You are giving an imitation of the Winged Victory poised for flight." He drew forward a deep chair.

"I was wishing that I had not been the first arrival at your steak party," she admitted as she sank into the inviting cushions.

"First arrival or last, what difference does it make except to me? Why worry? The others will come along in a bunch. While we are alone I'll ask a question. Has Kenniston Stewart explained why he let that annulment go through?"

"Hal Harding, if you mention that name again I'll go home if I have to swim."

"I bet you could do it, you won't have to swim, Cindy. You answered my question with your reply."

"What is it, Simpkins?" he inquired of the man in a white cotton coat who was hesitating in the doorway of the playhouse as if uncertain whether to approach.

Cindy's heart zoomed and grounded. She couldn't be mistaken. Hadn't she watched that slicked black hair with the one deep wave for what had seemed hours as the limousine hurtled on? He was the clown who had stolen the car. Her heart made like an Indian war drum. Now that she saw his face without the clown make-up he was the tough whose picture she had snapped at the beach. How had he managed to double back here with what had seemed the entire police force in pursuit? Watch your step, she warned herself. He mustn't suspect that you recognize him. She looked up with what she hoped was casual indifference as he approached.

"The folks you expected phoned after you left, Mr. Harding, that a fire had started up the shore and they were going to that," he said.

"*All* of them?"

"Yes, sir. One phoned the message for the bunch."

You're lying. You were briefed to say that, Cindy

thought. It is unbelievable that all the guests would sidestep the party. Hal must think me gullible.

"What do you know about that? A wholesale walkout. Sorry I got you here under false pretenses, Cindy," Harding regretted. "We'll have a cold drink, then we'll shoot for the fire. What's yours?"

"Nice, tall, iced orange juice for me. Sounds like the King of France and his forty thousand men. I walk up the hill to the playhouse and then walk down again." Nonsense but she needed time to think.

"Orange juice for Miss Clinton. Mine as usual, Simpkins."

As the man turned away she asked:

"Isn't he a recent acquisition? Can't remember seeing him here at any of your parties. How long has he been at The Hundreds?"

"About a week. He's good but I suspect he's a drifter. However, I'm enjoying him while he lasts."

"He looks efficient." Efficient at stealing cars, she added to herself. "To make the occasion perfect how about producing the 'South Pacific' album and turning on the phonograph in the playhouse? I can't think of anything more delightful than to sit beside this sunset-tinted pool and hear Ezio Pinza sing 'Some Enchanted Evening' especially for me." She crowded back the memory of the night she had heard the air perfectly whistled. Ken Stewart was out of her life forever.

" 'Some Enchanted Evening' coming up. It is at the house. I'll spring down and get it. All you have to do here, Cinderella, is to wish for something and it is yours. I'll be the fairy godmother. The only thing I won't produce is a pumpkin and mice to carry you away."

Her eyes followed him as he entered the path that led down to the main house. She hadn't liked his eyes when he had said that about the pumpkin and mice. Am I crazy or just bursting with conceit when I suspect him of conniving for an evening alone with me? The presence of that man Simpkins gives me the jitters. I'm afraid of him. Suppose for any reason Hal should not come back? I know that's a cockeyed thought, but nothing is too cockeyed to imagine after my experience Friday night. I *don't* trust Hal Harding. I know now that deep down in my mind I *never* trusted him. I've got to make my getaway and alone. How?

# TWENTY-SIX

THE SUN was going down in a fantastic splurge of color. The pool reflected pink and violet tints, but she wasn't seeing it, she was remembering that the bar in the playhouse was well stocked; that it wouldn't take the man Simpkins long to prepare the drinks. She must escape before he returned and while Hal was collecting the albums for the phonograph.

How? Hitchhike along the highway back of the playhouse? No dice. It would leave her across the harbor from The Castle, besides Hal could easily overtake her in his car. She must do something and *quick*. The caretaker's outboard? Could she get it? She must. It was her one chance to escape.

"I never waste a moment in indecision." The statement credited to Eleanor Roosevelt flashed through her mind. Indecision was out. She must get away in that boat.

A door closing. At the playhouse. Simpkins was coming. Without a tray. To speak to her? Had he seen Hal leave? In some undercover way, had he discovered that she had been in the back seat of the stolen limousine? Was he coming to warn her not to betray him?

She ran. Charged down the path that loped lazily toward the shore. Was it he calling? Think success and you invite success was one of the planks in her platform for living. Now was the time to give it a workout.

"I know I can. I know I can get away in that boat," she told herself over and over as she raced on. Luckily she would be out of sight of the large house until she reached the pier.

In the shadow of a spreading oak she stopped for breath, to listen and look. The caretaker's boat swayed at the landing. The power runabout in which she had come, with its gleaming chromium and glass windshield, its brilliant red trim, was moored perhaps fifty feet off shore. A smaller motorboat pulled and tugged at a near-by mooring. Her one chance was the outboard. She kicked off white sandals. The sound of heels on the planks might betray her. All set. Now think success and invite success, she prodded herself.

"I know I can. I know I can make it," she chanted as with sandals clutched in her left hand she ran forward.

No one in sight at the boathouse or pier. She didn't dare look back. She flung her sandals into the outboard and with fingers that felt all thumbs tried to loosen the painter. The darn thing stuck. Tight as the twine tied round the bag of jewels. She had untied that. She *would* do this. At last!

She jumped into the boat, adjusted the gas control, pulled the rope. The motor started without a hitch. Must be a recent model. She seized the steering handle and backed away from the pier. Throttled down to half speed and in spite of her frantic urge to get away came about slowly till the boat was headed for open water. The wake of the outboard set the two powerboats jerking at their mooring lines. Someone shouting. She looked back. Hal Harding was running down the avenue between the flaming maples. She waved. Made a megaphone of her hands, called:

"Sary phoned. 'Come home. Quick.' Couldn't wait." Let him make what he would of that. He stopped for an instant as if in amazed unbelief, then ran forward call-ing:

"Macey! Macey!"

The shouts came fainter and fainter as the outboard rounded a jagged promontory.

So far so good, she told herself and dropped into the stern seat. She exercised her tense fingers and took a fresh hold on the steering handle. This boat didn't kick up as much sea as the red runabout.

Now I can relax, she thought. Doubtless a psychiatrist would call my fear and getaway an infantile pattern of conduct, failure to mature emotionally. I call it a hunch.

I'd better stop pigeonholing my reactions and plan. I can see The Castle and Mrs. Drew's place the other side of Pirate's Cove. There is a fire up the shore. No mistaking that red glow against the sky. Perhaps I was unjust to Hal. Perhaps his guests did walk out on him—even so, that doesn't cancel the menace of that vicious Simpkins. Why was he coming from the playhouse without the drinks Hal had ordered if not to warn me not to tell that I recognized him as the clown who stole the car? The probability gives me what Sary calls the hibby-jibbies. I'm glad I had the nerve to beat it.

This boat is the only moving thing visible between that shore and the broad Atlantic. I've never been in just this spot before. I don't know how far the reef extends. I'd hate to get hung up on it with the tide going out. What are those gray wisps floating across that gorgeous sky? Fog? It can't be, her mind protested. Perhaps it can't, but it is coming in fast.

Wisps broadened to patches till the sky was a gunmetal gray. The sea turned dark and oily. Fog rolled in. Streaked with blood red from the setting sun it held the menace of a horror effect thought up by Dali. On it came, thicker and thicker. It blotted out landmarks. The gray silhouette of the shore dimmed. Vanished. If she could make the channel, then the harbor, she would be safe. It would be full of craft driven in by a warning weather broadcast.

Boom! Boom! Boom! Surf beating against the ledge. She was headed for it. She turned sharply starboard. Now she didn't know where she was. She listened for a guiding sound.

Muffled voices dead ahead and the velvet purr of a powerful motor. She would follow at a respectful distance, the boat must be going somewhere. Better reduce speed, or there might be a collision. Fog lay like a wet blanket across her shoulders, dripped from her nose. Perhaps the caretaker kept a slicker aboard. She couldn't take her hand from the steering handle to hunt for one, or the boat might swirl into a do-si-do and she would lose the guide ahead.

The last time she had looked for a covering to keep her warm she had plunged up to her neck in trouble. Had Bill—Ken Stewart—returned the robe to the owner of the black limousine? The clown who had stolen it had outwitted the police and made a safe getaway. She should have warned Hal that the man working for him was a criminal. She had thought only of her own danger when making her escape.

Her shiver was combined of cold, dampness and memory. She visualized the eyes between the slits in the black mask on the chalky face when the clown had danced with her. Idiot, why live over that? Couldn't she think of something happier—

She sprang to her feet. A huge dark shape was almost upon her. The boat she was following had come about and—

"Look out!" she screamed.

A light flashed. Too late. A crash. She tried to snatch at something before she plummeted into the sea. An absurd thought went with her. "I wish I'd put on my sandals."

A glare blinded her as she rose to the surface. Arms reached for her—she didn't know how many—and pulled her into a boat. Light enveloped her.

"I'll be damned, a woman!"

"Why in hell did you stand up when you saw us comin'?" the rough voice went on. "Ought to have known you'd pitch over. Were you drifting alone in a boat in this fog? Perhaps you weren't alone. Heck, have we got to fish for *another* guy?"

Cindy shook her head. Moisture showered from her hair. She had no idea to what type of men the rough voices belonged or in what sort of boat she was seated. All was deep shadow beyond the blinding light focused on her. She had an uneasy conviction that Hal Harding and his playhouse would be a haven of refuge in comparison with the present situation.

"I was alone," she panted, "on the way to the village when the fog caught me and I lost my bearings. What will happen to the outboard I was in? Can't you find it? It—it was borrowed."

"Not in this fog. Tough luck for the owner. It will beach somewhere—tide's going in—unless it goes out to sea."

"That's a cheering thought." Her breath was coming normally. "If you will leave me at the harbor pier—"

"Leave you nothing. You don't think we'll poke round in this pea soup to land a dame, do you? You'll go where we're going—and like it."

"The boss'll fire you if you bring anyone along," reminded a voice.

"What else can we do? Toss her overboard? There it is again. Steer for it. Quick."

A searchlight swept the water, picked up the powerboat and lingered. It revealed the figures of three men, two forward, and a third who stood near her.

"Toss her overboard." The words echoed through Cindy's mind and sent an icy shiver slithering down her spine. I don't believe he would, she reasoned, they wouldn't have stopped to pull me out of the water if they were that kind. Now what do I do? Think success? How can I think success when I don't know what to think? Would I be better off if I jumped overboard? No. I survived the limousine crash. I'll have faith that I will come out of this.

"*Faith,* your fortress against fear."

The clergyman's sonorous voice rolled through her memory and counteracted the chill. At least this boat has a destination. It is going to something that is big enough to show a huge searchlight. Are my teeth chattering because of fear or cold?

"Have you a slicker I could put across my shoulders?" she ventured. "I'm very wet."

"Sure you're wet." Came the sound of a locker being opened. An oilskin was flung at her feet.

"That will fix you all right," the gruff voice assured.

They can't be desperate characters or they would let
me freeze, just to get rid of me. The thought helped.
Snuggled in the slicker which felt and smelled clean she
sat in the stern. Nothing to do but sit tight and wait. No
use trying to signal another boat, the fog was so thick
she couldn't make out objects a foot ahead. Crazy of
these men to keep pushing on. Why didn't they anchor,
set lights and wait? Because it was desperately important
that they reach their objective?

It seemed hours that she huddled there. After a time
her eyes became conditioned to the fog. She was in a
speed runabout not quite so large as Hal's, with dark,
almost black finish. There was a man at the wheel
forward, one behind him acting as a lookout, and a
third who had questioned her and appeared to be a
crew member at large. At regular intervals the big searchlight picked up the boat and the course would be
altered to sail into it.

"Almost there." The man nearest Cindy groaned relief. "This is the toughest trip we've ever made. One
more like this and I'm through. You can split my share
between you and—"

"Shut up. We've got a passenger," a muffled voice
reminded.

Cindy closed her eyes. Not a minute too soon. A light
flashed in her face. She opened them.

"What's happened? This slicker is so warm—I must
have been asleep. Are we there?"

"Where's 'there'? Damned if I know." Three guffaws
in unison followed the question and answer of the man
who had been beefing about the tough trip.

"I don't know where 'there' is, Skipper. You said I
would have to go where you were going. From that I
assumed you were headed for somewhere."

"We're headed for somewhere, all right, and here we
are. Pretty work, Skinny—watch out!" he yelled, but not
before the bow of the boat had hit a resisting surface
with a force that set it plunging and rocked the three
men on their feet. A light from above enveloped them.

"What's the idea? Trying to stove a hole in the side?"

The voice muffled by fog sounded far away. "Come aboard, report, and collect your dough. Catch."

The man at the bow caught the line that came coiling down like a mammoth serpent and made it fast. The three men went into a huddle.

Were they planning to dispose of her? Would they make her walk the plank? Fortunately the sea was quiet if they intended to set her adrift in a boat.

"What you waiting for?" an eerie voice demanded.

The man who had first interrogated her went up the three steps of a ladder on the side of what appeared to be a yacht, stepped lightly over and disappeared. The powerboat rocked and swayed lazily and made sucking sounds as it bumped against the larger craft.

"Send the dame up." The ghostly order came from the haze above.

"Does that mean me?" Cindy asked. Anything was better than this grueling uncertainty.

"Yes, ma'am." The voice was respectful. "See the steps? Can you make it?"

Can I? It's a must, she prodded herself and hesitated. She wasn't so sure that what awaited her above was an improvement on the uncertainty she had been enduring.

"If you're going, get a move on," one of the men prodded. "We can't wait here all night for you to make up your mind."

"I'm going." She had been up the swimming ladder of a big boat many times before but not under these circumstances. Could she make it?

One step up. Two. Her wet stockinged foot slipped on the third. Hands caught her under the arms and lifted her to the deck. Panic, sheer panic, the sense of impending danger tightened her throat. What lay ahead in this impenetrable gloom?

# TWENTY-SEVEN

"THANK YOU. Thank—" her voice stuck in her tight throat. What difference did it make? Apparently she was speaking into uninhabited space. The person who had lifted her to the deck had disappeared. What next?

Next is to find out where I am, she answered her own question. Now that my heart has stopped racing its engine and my eyes are becoming adjusted to the fog something tells me that I have landed on a luxury yacht. I can see opalescent globes through the mist, lights undoubtedly. I must be on the aft deck. Those shapes shrouded under tarpaulin covers are seats, they suggest tea or cocktails at five. Tea. Golly, nice hot steaming tea. Now I am dreaming.

"This way." The voice came out of the mist behind her. A ghostly hand touched a ghostly cap. "The Captain will see you."

I'm a sad sight for the eyes of the skipper of this sensational craft, she thought, as she entered a luxuriously furnished salon vibrant with color and caught her reflection in a long mirror. Little tight curls capped her head; the once pale blue cardigan hugged her figure like the jersey of an Apache dancer she had seen on the screen; her wet skirt swished against her legs as she moved; water squished in her stockings at each step. The sailor leading the way—who, now that he was in the light, seemed anything but ghostlike—knocked on a door.

"Come in."

As they entered a cabin which appeared to be an office, he announced:

"Here she is, sir."

Another man. Cindy's hopes grounded. The beautifully appointed staterooms that opened from the salon—only one door was closed—suggested a woman owner. Miracle of miracles if it should prove to be Mrs. Sally Drew.

"Here's the lady, sir," the sailor reminded.

The man seated behind the desk absorbed in checking a pile of what appeared to be indices looked up. Cindy closed her eyes and opened them wide to be sure that what she saw wasn't a vision induced by wishful thinking. Mrs. Drew's secretary, Laurence Lloyd, was returning her incredulous stare.

"Mrs. Stewart!" He was on his feet. "You are Mrs. Stewart of The Castle, aren't you? How did you get on this boat? You shouldn't be here." His brows met in a portentous frown.

His startled greeting brought back the sense of distrust she had felt the afternoon she had met him at Mrs. Drew's. Perhaps Lyd Fane's acid "If he *is* a secretary," had prejudiced her. Added to that the instant of stillness when she had introduced him to Bill Damon had given her a chilly premonition of trouble. Watch your reaction, she warned herself, you are in too precarious a jam now to show that you don't like him.

"Where I came from is a long story, Mr., or is it Captain Lloyd?"

"I'm Captain here. Go ahead."

She told of faring forth in the outboard—omitting the reason—of losing direction in the fog; of the collision with a powerboat; of pitching overboard; of the rescue.

"Go on."

"And here I am, that's all. There isn't any more, yet. You must have heard the crew's version of my adventure. The men were very kind."

"Why not? They knocked you overboard." He came from behind the desk and looked at her from dripping hair to shoeless feet. "Your clothes are soaked."

"The sea is quite full of wet water tonight." She did

her best to suppress a nervous chuckle at her foolish retort but he heard it.

"That was a stupid remark of mine." She remembered his habit of pinching the lobe of his left ear. "I don't know what to do with you."

"I can answer that one. Send me home."

"Impossible. I'm under orders to sail on receipt of a radioed message which may come at any minute. I can't spare a boat or a man."

"The boat that knocked me into the water can take me back. It would be just restitution, wouldn't it?"

"Sorry. That speed runabout belongs to men who live way up the coast. They have been on business for the owner of this yacht."

Business for the owner. Again she remembered the growled, "You can split my share—" What kind of business? That remark would indicate that the crew was not allergic to the mighty dollar—if not so mighty as of yore, she reminded herself.

"I'll pay *anything* if they will take me home." The absence of bargaining in that reckless offer would have made her father's senior lawyer pale with horror.

"Sorry. The boat has gone."

"*Gone*. Why didn't you let me know before it left? Perhaps the crew wouldn't be averse to extra money. Who is, these days? Can you stand there and say you won't *try* to get me home? That I will have to stay on board and go where this yacht goes? It's a hang-over from the dark ages. It belongs in a horror movie. It's unbelievable."

"That's right, but it's the way it's got to be. We may have to up-anchor at any minute."

"In this fog?"

"We are equipped with radar."

Now what, she thought. As if in answer memory played back a record of Hal Harding's voice.

"She canceled because she has invited friends to dine on the yacht tonight."

"You can't go," she declared triumphantly. "This is Mrs. Drew's boat or you wouldn't be here. I was told that she is entertaining at dinner on board this evening."

"That's out because of the fog."

"But man, look at me. I can't live in these wet clothes."

"That's a cinch. There are clothes in one of the staterooms. The owner keeps an outfit here. I think you could wear them." He drew a bunch of keys from the pocket of his dark blue coat. "This way."

"I *can't* wear another woman's clothes."

"Take 'em or leave 'em, it's up to you." His hand went to his pocket as if he were about to replace the keys.

"I'll take them."

"They are quite swank clothes," he volunteered as he stepped before the one closed door in the salon. He unlocked it and threw it open, snapped on lights.

"Go on. You needn't be afraid. There is a bolt inside," he encouraged and turned away.

In the room Cindy slid the bolt and leaned against the door. She brushed her hand across her eyes.

"This experience from the time I fared forth in Hal's outboard has a dreamlike quality. Here's hoping it won't turn to a vicious nightmare," she said aloud, and took inventory of her surroundings to prove that she was awake.

The walls were applewood. Bedspread, covers of two chairs, dressing table and hangings beside the porthole were of aqua linen. A thick rug repeated the color. Toilet appointments were clear lucite.

She opened the porthole. Through it came the sounds of water lapping against the side of the yacht, the creak of the anchor chain, the smell of the sea. She counted the strokes of the ship's bell.

One! Two! Three! Four!

Only six o'clock? She had thought it must be midnight. It was after five when the outboard shot away from the pier at The Hundreds. It was too early for Sary to begin to wonder why she hadn't come home. Only Hal Harding knew she had started out alone in the boat. Perhaps he was so angry he wouldn't tell. There had been one other. Simpkins had seen her.

The wind had changed. The air coming through the

porthole was cold. Gave her shivers. Distasteful as was the thought of wearing another woman's clothes without permission, she must change from her own wet garments.

So suddenly that it stopped her breathing for an instant she remembered the message, the warning Sary had found in the red skirt. She drew a pulpy mass from a pocket of the dripping once-blue cardigan. It disintegrated the moment she touched it. She rolled the soppy fragments between her fingers. Nothing left. Not a scrap to show whence it came. The only proof she could offer that she had received it was the memory of the crudely printed words:

> "Keep away from the seat on the point.
> Stop flashing lights. DANGER."

She said them over and over as she changed to dry clothing.

Half an hour later she regarded herself in the long mirror in the door which opened on the shower. She had selected what seemed the most easily replaceable separates from the wardrobe: navy gabardine slacks, an orange-yellow cummerbund to hold them tightly at the waist, and a white silk blouse with long sleeves and Eton collar. Each garment was too large but she had leaned heavily on safety pins to make it fit. Orange-yellow sandals completed the costume. Her hair was fairly dry and had been brushed till it lay flat and gleaming on top, and curled at the sides and neck.

She shook her head at the allure of a bottle of choice perfume on the dressing table. It was her favorite scent. But it was bad enough to borrow a woman's clothes without a "by your leave," it would be nothing short of criminal to take her perfume.

What was she supposed to do next? Nothing in sight from the porthole—her chance to dispose of the wet clothes she had tied in a bundle with the gay kerchief. She leaned as far out as possible, heard the splash as it reached the water. It was a wrench to part with the monogrammed cardigan, she loved it, no use keeping it, it was ruined. The knobby bundle was bobbing on the surface. Of course it would sink, it must. She couldn't wait to watch it. She must make the next move.

What is the next move? Would she be invited to join the secretary—Captain—at dinner? The boat was still at anchor. Perhaps he had seen light and was preparing to send her home, perhaps Mrs. Drew had decided to come on board with her dinner guests. If there was a chef he must be tearing his hair at the off-again-on-again orders.

"I must find out sometime what is ahead. Here I go," she said aloud.

She drew the bolt. Her fingers tightened on it. The sound of a motor. Had the powerboat in which she had arrived returned? Had Lloyd had a change of heart and recalled it?

She snapped off the light before she peered from the porthole. The change of wind had blown the fog back to sea. The stars were out. A powerboat swayed and bumped against the side of the yacht. The owner and her guests? No. There were two men in it. Another was coming over the side.

Who were they? In some way had they heard she was here? Was it a rescue party? No sound of voices. Queer. There was something wrong about this yacht. When she had asked Sary about a Sally, she had said:

"Want to know somethin'? Every little while a big boat anchors off Rockledge shore an' signals. I guess she goes off in it. Kind of mysterious."

Was the man coming aboard a government agent? Suppose he found her here? Added to the police court appearance it would be difficult to explain. There would be no Ken Stewart to rescue her this time. Better get out and face the music.

Someone at the door. A key turned. Too late. She was locked in.

Locked in!

The dream had changed to nightmare. Lloyd could have sent her home in the boat that had brought her here. He had let it go without her. What did it mean?

Head pressed close against the door she listened for voices on the other side. Not even a low murmur. Quiet as the grave. The only sounds came through the open porthole, the suck of a rocking boat; low voices; the creak of a chain as the yacht swung at anchor; a starting motor; the powerboat was leaving. Where was the man who had left it to come aboard? Had he been enticed into the Captain's cabin for a pacifying drink? Who had locked this door? Was someone afraid she would be seen?

Afraid of her? That was a thought. Lloyd had refused to send her home; had declared, "At any moment orders may be received to pull up anchor, fog or no fog." If those facts didn't add up to mystery what facts would?

Mystery. Sary's word again. *Mystery!* There was a mysterious cache of jewels in the turret room of The Castle. Could the outfit on this boat be connected with that? Now I am crazy. Sally Drew, the owner of this yacht, is a businesswoman, silent partner of a big cosmetic concern, isn't she? Where would she pick up a lot of Oriental jewels to hide?

Was she the owner? Laurence Lloyd had not once admitted that this was Mrs. Drew's yacht. One of the men in the powerboat that had picked her up had growled, "You may split my share between you," and had been ordered sharply to "Shut up." Later the crew had been told to come aboard and collect their "dough."

Suppose this was Sally Drew's boat? Suppose she was not a silent partner in a big cosmetic company—Ella Crane had started the rumor and time and again her statements had been proved to be products of her prolific imagination—suppose Sary was right and the tenant of Rockledge was a mysterious person?

The question sent her thoughts racing backwards, to the afternoon she had made the neighborly call; to Alida Barclay with her hand pressed against the wall in the colorful living room; to the Oriental tray and eggshell china; to Rena who had served tea; to her companion on the beach, the man with the tilt—

Her heart flopped over with a force and suddenness that stopped her breath, sent her thoughts scurrying on. Already she had decided that the tilt of the hat of the man in the snapshot was identical with that of the shadow she had seen slip out the patio door the afternoon she had met the bracelet man; had he just planted the bag of jewels or had he come to retrieve them and been frightened by her sudden appearance in the hall? The face of the man in the snapshot was that of Simpkins who was working for Hal Harding. His hair was exactly like that of the clown who had stolen the limousine—who was playing around with the maid at Mrs. Drew's house.

Add that up and what do you get? she asked herself. Her blood turned to ice, her mind answered:

"A bunch of crooks!"

# TWENTY-EIGHT

"CROOKS!" she repeated under her breath. "You are locked in the cabin of a boat owned by a bunch of crooks. What do you do now? Get out, of course—and *quick.*"

Cautiously she tried the door. Locked on the outside. She had drawn the bolt when she thought of joining Lloyd. The hum of a motorboat. Was it returning for the man who had come aboard a short time ago?

"Catch."

The thud of a line followed. Voices. Gay, laughing voices. She peered through the porthole. Mrs. Drew and her guests? Would they come to this stateroom to leave their wraps?

The plot thickens, she thought and wondered that she could be so flippant when she was in what could be a perilous situation. Lloyd had refused to send her home. He was a crook as was the owner. The guests might be more crooks. She'd better hide somewhere until convinced that it would be safe to explain her presence aboard or find a way to escape.

No time to stand here deliberating. Someone was coming up the side. Too dark to see whether it was a man or woman. She soundlessly opened the door to the shower. The door directly opposite must lead to another stateroom. Gently she turned the handle. It did, to a room decorated in green. She stepped in and closed the door behind her. A door to the salon was wide open. It would be a risk to close it. She tiptoed across to the closet. Empty. Could she squeeze in? She could. Not a

218

minute too soon. Her heart did a hop skip and jump. Voices.

"How charming." That couldn't be Ally Barclay speaking. Things didn't happen that way outside of books. "Does the dinner table fold into that beautiful cabinet?"

"Yes, Mrs. Barclay." Mrs. Drew's prissy voice. "I thought it would be pleasant to dine before we sail, then the last wisp of fog will have vanished. You and the Counselor were good sports not to be frightened by it. I am so used to being at sea in all sorts of weather that I never think of danger. Leave your coat here," the voice came now from the threshold of the green room. "Come into the salon when you are ready. I'm next door if you need anything."

"Thank you."

Would Mrs. Drew miss her clothing, Cindy wondered. The sound of the salon door of this room closing? She listened. Widened the crack to which her ear was pressed. She would take a chance.

"Mrs. Barclay," she whispered.

A crash. A lucite brush dropped on the glass top of the dresser? Silence inside. Outside the purr of an engine. Was the motorboat going that had left Mrs. Drew and her party?

"Mrs. Barclay," she repeated softly. "Cindy Clinton. Here."

A key turned. Had it locked off the shower? The faint sound of a sliding bolt. Had that shut off the salon? A second later white-faced Alida Barclay in a thin amethyst wool coat and skirt stared back at her as if she couldn't believe her eyes.

"Cinderella Clinton," she breathed the name. "Where did you come from?"

Cindy held up a warning hand as she stepped from the closet. She whispered a brief explanation.

"Now what shall I do?"

"Give me a minute in which to think. My mind is rocking like a porch chair in a high wind."

"Hurry. Hurry. Decide something. If I step outside

this room and Mrs. Drew sees me in her clothes she may think I stole them before I have a chance to explain."

"That is not the only reason you must keep out of sight."

"Then you suspect them, too? I'm sure the owner of this yacht is a crook and Lloyd and the crew are up to their necks in crime, Mrs. Barclay. Watch your step. You are in danger."

"No. Seth and Ken Stewart are aboard. You must lie low, Cindy, not only for your own sake, but because your appearance might throw a monkey wrench into our plan. Get back into the closet. Stay there. We will pick you up some way before we leave. Quick. Someone's coming."

Humming softly she drew the bolt soundlessly. Snapped off the light. Opened the door to the salon.

"Leave it open, please, Mrs. Barclay." Mrs. Drew's voice. "It will give us more air."

Men's voices. Ken Stewart's set Cindy's pulses quick-stepping and her heart racing. Why was he here? Of course he would be. Hadn't the owner invited him to sail with her? Seth Armstrong speaking. Lloyd answering. Where was the man who had come aboard before the owner and her guests had arrived? He had not returned to the boat that brought him, it had left directly after he came over the side of the yacht.

What had Alida Barclay meant when she said, "You may throw a monkey wrench into our plan"? What plan? Come to think of it she hadn't seemed surprised when told she suspected that a gang of crooks controlled this yacht. Perhaps she knew it. Perhaps she, her brother and Ken Stewart were here for a purpose?

"The jewels in the turret room."

The words shot to the top of her mind like bubbles in a glass of champagne rising to the surface. Had Ken Stewart been investigating whence that cache all this time? He had spent days in Washington, but that was before she had discovered the hidden loot.

She relived the moment in police headquarters when he had extended his billfold to the chief for inspection, his "Take a look at this." Recalled the official's startled,

"Goramighty, it was you, Col—" saw again the warning lift of Ken's hand which had broken off the sentence. Curious how a mystery began to untangle when one caught the right end. Probably that same police department had supplied "Brother Joe." No one else had appeared to guard the hidden loot in The Castle.

Cautiously she widened the crack. Why stay cooped in this closet when possibly a melodrama was about to be unreeled outside? Ally Barclay had left the door partially open. Could she slip behind that? This stateroom was dark. She had made it. Through the crack she could see the end of the salon with a table set for four. Crystal sparkled. Silver shimmered. From the sounds it would appear that cocktails or sherry were being served.

"I didn't find out whom you were representing at the Bal Masqué, Mrs. Drew—" Ken Stewart's voice.

"I left before the unmasking. I wasn't used to my costume, and when it threatened to come apart on me I departed."

"Did any one of you discover the identity of the clown who cut in so often on the girl selling papers and her news? I wondered if it was a case of love at first sight."

"I didn't notice him. I wasn't the newsgirl, Colonel Stewart. I wore a purple East Indian costume."

"The one you brought from Calcutta—Patty Gould?"

"Max!"

The hoarse exclamation brought Cindy from her hiding place to the threshold. She could see Mrs. Drew's ghastly face—her pallor accentuated by the brilliant green of her frock—as she stared at the man in uniform who had stepped into the room. Light struck the large lenses of his spectacles with uncanny effect. It highlighted also the small, shining bald island on top of his head surrounded by graying hair. The silver bars of a captain glinted on his shoulders, a broad and colorful array of service ribbons adorned the breast of his tunic.

"I see you recognize me, Patty, my love." A gargoylish grin distorted his face.

In the split second of silence that followed her horrified exclamation Mrs. Drew had pulled herself together.

"I don't know what you are talking about. Lloyd, how came this man aboard my boat?"

"Your man Lloyd will keep his mouth shut till I get through talking." The voice was that of a person accustomed to command. "You called me 'Max,' didn't you? That is my name, isn't it?"

"How do I know what your name is?" She was magnificent in her disdain. "I was startled for a moment. You looked like a brother I lost in the war. He was a Captain. Lloyd, put this person off my boat."

"No one will put me off this boat till I have collected my half from the sale of our possessions you brought to this country, Mrs.—Drew. Am I right in the name? I understand you have had several since you discarded mine. I have been half crazy with anxiety about you—didn't give a damn for the treasures—now that I see you and know what you are, so far as I am concerned you died the day you left me." He removed his spectacles and polished them with a handkerchief.

"You'd better come clean, Patty, *my love.*" His voice lashed. "Each person in this room knows you've been smuggling during the last two years."

"How did you know—" As if realizing she had betrayed herself she whirled toward Ken Stewart in a passion of fury.

"*You* did this. You heard that broadcast of missing persons at White Pillars. At cards you tricked me into showing my skill. *You* got in touch with this man who claims to be my husband. *You—you—*" Fury choked her voice.

"Better stop where you are," the man in uniform reminded coldly. "With every word you're plunging deeper into confession. I'm not here to claim you as my wife. I don't want you. I want my half of our joint property or my share of the money you got for it and I won't leave this boat till you sign over my rights."

Her eyes flashed from one to another like those of a trapped animal. Stopped at Laurence Lloyd. Narrowed.

"Why haven't you said a word in my defense? I wonder if all this time you have fooled—"

"You and the crew of this boat are under arrest, Madam."

Cindy's heart shot to her throat and choked her with its heavy beat.

The white-haired police chief in person. He stood in the doorway that opened on the deck. He was the man who had questioned her at headquarters. Would he suspect she belonged to this gang? That was a lovely thought.

"Arrested." Mrs. Drew looked him up and down as if he were some strange animal which had wandered into the lounge. *"Arrested? For what? Because I deserted that man in uniform? All right, he was my husband, but you don't arrest people for desertion in the State of Maine, or do you?"* There was a hint of amusement in the last question.

In the instant of tingling silence which followed Cindy forgot that she should remain out of sight and stepped across the threshold. Safe enough. No one would notice her in this crisis. She glanced surreptitiously at Ken Stewart. He was staring at her as if he couldn't believe what his eyes were seeing. It was but a second before they returned to the white-haired police chief who had produced a paper from the breast pocket of his brass-buttoned dark blue coat.

"The charge of desertion does not appear in this warrant. You are accused of smuggling stolen goods into this country."

"Laurie!"

"No use to appeal to your captain for help, Madam. The broadcasting radio of the yacht has been put out of commission. You can't warn your accomplice on shore. Already government men are at work in your house with mirrors, torches and probing rods to find the loot hidden behind walls and in furniture. We've let you run your rig till we knew there was plenty of evidence. That covers it. The persons present not under arrest are advised to go and *quickly*."

Alida Barclay came to the stateroom for the topcoat
Cindy was holding out to her.

"My heavens, in the excitement I completely forgot
you, Cinderella. I'll go first. Follow in a minute. Our
hostess is so engaged she won't notice."

She did.

"Who's the woman in my clothes?" Mrs. Drew demanded as a figure in navy, orange and white flashed by.

"I'll explain later," Cindy heard Lloyd say before in
her headlong flight she collided with Ken Stewart who
was helping Alida Barclay over the side. A light from
below illumined them.

"Here I am!" She announced the evident fact breathlessly. "I was so afraid you would leave me."

He waited till Alida called, "Next," before he seized
her shoulder in a grip that hurt.

"How long have you been on this boat, Cinderella?"

The hint of suspicion in the demand coming on top
of the evening's excitement and threat of danger infuriated her.

"Something over two thrilling hours, I'd say," she
answered airily. "Sensational yacht, isn't it?"

"Did you come on board with Lloyd?"

"Ask him. Now, if you will step away from the exit
I'd like to leave, Simon Legree."

"Go ahead."

He held her arm till her feet were firmly on the
ladder. The tide was higher than when she had come
aboard. Only two steps and she was in the motorboat.
Ken Stewart followed. He picked up a slicker.

"Stand up. That blouse is thin. Quite a sea running.
You'll be drenched. Put this on."

She stood but raised rebellious eyes to his. Her lips
opened to resent his lordly order. Closed. Why make a
scene?

"White Pillars, Scott."

"Yes, Counselor," the man at the wheel responded.
"It's going to be rough, sir. The tide against the wind
which has risen has cooked up a choppy sea."

"Choppy is right. Get through this as fast as you can,
Scott.

"Cinderella Clinton, where in heaven's name did you come from?" Seth Armstrong demanded, even in the dim light she could see his cheeks puff and deflate. "When you dropped into this boat I thought it was an hallucination induced by an overdose of excitement."

"It couldn't have been a patch on my brain storm when she stepped from the closet of the stateroom in which I left my coat, Seth. Tell us what happened, Cindy. I couldn't get half of it from your excited whisper."

She told them, omitting the reason for faring forth in the outboard. Her story was punctuated by sudden silences when the bow of the boat bore down on a breaking wave throwing geysers of white spray.

"Why were you alone on the water so late?" Ken Stewart demanded.

She watched the red light of his cigarette glow and fade as she counted the faint strokes of a distant ship's bell. Only eight o'clock? It seemed years since she had raced down the path from the playhouse at The Hundreds.

"I felt an urge to get away from it all," she answered lightly.

"And you succeeded, I'll say. I'm worn to an emotional frazzle by the late events," Alida Barclay declared. "Fortunately there is only one more."

"Ally!" Her brother's low warning was accompanied by the motion of his hand toward the man at the wheel.

"Righto, Seth," she agreed in a voice as low as his. "Cindy, you must be exhausted. I hope you didn't take cold. How long were you in those drenched clothes?"

"It seemed an aeon or two but I wasn't even chilly. Smell the sea. I love it. The sky is clear. Millions of stars. And now that I am on the subject of stars, have you heard that reservations are being booked for interplanetary trips to Mars, Saturn, Jupiter and the Moon leaving a space-port on March 15, 1975?"

"What a corking idea for a twenty-fifth wedding anniversary trip for a man and gal married this year. Children would be old enough to leave at home safely by that time."

"It would depend a little on how many there were, Ken." Ally Barclay laughed. "You're shooting through the years faster than a rocket can shoot through space. Is it that you hear the ring of wedding bells, Colonel?" she teased. "Thanks be, we're out of that choppy sea. I couldn't have taken much more of it. We'd better land Cinderella at The Castle first, Seth."

"I'll see that she gets home safely, Ally. I left my car at White Pillars," Ken Stewart reminded.

"The air force has spoken," Seth Armstrong declared and chuckled.

Perhaps the Counselor wouldn't be so amused if he knew how she resented the dictation of the "air force," Cindy thought as after removing the slicker she stepped from the boat at White Pillars landing.

"Come in for a snack," Alida Barclay invited. "Do you men realize that we didn't get as far as dinner? Did you have anything to eat on the boat, Cindy?"

"Eat! No. I was too busy planning how to get away to think of food. I must go home. Sary will be expecting me. Colonel Stewart should stay—"

"Colonel Stewart is taking you home, Cinderella. Come on."

"Ken, report to me tomorrow, tell me where and how you ran down the husband. There is still one piece of the puzzle—"

"Even trees have ears, Ally," her brother reminded. "Good night, Cinderella. Good night, Stewart. God be with you. Something tells me you'll need Him."

When they reached the long green car at the side of the drive Ken Stewart produced a robe from the back seat.

"With the top down you'll need this. Put it over your shoulders. Comfortable? Let's go."

They had passed through the village before he spoke again.

"I know now how you came to be on the yacht. My apologies for suspecting that you had gone aboard with Lloyd. He's a tiptop agent, but—let's be charitable and say unreliable when it comes to an attractive female of

the species. Ready to tell me why you were in that
outboard alone in the late afternoon?"

"No."

"I thought we might trade experiences, that you would
be interested to hear what led up to the appearance
tonight of the abandoned husband."

She sustained it as if from an electric shock, resentment
forgotten.

"I am, oh, I am. Terribly interested, but—I don't want
to tell why I borrowed that boat—I did borrow it without asking—it's a comfort to know that if it's lost I can
pay for it—the reason I took it may have been entirely
cooked up by my imagination."

"That's enough for the present. Perhaps sometime
when we are friends again you'll tell me the whole
story."

"We'll *never* be friends, *never*," her breath caught in
a strangled sob.

"Never is a long time, darling. Want to hear the
story?"

"*Please.*"

"Alida Barclay did a piece of detective work abroad.
When the head of the customs department heard she
had a brother in this town he contacted her and asked
her help. Save your startled '*Really?*' You'll need it
later. You heard the chief of police of this district read
the warrant, so you know what she was sent here to
unearth. It was weeks before she suspected Mrs. Drew.
She told me you caught her tapping the living-room
wall at Rockledge. From what the chief of police said, it
wasn't a patch on the tapping going on at the present
moment. She had been tipped off that there was storage
space behind sliding panels. She was trying to find a
spring that would open one. That same day you introduced me to Lloyd. He is an agent with whom I worked
on a case."

"You said you never had—"

"Heard the name Laurence Lloyd. Right?"

"Right. Forgive the interruption. Go *on*. I'm so tense
my toes have curled under in Mrs. Drew's sandals. It

seems as if the stars were nearer, as if they had leaned down to listen."

"If they have, they haven't heard anything yet. Remember that a couple of days later I went to Washington? It was to renew my credentials—I served in Intelligence before the airlift—so I would have a right to help Ally run down the smugglers."

She remembered how she had missed his companionship, and set her teeth hard in her lips to steady them.

"The night of the dinner at the Armstrongs' I watched the faces of the guests in the living room as the announcer of the Missing Persons program described the wife for whom the Captain of Infantry was searching. I noticed Lydia Fane's loss of color, her tilted coffee cup—that means a story—but I was more interested in Mrs. Drew. A spasmodic twist of her eyes when the wife's expertness at bridge was mentioned set me on her trail like a bird dog on a scent. I asked her to be my partner at contract—I told you she was dumb at the game, too dumb to be true, but I didn't tell you that I let her fumble halfway through, then signaled for a certain play that only an expert would understand. She fell into the trap and came across triumphantly. That tied it. I had found the runaway 'Patty.'

"The morning after—the day of the discovery of the bag of jewels in the turret room—I long-distanced Washington and was put in touch with Captain Max Gould who was trying to find his wife. We arranged for him to come here and check. Ordinarily, I wouldn't butt in when a woman deserts a husband, it's the business of the couple—but in this case I was convinced that the missing lady was wanted also by Uncle Sam. When she left her husband she had these jewels and objects of art. To my mind that tied her up with the smugglers. There were plenty of contributing clues to back me up. I discovered that long ago the Captain had decided she had sold their treasures. That fact helped. That's the score so far. Only one piece of the puzzle missing now. Who has passed on the loot after it was landed at Rockledge?"

"I'm sure I know," Cindy declared eagerly.

She reminded him of the shadow with the tilted hat

brim she had seen in the hall of the The Castle; went back to the man on the beach with the parlormaid from Rockledge; to the lacquered black hair of the clown who had stolen the limousine; told of her startled recognition of him when she saw the servant at Hal Harding's playhouse this afternoon. She felt his quick look at her and wished she had omitted that last item of identification.

"I believe that he had hidden the jewels in the turret room the afternoon I saw him in the hall," she concluded.

"Could be, though I would hesitate to accuse a person of crime on the sole evidence of a tilted hat brim. Now that so much has been uncovered the finish will come in a burst of speed. I shall be glad to have it cleared up. I've been called to Washington."

"Not back into the service?" That wail sounded as if she cared. "I thought you intended to stay here until you finished your book." That was better. The statement held just the right amount of tepid interest.

"I'm not called back into the service. I had planned to stay here and finish my book, but, the Inn closes early and—"

"This country is gorgeous through September and October." Why was she trying to sell him this place when she would be glad to have him go?

"It must be. There's The Castle ahead. I'm coming in, Cinderella. I have a plan to present to—"

She clutched his arm.

"Stop! Quick. A light flashed in the turret room. The rest of the house is pitch black."

# TWENTY-NINE

"I DON'T understand the absence of lights. Where are Sary and Joe?" Cindy whispered.

"We'll find out. I'll park the car in the shadow, lock it and dim the lights. I don't dare leave it dark for fear of an accident. If I drive nearer the house, we may be heard. Come on. Walk on the grass. Have you a key?"

She nodded. Her throat was so tight from excitement she couldn't produce a whisper. Were they on the trail of the person who had hidden the jewels? Could they trap the man with the tilted hat and lacquered hair? He had made a miraculous getaway when the limousine had crashed into the roadblock; "I don't know how he done it unless with mirrors," the sergeant had declared truculently. Another flash in the turret room so quickly gone she wondered if she had imagined it. The front steps at last. Ken Stewart held out his hand.

"The key." His whisper started icy tingles along her veins.

He opened the door. Closed it soundlessly. In the dark hall they stood motionless. Listened.

"Footsteps. Hear them?" The faint distant creak of a floor board brought with it the memory of the many times she had shivered with childish fear in this very spot imagining she heard the smugglers. "Whoever it is appears sure there is no one in the house."

"I'm going up," she whispered close to his ear, "to lock the door to the stairs. Lock him in."

"*No.* I'll rout out Joe and we'll nab him. He won't have a chance."

"We *can't* spend time locating Joe. He may be knocked out somewhere, must have been, or the person in the turret room couldn't have entered the house."

She twisted free from his tightened grip, kicked off Mrs. Drew's sandals and ran swiftly up the stairs. Lucky she knew every inch of this house, she thought, as she felt her way in the Stygian gloom of the upper hall. Why hadn't Sary left lights? Perhaps she had. Perhaps the man in the turret room had put them out—or his accomplice had.

Accomplice. That was a thought. The door to the stairs. At last. She listened. Came another creak of the floor above as if someone were walking carefully. With a little prayer that it wouldn't squeak, she slid the bolt cautiously. Now to get downstairs before a hand could grab—

An iron grip closed on her shoulder. She caught at the fingers covering her mouth. A seal ring. Ken Stewart had followed her.

"Did you lock it?" he whispered.

"Yes."

They crept down, stopping every few stairs to listen.

"Hear that? He's at the door to the hall trying to get out. It's bolted. He'll have to come down the secret stairs." At the door of the old kitchen she caught his hand in hers.

"Hold tight to me. I know the way. We'll c-catch him. Could you flash your cigarette lighter just once till—I can feel your 'No' headshake. I'll find what I want without it." With hand outstretched before her, she crossed from the desk to the old oven. She stood still. Listening.

"That's Sary. Putting her key in the front door. Stop her. *Quick*," she whispered. She saw his dark shadow move toward the hall. Heard his stifled, "Stay out."

On the step he pulled Sarah Ann Parker close to the door.

"Don't speak," he warned. "Someone in the turret room."

"Lot I care who's in the turret room," her low voice was hoarse. "I was called on the phone an' told a boat

had been found on the beach with Cindy's sandals; that
a cardigan with her initials had been picked up floatin'.
I knew I hadn't ought to, but I made Joe go with me. I
saw 'em. They were hers. I don't care if I don't live any
longer with her g-gone. I've just been hangin' on till she
married an' had a baby I could love." She pressed her
head against his shoulder and shook with dry sobs.

He put his arm about her. Whispered close to her ear.

"Cindy is inside, Sary." She jerked up her head. He
warned. "Don't speak. That was a yarn to get you out of
the way and—"

"But I saw—"

"Never mind what you saw. She's inside. A light
flashed in the turret room. We heard footsteps. Where's
Joe now?"

"He was here a minute ago."

"We'll find him. Come in. If you stumble over anything I'll—"

"You won't have to break my neck. I know every inch
of this house light or dark. Want to know somethin'?"
Sarah Ann Parker was herself again. "If you make a
sound it's *your* neck'll be broken. Come in."

"You here, Cindy?" The low query was strained and
breathless.

"Yes, Sary. Ken. He's opened the turret room door to
the secret stairs. Listen."

"O.K. Sary, find the light button. When I say *go*, snap
it, understand?"

"Sure, I understand. Here, grab this warming pan, he
may be ugly."

"Keep it. I'd rather have my two hands. Cindy, go
back by the door. You—"

Came the sound as of a truckload of hardware clash-
ing, crashing down stairs, accompanied by a cannonade
accompaniment of *thud! thud! thud!* Simultaneously
light flashed on; pumpkin-yellow walls glowed; copper
shimmered; the cupboard banged open with a force that
sent treasured plates of mulberry and black Canova to
the four corners of the room. A figure shot out from
behind it, with a grayish-white bag clutched in its arms,
a hat with a tilted brim tipped over its face.

"Enter, Mr. Simpkins! I was expecting you." Cindy's voice and laugh were high with excitement. "There are ladies present. You really should remove your hat, Mr.—"

"Cindy, come here." Ken Stewart grabbed her arm but not before she had snatched the felt hat. She stood as if turned to stone.

"Hal," she whispered incredulously. "Hal Harding!"

As if he realized the absurdity of his position flat on the floor staring stupidly up at her, Harding rolled to his knees, and with a grimace of pain struggled to his feet.

"Whoever planted that assortment on the stairs is wasting her time in this village, Sarah Ann Parker. She should be in the FBI." He tenderly massaged his right hip as he talked. "Too bad I couldn't finish the job of protecting you, Cindy. I intended to get the stolen property you have been hiding out of the house to save you the unpleasant notoriety of appearing in court to testify why you are aiding theft."

"Me? I—aiding theft? You're crazy. That bag was hidden in the turret room by—"

"He doesn't need your explanation, Cinderella. He knows who hid it there."

"I do, do I?" Harding's menacing step forward matched in vicious intent his truculent voice. "You've interfered in my affairs, Damon or Stewart—whatever you happen to be calling yourself now—for the last time. You—"

"Not quite the last time." Ken Stewart's cold voice sent icy inchworms of apprehension looping along Cindy's veins. "Unfortunately—I didn't want the job—I shall be forced to testify that I have known for some time that you are the liaison man between Mrs. Drew's importations and the gang that comes to your place to collect the smuggled loot."

"No. Oh, *no!*"

"Liar!" Cindy's broken protest was lost in Harding's shout. A little foam had gathered on his lips. "You've cooked up this yarn because Cindy loves me and *you* want her. 'Peter, Peter, had a wife and couldn't keep her,' that's you. I don't know the Drew woman. Never saw her until I met her at the Armstrongs'."

"No? How come you picked up her favorite pet name, 'sugar'? I heard you call Cinderella that the first time we met, remember? When Mrs. Drew came out with it at the Armstrong dinner, it fitted like the missing piece of a picture puzzle. I knew you were the guy I was looking for, that you were in cahoots with the smugglers, that you had picked up the name from constant association with Sally Drew. If you knew nothing about the woman why try to prevent Cindy from calling on her? You knew the outer measurements, interior and deck arrangement of her boat because you had sailed on it with a former owner, you said. Phooey! You've sailed with her, and you declared you never had met her, that statement will take a lot of explaining in Court."

Harding flung himself on the speaker in a fury of hate.

"You—you—"

"That's enough of that, Mister." A burly man in a red and black plaid lumber jacket caught his hands and pinioned them behind his back. Had "Brother Joe" materialized from the air, Cindy wondered.

"What do you people think you're doing?" Harding twisted his arms and Joe released his hands. He nervously adjusted the collar of his blue shirt and settled the striped tie. "Someone's been kidding you. I was tipped off a conspiracy was brewing to drag in Cinderella Clinton's name as accessory to a smuggling enterprise, that she had received and hidden stolen goods. I came in secretly to get the bag out of the way before she could be accused."

"Secretly. Sakes' alive, 'twas you, Hal Harding, who phoned me to go look at Cindy's clothes, picked up on the ledges, and your boat with her sandals, so's you could get into this house, said I'd better get my brother to go along. Most broke my heart tryin' to make me think she was gone, you—"

Ken Stewart caught Sarah Ann Parker's arm and forcibly drew her back from what threatened to be assault and battery.

"You found the things I told you you'd find, didn't you?" The contemptuous demand brought a nod and broken "Yes" in reply.

"You acknowledge that's true. The facts had been phoned me." Harding touched the bulky gray-white bag on the floor with the toe of his shoe. "Here are the stolen jewels. If you don't believe they are jewels, open the bag. To substantiate the fact that Cinderella Clinton hid them—"

"You heel! You rat—"

"Leave him lay, Colonel. We've got plenty to jail him."

The voice checked Ken Stewart's forward lunge. Cindy brushed her hand across her eyes, shook her head as if to clear them. It couldn't be the man Simpkins leaning nonchalantly against the side of the doorway with his right hand thrust into the pocket of his brown tweed coat. It was. She looked down at the soft hat clutched in her right hand, the hat she had pulled away from Hal's face; the hat with the tilted brim she had been so sure had been worn by the shadow who had vanished from the hall the afternoon she had met the bracelet man at Ella Crane's shop. Memory broadcast Sary's voice:

"Hal Harding came through the garden looking for you, just as I was leavin'. When I told him I expected you any minute he said he'd hang round till you come."

Was it possible he had hidden the jewels that afternoon? Had been in the house when Sary returned, had slipped out without being seen? But he had declared only a few hours ago that he had not worn a hat this summer. A red herring drawn across his trail? It was unbelievable, not only that he would be dishonest, but that he with a large inherited fortune would need money from such a source. Why didn't someone speak? Was the man in the doorway a black magician whose spell had turned each person in the room to stone? Hal Harding's eyes looked like nothing so much as huge light blue glassies bulging from their sockets.

"Simpkins," he cleared his hoarse voice. "Simpkins, have you been fooling me? I'll get you for this."

The man in the door way straightened from his nonchalant lounge and entered the room, his right hand still in his coat pocket.

"Your mistake. Take it easy. There's a car waiting outside. Come along and tell your story. You'll find your gal confederate, Rena Foster—the newsgirl at the masquerade—waiting to tell hers."

"Now you've made your mistake—Simpkins. I go nowhere till I have a lawyer—"

"Counselor Armstrong was your lawyer in your divorce cases, wasn't he? He'll be waiting for you."

"Let him come here. I'm *not* going—"

"Joe!"

The authoritative voice rocked Cindy's conviction that she was awake and not dreaming. The man who had taken command of the situation couldn't be the tough whose picture she had snapped; he was—the features were the same, but—

"Come along quietly, Mr. Harding," the voice of the man she had thought of as Simpkins broke in on her confused reflections. "Bad enough to bring this trouble into Miss Clinton's house—look at this mess of broken china—we don't want to add to that unpleasantness by knocking you out."

He was going quietly. Cindy laid her hand on his arm.

"Hal. Hal, I—I don't believe you stole those jewels," she affirmed brokenly.

"Thanks, *sugar*. That must be the reason you ran away from the playhouse this afternoon, you *trusted* me." His voice was brittle with repression. "Let's get going. Quick."

As he and "Joe" left the room the man called Simpkins stopped beside Cinderella.

"Believe it or not, Miss Clinton, I was about crazy when they told me you were in that limousine I put on the act with. It was my car, by the way. I started to tell you at the playhouse this afternoon, but you ran away before I had a chance." He ran his hand under the collar of his beige shirt as if it were choking him. "When I think of what might have happened—"

"That didn't." Stewart's hand rested lightly on his shoulder as if he liked him.

"Thanks, Colonel. Sorry to take you away from her—here," he grinned, a likable grin, as he made the correction, "but you cracked this case, you've got to come. There's a lady waiting for you."

"Go ahead. I'll be along in a minute." Ken Stewart turned to Cinderella. "This does it. I told you it would finish in a burst of speed." She caught his sleeve.

"Give *me* a minute. Have you known all this time that the person to whom I referred as 'the man with the tilted hat,' was an agent working on the smuggling case?"

"Remember the evening I stepped into the old kitchen via the window?" She nodded.

"Remember I told you then that I had seen the lights of a parked car near The Castle? It was the man whom Harding called Simpkins waiting to contact me to tell me he was working on the case. I must go. We have a date tomorrow evening, Cinderella. I won't have a moment free until then. She hasn't had dinner, Sary. Make her eat something. Good night."

Sarah Ann Parker's eyes followed him as he left the room, came back to the collection of articles on the floor which had preceded Harding's catapult from the secret staircase.

"So, that's where your tennis cups were exhibited, Cindy? And Hal thought I laid the trap. Perhaps you wouldn't have done it if you'd known who you'd catch." She sniffed. "Look at your great-grandmother's beautiful Canova plates, scattered and most of 'em broken. If only I'd thought quick enough to pull open the cupboard. I hope you think your idea was worth it."

"Like the Northwest Mountie, I got my man. Sary, I can't believe that Hal—" her voice broke.

"There, there, child, put him out of your mind. Sakes alive, what you got on? So much excitement I hadn't noticed them blue slacks and white shirt before. They hang on you like a size forty-five on a size thirty-eight scarecrow. Where'd you pick 'em up?"

Cindy told her, gave a thumbnail sketch of her adventures. Sary's eyes threatened to pop from her head. She concluded:

"I'm going up now to shed these borrowed clothes. We'll have them cleaned and pressed and return them to the owner. I wonder where she'll be?"

"We'll know soon enough. Come to the kitchen after you've changed. Colonel Stewart told me to get you something to eat. Wouldn't you know he'd think of that? Didn't you tell me that when he was a boy he was always bringing home lost kittens and dogs to care for?"

"I happen to be neither a lost kitten nor a dog, Miss Parker."

"Want to know somethin'? I'll bet he doesn't think you are. There's half a cold chicken in the icebox and the makings of a fresh peach shortcake. Hurry down. I'm starvin' myself."

# THIRTY

THE FIRST DAY of September. What would the month bring, Cindy wondered. Already it had added autumn tang to the air, had brought deeper, more vivid color to the flower border in the patio: the strong yellows and reds of calendulas and zinnias; a rosy cloud of feathery chrysanthemums, flanked by snowy white, which in turn snuggled against a deep rose-colored variety; monkshood and tall blue asters; enormous dahlias, pink, yellow, crimson by the majestic score; a bronzed grackle instead of a robin bathing in the shallows of the pool.

All this and heartache too, she thought as she looked at Tom Slade in citified gray flannels sitting across the glass table laden with silver and china. When Sarah had reported the telephone message that he was coming, she had declared that the poor boy needed hot tea since he was just out of hospital. He hadn't cared much for it. He glanced up from the silver spoon he had been tapping against a saucer.

"Sure you mean it, lovely?"

"Tom, Tom, dear, I—I wish I didn't. I honestly wish I could say I loved you enough to marry you. I do love you, but not that way."

He leaned forward eagerly.

"If you love me at all, how do you know you wouldn't go all out for me if we were married?"

She shook her head.

"I married once without any kind of love—if one can call a ceremony not performed by a clergyman or an accredited officer of the law marriage. I won't marry

again until I—I feel that I'll *die* if the man I love
doesn't love me." How could she have let herself go like
that? Her voice had shaken.

"That's the answer." He rose and as she stood up,
placed his fingers under her chin and raised it till he
could look into her eyes. "I doubt if you have to die,
lovely. Don't drop those spectacular lashes. You can't
hide your heart from me. Don't you think I love you
enough to want you to be happy?" He reached for a
glass of water.

"Funny, since that spill my voice gets roughed up
easily. I'm starting over the road early tomorrow for
home and work, plenty of work. The government agent
who beat it with the black limousine has had my convertible repaired and has paid the hospital bill. Fair
enough."

"That doesn't compensate for your suffering. Tom, do
you think you ought to make the trip now? Wait until
you get your strength back."

"What do you mean, *my strength back?* Not insinuating that that little accident has made a sissy of me, laid
me up permanently, are you?"

"Don't beat me, Thomas." Her laugh was shaky.

"Then watch your step, woman. Want to know somethin'? Jupiter, but I'm going to miss Sary—there is a
rumor that the Fane girl has a husband in the army."

"I suspected it the night of the Armstrongs' dinner
when the Missing Persons announcer told of the Captain who was trying to find his wife. She turned ghastly
and almost upset her coffee cup."

"They say—correction, Ella Crane says—she is going
back to him now that it looks as if Hal Harding
would be removed from circulation for a time. She has
been on his trail."

"Then you have heard about Hal, Tom?"

"Sure. I was at the hearing this morning while testi-
mony was being presented pro and con."

"Why, why did he do it? He didn't need the money."

"That's the catch, he did. Divorcing two wives because each time you've seen a gal you like better is
expensive business. The smuggling gang has been

snitching jewels and priceless *objets d'art* abroad, selling the loot here and sending cash back to finance the overthrow of a certain government. It got a whopping percentage. He kept out that bag of jewels to finance himself. That's where he stumbled."

"How could he get so out of character with his background and his life? It's tragic."

"Leaving out the crime of dishonesty, how could a man of his intelligence—that's what gets me—have been so *stupid* as to tie up with an enterprise like that? It was like touching pitch—if he tried to get rid of it old debbil blackmail was at his shoulder—he had the choice of two evils, paying through the nose the rest of his life, or being caught. Something tells me that Kenniston Stewart would rather not have it, but the credit of breaking this case will go to him. It seems that before he came to this town he had started to investigate Harding's past and present—"

"Before he came here? How could he have heard of him?"

"Ask him. I'm off. I won't say good-by, lovely. Just, I'll be seeing you."

She sank into her seat at the table, eyes on the house door which had closed softly behind him. His voice had broken on the last word. Why did love have to hurt? Why, why couldn't she have loved him instead of a man who didn't love her?

"Peter, Peter, had a wife and couldn't keep her." Hal Harding's rasping voice shot to th top of her mind. "Didn't want to keep her," if Hal but knew it, she corrected. "There's a lady waiting for you, Colonel," the man Simpkins had reminded. Of course, it was Ally Barclay. Was Sary right? Did he want to marry her?

"Cindy," Sarah Ann Parker's voice was followed by the slam of the door behind her. She looked down at the table. "Sakes alive, you two didn't eat any of my mushroom *canapés,* and Mr. Slade used to gobble them by the dozen. What happened?"

"He pretends he's in the pink, but I think he's still feeling the effects of the accident."

"I guess you're right. Perhaps there's some other trouble mixed in with it. He told me he was startin' for home tomorrow at daybreak, handed me a ten-dollar bill an' said, 'Sary, credit that to all the soda lemonades you've mixed and the brownies you've baked for me.' Nice boy, I felt kinder sorry for him." She sniffed and wiped her eyes.

"Sarah Ann Parker, stop it, or you'll have me crying." She helped place cups and plates on the tray. "Why the bandaged finger? What happened to it?"

"Darius came in early this morning with a red squirrel dangling from his jaws. I got the poor thing away from him an' then it sunk its sharp teeth into my finger. O-o-ooch, it hurt. Those little things fight back fierce, when caught."

"If the creature had had a sense of poetic justice it would have bitten Darius instead of you. It might have taught that black cat a lesson. You said you intended to drop in at Ella Crane's, I suppose you have all the details of the Rockledge activities at your tongue's end."

"Sakes alive, Ella is doing a rushing business, everyone in town is droppin' in. The women feel terribly sorry 'bout Hal Harding—one time or another he had 'em all with their tongues hangin' out, an' I guess from all accounts he's the one to be sorry for, the rest of the gang have been workin' the racket in other places for a couple of years. I liked him, but I never trusted him. Seems that the tough guy we thought was Rena Foster's beau was here to help catch the smugglers. Funny, ain't it, we should have smugglers at Pirate's Cove again? Seems kind of fitting."

"Fitting! Sarah Ann Parker, you have a perverted dramatic sense."

"So long's I've got somethin' dramatic in my make-up, it's all right with me. One thing came out at the hearin', Rena Foster confessed that when she came into the kitchen, the day you had that queer sleepin' spell—she thought we was all away an' come in with that big basket to pick up the jewels for Hal Harding—she waited till he left by the front way an' she came in the back door. In court she made sure he didn't get clear an' leave her holding the bag."

"Then she was working both sides of the street. Helping him against the woman by whom she was employed."

"That wouldn't worry her none. Want to know somethin', Cindy? Seems I've been suspected of spyin' on the folks at Rockledge, of flashing lights to the yacht and misleading it."

"You, Sary? Where and how did you hear that?"

"I met the man we'd thought was Rena Foster's beau on the street—he isn't so tough-lookin' when he smiles. I guess that face gets him the detective job. No one lookin' at him would think he was on the side of law an' order. He stopped me.

" 'See here, Miss Parker,' said he. 'Fools rush in where angels fear to tread. You were taking a crazy chance when you butted in on the smugglers. I happen to know that one night a couple in a boat tied to The Castle landing was ready to garrote you if you appeared.' Must have been the night you yanked off my bathrobe, Cindy—then he went on, 'Did you get the warning I slipped into Miss Clinton's pocket at the masquerade?' Kind of exciting, isn't it?"

"Exciting? The possibilities are hair-raising. Then it was the clown who tucked the note into my pocket? Sarah Ann Parker, was he right? Did you mix into the Rockledge mess?"

Her grin was half triumph, half admission.

"Twice I flashed lights that sent the yacht packin' in a hurry. I was experimentin'. Sakes alive, I suppose I won't have a chance to mix into anything like that again. Looks like the Devil an' his works have been cleared from this village. Life will drop back to be just one everlastin' round of cookin'—not that I don't love cookin'—dishwashing and movies." She lifted the laden tray.

"I forgot to tell you, Colonel Stewart phoned. When I told him you and Mr. Slade were talkin' very serious in the pat-i-o, he said not to call you, just tell you he'd be here about eight to take you dancing." She stopped at the kitchen door which Cinderella opened for her.

"Better wear the swishy blue taffeta, Cindy, and the two ninety-eight string of beads. Wonderful buy, wasn't it? You can fool me some of the time but not every time, Miss Clinton." The slam of the door behind her registered indignation.

Two hours later Sarah Ann Parker hovered about the table in the candle-lighted patio.

"You look awful nice, Cindy. 'Tisn't the dress I wanted you to wear, but I guess that fluffy net is more suitable for this warm evening than taffeta. Turquoise blue, isn't it? I'm kinder getting used to the sleeveless top, I like 'em when bare arms are as pretty as yours. The pink rose at the shoulder looks perfect enough to have come right out of the garden. How much shorter the days are getting. Can't hardly see the chaise longy pushed back in the corner." She poured coffee clear as dark amber into a porcelain cup.

"Drink this, child. You haven't eaten enough dinner to keep a bird alive. I've been runnin' on, tellin' you how nice you look to cheer you up. Not feelin' sad and sorry about Hal Harding, are you? He ain't worth it."

"Of course I am sorry about Hal Harding, Sary. I liked him until—lately. It's tragic to think that a man who had everything, education, money, personal charm, an outstanding war record, a fine family behind him, would make such a mess of his life."

"I guess he started wrong. Always had his own way. Couldn't adjust himself to marriage. Never reached emotional maturity, I heard that over the radio. Not about him, but a speaker said that what this country needs most is for folks to grow up, quit throwin' fits of temper or sulkin' if things don't please 'em. Then he went on to say, many of them who think they're men an' women are in the diaper or schoolboy stage mentally and emotionally."

"*Miss* Parker, I didn't know you ever listened to anything like that."

"You never can tell when a seed will drop into someone's mind and sprout. Maybe I'm growin' up, too. I wish you'd eat something more, Cindy. But, perhaps you'll have supper where you're goin' dancing."

"I'm not going dancing, Sary." She rose. She could

battle better on her feet. "I've planned to meet friends at the Inn for cards."

"Cinderella Clinton, do you mean you're turnin' down Colonel Stewart?"

"My, but you're a quick thinker, Sary." She picked up a long white coat from a chair. "I'm going in my car—"

"In that old jalopy? Call that a car? What shall I say to Colonel Stewart when he comes?"

"Oh, tell him I had a previous engagement."

"Just like that. I will. I guess 'twon't trouble him none, not with Ally Barclay round to take out. I hope the car breaks down an' leaves you in a wilderness a hundred miles from home, Cinderella Clinton." The screen door banged behind her.

Twenty minutes later, ten of which had been spent trying to revive an expired motor, Cindy regarded the decrepit jalopy beside the road. She would have to abandon it. Better stop at the next house and phone the garage to come and drag it home. Then what? Sary would tell Ken Stewart she had gone to the Inn. He would drive there for her. He had said they would go dancing and he was not one to give up easily.

She didn't want to hear his explanation of why he had come here under another name, had let the annulment go through, she thought as she trudged toward home in high heeled blue slippers that had not been designed for walking a country road. No doubt but he would bring up the subject. She couldn't bear it. She might betray the fact that she loved him. Then he'd feel sorry for her. Why did she have to love a man who didn't want her? Why long to have his arms about her? That last was sheer sentimentality. How did she know she wanted his arms about her? They never had been, had they?

She had made it. Curled up in the chaise in a dusky corner of the patio she glanced at the illuminated dial of her jeweled watch. Not quite eight. She wriggled off her slippers. That walk had finished them—and almost her feet. Dark as Erebus here. The night was so still she could hear every sound. Crickets had deserted the gar-

den. The light breeze was salted with the smell of the
sea.

A car stopping. Ken's? Sary would tell him she had
gone to the Inn and he would follow. Would he? Why
be so sure, with Ally Barclay in the offing? Numberless
men had married women years older, and been happy,
hadn't they? The front door opening. Closing. He had
gone. That ended that. He wouldn't forgive her for
side-stepping the date. He wouldn't come back. Now she
would steal upstairs. The screen door was opening. She
swung her feet up to the chaise. Ken Stewart was silhou-
etted against the light in the hall.

"I won't go to the Inn, Sary. I saw her car abandoned
beside the road. I have a feeling she will trek back to
The Castle, if she doesn't I'll go after her. Meanwhile
I'll wait here." The door closed.

Now that her eyes were accustomed to the dusk she
could see him—he was wearing a dark suit tonight. He
stood at the edge of the patio looking out at the garden,
whistling softly, "Smoke Gets in Your Eyes."

Miss Clinton, you're in a fix, she told herself. Better
come out of hiding boldly and laugh it off—

Something dropped into her lap. Something big and
black and satin-smooth. Something else with a bushy tail
that struggled.

"Darius! No! No! Drop that—" She leaped to her feet,
ran to the man standing as if turned to stone. Clutched
his shoulders with both hands.

"Ken! Ken!" She drew a long sobbing breath. He held
her close.

"What frightened you, Cindy?"

"Darius! Landed in my lap with a big fat squirrel."
She shuddered. "Sary said they are f-fierce—"

"They've gone. In different directions, darling. You
frightened the daylights out of them. I've heard that a
black cat brings luck. Now I know it. It sent you into
my arms to save you from wild beasts. Stay where you
are." He drew her back. "You can't go now. This is the
third rescue. Remember I warned you. Now I'll keep
you." He lifted her chin. Bent his face to hers.

"That kiss has been building up since the first impact of your eyes on mine," he declared unsteadily.

"It—it was so long I—I can believe it," she whispered with an attempt at gaiety. Head against his shoulder she looked up. Voice and eyes were grave.

"Then why—"

"Come in where I can see you."

There was no sign of Sarah as they went through the hall, but from the floor above came a man's voice singing:

"Once you have found her never let her go."

He laughed.

"Sary, her phonograph plus her sense of the dramatic. I don't need to be reminded not to let you go."

He followed her into the old kitchen, glowing with yellow and copper in the lamplight. Closed the door and shut out the music. She backed against the desk. He crossed his arms on top of the high back of the wing chair. The laughing brilliance of his eyes sent her lashes down.

"You needn't be afraid of me, Cinderella. The next time I kiss you I'll post a notice—I take back that rash promise. I know I can't keep it. When I phoned this afternoon, Sary said that Tom Slade was with you."

"He came to say good-by."

"A grand person. He sent me a memento of the summer."

"Funny thing for him to do, wasn't it?" She seized the chance to steady her throbbing pulses by getting away from the subject of themselves. "You weren't special friends, were you? Would I be out of order if I asked what it was?"

"A red satin slipper. He knew I had the mate. Said he thought they should be together. A statement with which I am in one hundred per cent agreement. Ten days from now I am due in Washington to receive a citation—"

"A citation. Wonderful, but aren't you coming back?"

"That depends on you. Will you go with me as my wife?"

"Ken, do you want me? Then why—"

"Come here. I can't talk when you're so far away." He caught her in one arm. "We'll have the rest of our lives for explanations, Cindy. There was no woman in my life before you—" he laughed and kissed her swiftly—"except that glacial Mrs. Kenniston Stewart who conducted my business so expertly. I loved you from the moment we met at Ella Crane's. Believe me?"

"Yes. Because I felt the same way, though I didn't know it for a long time after."

"You're so sweet and warm and alive, Cindy. Ready to hear my plan?"

"Ready? I'm on my toes with excitement."

"Here goes. We'll be married in the church here— we'll have to allow five days after we get the license— motor to Washington—as you suggested, it's a gorgeous time of year. We might stop on the way and book reservations for the interplanetary trip—" His laugh was buoyant, young— "Then return to The Castle where I'll finish my book, after which we'll settle where my work is to be and begin the real business of living. Does that appeal to you?"

"Sounds ideal. We'll have to consult Sary."

"Sarah Ann Parker has assured me that she can have the most luscious wedding cake ready in time."

"Then she knows—"

"That I love you? Who doesn't? Do you—now?"

"I'm beginning to get the idea, Colonel."

"That's progress." He held out his right hand. In the palm sparkled a diamond circlet. "I would like to put this wedding ring on your finger myself," he said gravely. "Do you dislike it too much?"

"Dislike it? Where did you get that strange idea? I love it. I wouldn't want any other."

"That does it. I have another ring for you. Remember I said I brought you a present from Washington? I quote, 'It's big, sensational, choice.' I'll give it to you on the way to the license bureau."

"Are we going there—tonight?"

"We haven't too much time. I bribed the license clerk to wait for us until ten. Where's your coat?"

"In the patio. My slippers are there. I kicked them off."

"You don't need them." He brought a pair of red satin slippers from a side table. "I left these when I came in. Sit in the wing chair." Before her on one knee he put them on. He held one satin-shod foot tight in his hand.

"Do they fit? Has the right Prince found your slipper, Cinderella?"

His unsteady voice, his demanding eyes drew her like a magnet. She nodded. Leaned forward. Her lips were soft and warm and clinging as she kissed him.

"A perfect fit. And the right Prince for all the rest of my life, Your Highness."

He swept her to her feet and into his arms. Pressed his face against her hair.

"Cindy, Cindy. *Cindy*. That's telling me." He cleared his voice.

"Remember, you didn't like that guy Stewart? Think you'll be happy taking his name again, Mrs. Kenniston Stewart?"

"Again? What do you mean by *again?*" Her tender eyes were alight with laughter as they met his. "Want to know something? Deep in my heart I never gave it up."